Porcelain - the Flesh of Innocents

Lee Cockburn

Clink
Street

London | New York

Published by Clink Street Publishing 2017

Copyright © 2017

First edition.

ISBN:
978-1-911525-31-8 - paperback
978-1-911525-32-5- ebook

Chapter 1
Prisoners

Twenty-two years previously

Fingers twisted her soft youthful flesh cruelly tight, the skin bevelled as the grip tightened and tortured; soft whimpers were barely audible, as to scream would only bring on more pain and prolonged torture. Teeth gritted as a voice rasped cruel words into her face, saliva dotted on the young girl's cheeks. She turned to avoid it, but this was not the thing to do. The slap was loud and the stinging pain instant. Her cheek flushed immediately. The second blow was a fist, rocking her back so viciously she could not keep her balance and she seemed to float backwards until she thumped down onto her tiny bottom. She could not stop herself this time and the tears came flowing down her cheeks. She cried loudly holding her face; her lip was already swollen, her nose bleeding, the swelling now visible and growing.

"Now look what you made me do you evil little bitch. You made me hit you, you make me angry - wanting! needing! All the time, mummy this and mummy that. I can't stand you, you little cow!"

The woman's face was contorted with disgust as little Amy's nose started to run, a mixture of snot and blood, a gloopy mixture that any other mother would rush over to and caringly wipe from their child's nose, offering arms of comfort for the pain and distress the child was in. Not Megan, she hated those kids from the day they were born; she hated them, hated them both, Amy and Nathan, her five-year-old twins.

"Now, where is that little shit? NATHAN, NATHAN!" Megan shouted at the top of her voice. "You get down here right now or so help me I'll fucking kill you, ya stupid little bastard."

The discoloured and stained door opened at the top of the stair and a slovenly, unclean, unshaven, middle-aged man came out of the room. His belly hung over his trousers. He lifted it up to pull up his zip and fix his belt as he started to come down the bare carpetless stairs, his feet making a gripping sticky noise as he clumped down.

"Oh, that's where he is. Do you want her up there just now too or do you want your tea?" Megan said with a sadistic look on her face. The smell of fatty food wafted through the house and clung to the already filthy walls and odd curtain still hanging, adding to the combined stench of body odour, urine, faeces and general filth.

He rubbed his belly and scratched his crotch, thinking for a moment, wondering if he could be bothered doing it again. His eyes darkened and his mouth contorted as he said "Yeh, bring that little bitch up too, am no' hungry yet".

Amy tried to run to the cupboard at the back of the room but she was whipped backwards violently as Megan caught hold of her hair. Her head stopped dead and her feet flew up forwards in front of her as she was lifted off the ground. Her mother dragged her up the stairs, the walls filthy with years of grime and neglect, stains marking every inch of the wall, blood, snot, alcohol, vomit and scrape marks from the children's futile attempts to fight against their so called parents and their inevitable ordeal.

Stale breath, unclean flesh and rancid toxic body odour filled Amy's nostrils as he lay on top of her barely holding up his hefty weight, her wrists held tightly with familiar hands as he took her innocence once again. Megan watched, her eyes filled with excitement at the scene being played out before her. She enjoyed watching them suffer, whichever way it came. She had resented them from the time she discovered she was pregnant. Her partner had left her the minute she told him and she was too far gone to have them aborted; she was so overweight she hadn't even noticed she was pregnant. Her chaotic lifestyle before and during pregnancy was one filled with drug abuse and drinking to excess.

Nathan's tiny little fingers pushed tightly into his ears as he pushed his face tighter down into his knees, trying to block out the noise of his sister being abused, slapped, pinched and violated in every degrading way. Pain rippled through his body from the same acts inflicted on him earlier. His mother's new boyfriend was practically invited to abuse them. He had deliberately befriended Megan for that very reason; he wasn't interested in her, she was merely a means to an end for his unhealthy desires. He had watched her over several months and used her to get to her children, although that didn't stop him abusing her with regular beatings and violent sexual exploitation as well when he got bored with the children.

At last the door slammed shut on the children and loud voices and sounds of twisted laughter moved away downstairs. Nathan got up immediately and went to his sister and took hold of her hand helping her to sit up. He wiped her tears with the sheet. Putting a protective arm around her they just sat there, locked in the dank dark room filled with the disgusting stench of wretched filthy bodies, theirs included, body fluids and copious amounts of rotten food. The bedclothes were stained dark yellow and brown with years of sweat and overuse, the ashtrays peaked into pyramid shaped ash piles. Round the walls were shelves upon shelves filled with the most hideous cheaply made porcelain faced dolls. Nathan and Amy tried to hide under the covers, to avert their tiny innocent eyes from the constant stare of a thousand eyes watching them. They were terrified of those dolls. There was no escape from them, the blue and brown piercing eyes would follow them round the room, haunting them, watching them, making sure they could never escape. Their mother Megan had moved into her late mother's council house in the Niddrie area of Edinburgh and had inherited the collection of tacky Spanish porcelain dolls that her mother had bought every time she had visited her favourite place in Benidorm.

The flats were high rise and their window was on the 13th floor which had no windows overlooking it, no means of escape and no way of being seen by any concerned passer-by who may happen to look up and see two wretched faces peering out. The twins were undernourished, scantily clad and unclean - pawns for the the vile reptilic people who were meant to care for them but who abused them unchallenged whenever they liked, as often as they wanted.

The door swung open. Twisted chip wrappers contained the crusts of a couple of pies, a few deformed nearly inedible chips that had been put aside and stale bread with margarine spread thickly on top of it. A mug of water accompanied the scant meal; it had so many rings of filth on the inside that they almost couldn't be counted. These were unwashed stains from coffee, milk and anything else that had been drunk from the cup in the last month or so. The children sat motionless, eyes wide, terrified, until the door closed again and they both scurried over to the food and stuffed it into their needy little mouths, desperate and starving. Regardless of the state of the food, it was food; that's all they cared about, they were starving.

Chapter 2
The Trial

Susan was told to take a seat back in the dock as the defence wanted to recall a witness. She sat there uncomfortably as a result of brutal injuries inflicted on her by John Brennan. Brennan was Edinburgh's most recent and notorious serial killer, his relentless pursuit of Susan to torture and kill her had left her scarred for life. He was the serial killer that Susan had slain in order to preserve her own life and that of the others that had fallen injured there with her that night. She had ensured he would never rape and torture anyone else ever again. She sat in the dock without movement as she listened to the rather damning evidence of the excessive force she had used on Brennan and the case seemed to be building up unfairly against her. She listened as the evidence was explained in full and graphic detail to the court and jury, the facts that the first or second blow to Brennan's head would have been enough to incapacitate any person and render them unconscious. It was the only way that would have allowed her to escape. The medical terminology of the damage that each blow had caused to Brennan was explained; his skull smashed into pieces, his brain exposed and brain matter scattered on the floor, blood spattered high up on every wall, a scene of utter carnage. On the face of it, Brennan's was a brutal murder.

The defence uncharacteristically recalled Detective Sergeant Taylor Nicks to the stand, hoping that her honest and sincere explanation of that night would remind the jury that Susan had been justified in her actions and just how desperate the situation had been for all of them, not just her.

Bringing her back to the stand would allow DS Nicks to re-emphasise in more depth the true horrors of what John Brennan had done to Susan and many other women, including DS Nicks herself. Taylor stood once again in her usual statuesque stance; tall, slim, with striking features, long wavy brown hair, brown eyes, tanned skin, a beautiful woman with only a hint of makeup. Her words were calm and unbiased as she emphatically reiterated the relevant facts to the court regarding the situation, the terror, the pain, the emphasis placed on the fear that Brennan had put upon Susan. He had made it his life's ambition to hunt her down, terrorise and torture her with the aim of finally murdering her. Taylor never once questioned the fact that Susan had killed him instead and deliberately so, and started to explain why she had to. She stated that Susan may have been able to escape, as the prosecution repeatedly pointed out, but Taylor's partner Kay was also in the room with them, badly injured and vulnerable, immobile on the floor. Taylor had also been injured by Brennan as she tried to save Kay's life and she too was unable to get up and get away.

She told the court, "Had Susan escaped that night after wounding Brennan, our lives would have undeniably been at risk, her actions and Brennan's demise absolutely saved our lives and had he escaped, he would not have stopped there, they never do!" Taylor's eyes were full of honesty and genuine emotion, her gratitude echoed in her words as she believed she owed her life and Kay's to Susan and her instinctive actions. She also silently pleaded with the jury to see that the situation was not black and white, every action had a reaction and Susan did not choose to be in this predicament.

"If Susan hadn't taken the action she took that night, we would have all been raped, tortured and eventually killed, all three of us, and he'd escaped once before and none of us could take the risk of having this happen again, for our sakes and other women, your honour."

She went on to try and describe the scene that night, trying to get the jury to see it from their eyes, the terror, the certainty of the events that were to follow - rape, assault and maniacal violence. Had Susan not acted instinctively and with the force she did, Brennan would have overpowered her and would have most certainly killed them all.

When Susan eventually got to the stand, a very lonely place for anyone, she was ashen-faced, reliving the nightmare again was obviously taking its toll on her. She stood trembling, her leg moving involuntarily, as she recollected the prolonged abuse, assaults, terror, rape and degradation she had suffered at the hands of this monster. She listed and showed some of the physical injuries that she was able to show to the jury, her tears and emotion clearly genuine and on show for all to see. The jury members listened intently, their faces showing disgust and sympathy as Susan spoke and revealed her scars. There was not a hint of her trying to gain sympathy, every emotion was real and the jury could see the true torment that she was having to relive. Susan stopped talking and took a deep breath as she got to the final account of that fateful evening. She clasped her hands and looked honestly at all the faces staring silently at her from the jury box, every one transfixed with her words, some sitting open mouthed at what had happened to her, her bravery and that she was even there to be able to tell her story at all.

Susan slowly opened her mouth. She spoke softly as she said, "I ran into the room. My wrists were blistered and bleeding, where he had bound me tightly to the bed to deal with me later. I had a baton in my hand that I had found in the bedroom and I saw the two women lying there, both badly injured, blood everywhere, and I knew what he was going to do, as he had done it to me. I knew he was going to rape them and finally kill them! I had to stop him, I had to stop him, stop him forever! So I hit him once, then I hit him again and again, harder and harder and I just couldn't stop. It was like instinct, I was terrified that he would turn round and grab me from where he lay. I didn't think of the damage I was causing to him, I just needed him to stop and if that meant killing him, then that was what I had to do!"

Susan stood silently for a moment, her hands gripping onto the surrounds of the highly varnished box she stood within. Her grip faded as she slipped down and thudded heavily to the ground. The court officers ran quickly over to where she lay and DS Taylor Nicks also rose from the back of the public stand and made her way to be by her side, as did Andrew, Susan's partner. The stress of recounting the cruel events had caused her body to relive the terror of that fateful evening. Her body had chosen to shut down in order to escape the cruel torture of reality. She came to suddenly, embarrassed at the situation, because in no way did she want to be seen as weak or false. She was asked to take a little time to recover but refused and demanded to be allowed to continue there and then.

"Sorry sir," she said sincerely to the presiding sheriff. "I don't know what happened but I am ready to continue now and it won't happen again," she assured him.

Numerous questions were asked of her, to which she answered honestly and she was asked to clarify a few points and that was it, the show was over and now it was time to wait, wait for her fate to be decided.

All of the witness evidence had been heard and the jury were sent away to deliberate. Susan was taken down the stairs to a bleak and empty cell with a concrete slab for a bed. It had a plastic coated blue mat placed on top of it and a solid metal non seated toilet in the corner that she had to press a buzzer for if it needed flushed. She sat alone in the cell and slowly bowed her head in her hands and wept, tears streaming down her face like miniature rivers. She could not believe her life had come to this, her once comfortable and peaceful happy life and all because of him.

"All Rise."

The sheriff entered, his wig sitting high upon his head, his gown and presence was formidable for anyone who had ever stood before him, awaiting judgement. He gestured with his hands for everyone to sit, and all within the court silently obeyed. The formalities were addressed and he then turned to the jury for their verdict. Susan, Andrew, DS Taylor Nicks, DC Marcus Black, DC Fran Andrews (another victim), Kay – who had to use a wheelchair due to the serious debilitating injuries inflicted on her that night at the hands of Brennan – and all of the others who had given evidence against him, stood there hoping for the right and just outcome of this trial.

Susan held her breath, closed her eyes and stood trembling on the spot, her whole life depended on this moment. Would he finally win after all he had put her through, even from beyond the grave? He held her future life in the balance, that sick, sadistic pervert, John Brennan. Her lips spoke his name under her breath, a little startled that her thoughts slipped out verbally, and hoped she hadn't been heard, as the head juror stood up and faced the sheriff.

The woman who stood, spoke confidently and clearly, but quite softly as she read out the verdict. "We find the defendant, NOT GUILTY OF MURDER. We find that the accused acted lawfully and through necessity, committed a justifiable homicide in self-defence of her own life and the lives of the other two women, that she knew were helpless and could not escape with her."

There was a loud sigh and an overwhelming sense of relief from within the courtroom, from those involved and from members of the general public that had followed the trial. Those involved hugged one another, pain still etched on their faces. For once the British justice system had taken the side of the innocent over that of the criminal! They all then looked up at Susan, who just stood there with her hands covering her mouth iQn disbelief, and a deep sense of relief that her harrowing ordeal was finally over. She was free from him and the fear she carried with her, free to start to rebuild her life, a new life with her new love, Andrew, the man who had risked his life to save hers, through love and protective instinct.

Taylor hugged Susan with affection and respect as she walked into the body of the court, rather than back down the bleak stairs to the cells. Taylor owed her life to Susan; everyone that was there that night did, although Kay was still in a bad way.

"Good luck you, please keep in touch and come and see us sometime, we'll be there, we're always there. Oh, and Andrew, you better look after her, don't let her out of your sight." She gave him a hug too but did not want to dwell on the enormity of the decision made by the court and the significance of the result.

She knew they had to get back to work, back to reality, the endless stream of damaged souls that crossed their paths every day. She even wondered what would be next. It would certainly take some event to top that of Brennan, a man that she'd never forget.

Andrew smiled at Taylor and then at Susan, and said, "No, I think she'll be the one that'll protect me," and he meant it, because Susan was a different person. She had vowed to herself never to be the victim again, ever!

Chapter 3
Innocent or Not?

He tried to get up, struggling to get to his feet as the bat struck his other knee with equally brutal and damaging force. As he buckled to the floor, the bat crashed into his ribs, smashing them so hard that he fell over onto his side. Saliva hanging down from his mouth, he struggled to get a breath as he moaned out loud, putting his hands up in a futile attempt to stop any further assault from the masked stranger that stood in front of him, looking straight into his eyes.

"What do you want from me, why are you doing this to me, what have I ever done to you?" The man's quavering voice asked of the ominously silent figure staring right at him.

A small but strong hand gripped on to his face twisting it out of shape, nails digging right into his skin, blood oozing out as they forced deeper into his flesh with pure hate and venom. They deliberately pushed close to his eyes, cruelly taunting him. The stranger took a step back and began to kick him like a crazed animal, his face, his neck, all over his body. A boot stamped down hard on his chest and his stomach. As he lay there winded and in severe pain, the man sensed hesitation from his attacker. He felt his leg being moved forcefully over as he lay on his back, the pain now coursing through him and he feared what would happen next. Suddenly he felt an excruciating pain in his groin, as the bat slammed down on his genitals with such force it seemed to crush them against his pelvis, then another, then another. He was now rendered completely unable to move, barely conscious as he was rolled over. He could feel his belt being unbuckled, then the hands wrenching at his trousers and underwear as they were sliced with a blade. His mind raced in terror at what could be coming next, fearing the worst that he may lose his balls, then he felt a ripping, tearing sensation and searing pain, sickness to the pit of his stomach just before he lost consciousness. A merciless grin was etched on the attacker's face as they stood up, their last kick forcing the weapon deeper into his anus, before they turned away with a sense of satisfaction.

Carefully they cleaned up the scene, even wiping the victim's face where their hand had gripped him so brutally, making sure they hadn't left a single trace of themselves on him, not leaving a clue about who or what they were. His pad had been pristine prior to this unwanted visit, expensive tastes, no warmth or homeliness, very clinical with modern hi tech audio equipment, and masculine fixtures and fittings, now all sprayed with blood spatter from the assault that had just taken place.

The stranger looked around the room, taking in the surroundings. A sense of empowerment and satisfaction warming them deep inside as they looked down on the wounded animal in front of them.

Putting on gloves they thumbed through the DVDs that lay close to the bed, no markings on them, just countless black cases. There was no fear over the length of time they had been in his house, because if the police were coming, they would have been there by now. The stranger was well-versed on police procedure. The chosen DVD was pushed into the player and the telly was clicked on. The stranger hesitated prior to pressing play, an inner apprehension holding them back. The 50-inch mounted Sony HD television came to life and the surround sound speakers made the screams of the very young female child more painful to hear, the obvious fear and pain she was in sending shivers down their back as they paused the film on the harrowing scene. The face of the beaten man was clearly visible as the perpetrator of the crime taking place. Nausea overwhelmed the stranger as they stood up and selected a calling card out of a bag and left it beside the television, taking care to position it in full view for when the police arrived.

The flash lit up the room as the stranger stopped to take a souvenir, a photograph of the first vengeful retribution. Lifting a mobile phone from a table near to where the man lay, now trussed up to prevent his escape, a finger punched in 999. One final look round the room and they were gone, like a ghost in the night.

Driving away, sirens could be heard making their way to respond to the silent treble nine call just received in the control room.

Chapter 4
Who and Why?

DS Taylor Nicks strode confidently into the room, smartly dressed in a figure hugging two-piece suit; long, slim, toned legs; fitted blouse carefully crafted to draw attention to her perfect feminine shape. She smiled at her colleagues as she made her way to her desk. They resembled meerkats as she passed them by. DC Marcus Black was already at his desk working away in front of his favourite family photo. A conscientious, hard working individual, Marcus was very handsome with rugged and chiselled facial features and a toned athletic physique. He was also a really decent guy. He raised his head as he saw Taylor approach and greeted her with a genuine smile, which stretched across his face as she gave him a playful shove in the back. Their bond was very strong as they had worked together for many years. They had built up a good relationship and friendship and trusted each other implicitly.

"Hi, how long have you been in? You always make me look really bad, always being in before me."

He just smiled at her, knowing she didn't really care and would never change her ways just to look good. She enjoyed life too much to waste a moment of her private life at her work's expense, unless there was something special going on, always living life on the edge.

"Great result yesterday with Susan. Can you imagine if that had gone the other way, that would have been a travesty, which I was actually thinking might happen."

"Totally the right decision though! What would society be if she had been sent down. He deserved everything he got and more, and thank goodness the jury thought that too!" Marcus replied. "How's Kay holding up, is she any better?"

"Not so good. Her injuries are healing but her head isn't in a good place right now. She's finding it hard to come to terms with what happened, and she seems to be disappearing into herself lately."

"No wonder though, she nearly died."

Kay was Taylor's current partner. They hadn't been together very long but their short time spent with each other had been an incredibly intense affair, filled with passion, lust and desire. Kay had never been with a woman before and Taylor had always shied away from any sort of relationship, but Kay was different. Unfortunately, that hadn't been enough, even with their strong feelings for one another. Taylor had faltered and had had a passionate encounter with one of her team during their last enquiry whilst hunting Brennan. She had been tempted by her fit and very attractive colleague Fran Andrews, a feisty, good-looking woman, who had openly flirted with Taylor, something Taylor very rarely could resist.

"Anyway, enough doom and gloom, what have we got today, anything worthwhile?"

Both knew that, after hunting for Brennan, the sheer enormity of that enquiry would be hard to beat in terms of interest and excitement.

Marcus pulled up his keyboard and showed her the job down to Newhaven in Leith, an old fishing village very close to the sea and the harbour. A popular residential area with a massive regeneration programme ongoing, with hundreds of new-build luxury flats being built on reclaimed land.

"You should have seen the state of this guy when they found him. Someone must have really hated him to take the time and effort to do that to him."

"Do what?" Taylor urged him to tell, attention already totally focussed on what he was going to describe. Her intrigue for the cruelty of human nature never faltered.

She still saw things all too regularly that she couldn't believe had happened. She nudged Marcus hard with her elbow as he deliberately hesitated in sharing the gory details with her. He started to describe the scene and the injuries inflicted on the victim, mainly deep cuts and bruising. Taylor looked at him as if to say, is that all? Until he described the complete destruction of the victim's genitals and the graphic description of where the weapon had been lodged, causing severe haemorrhaging and internal damage. Taylor winced as Marcus described the scene to her.

"What the fuck, who is he, is he known to us?" she questioned.

"He has never been charged with anything, but his name has been mentioned in several intelligence logs relating to child pornography, images and the like, nothing solid that would tie him to anything, not overly hardcore, and nothing that could be attributed to him back then during the enquiry."

"Revenge do you think? No one does that sort of thing to anyone without reason or some personal motive."

"It gets better." Marcus pulled up a list of evidence taken from his house. "DVDs, memory sticks, hard drives and a plethora of sex toys, most of which had been kindly laid out in plain sight for the police to find."

"He's the victim, why have they gone snooping around his stuff?" Taylor scrunched up her face.

"The person who visited him, left his giant telly on with a frozen image of hardcore child pornography displayed there for us to see, and guess who was the star of the movie?"

"What do you mean, us?" Taylor exclaimed.

Marcus answered, "Whoever was there, called 999 knowing the police would attend. They didn't want him to die and they wanted us to find all of this stuff, and with all that on display we were able to apply for a warrant and they granted one straight away - and rightly so! This guy appears to have been right in the centre of a well-organised, hardcore paedophile ring but had never been caught, until now, now that the perpetrator gave us a little help."

She slapped the desk pretty hard – this investigation now offering up two very different strands of enquiry for their team to look into. Who carried out this atrocious crime and why, and was this just the beginning? What else had the victim been involved in?

Chapter 5
Next

He closed the door behind him and the sigh of relief to be home was obvious He leant back against the door and was thankful that his long and boring day was over. He may be a managing director of a successful insurance firm based in the centre of Edinburgh but he hated the restriction of so called normality and the inability to talk to anyone about his desires and what went on in his secret life. That was until he got home to his computer, his window into the unrestricted world wide web, filled with sin and lack of regulated control and restriction for those who knew how to work their way around any inbuilt security filters. He could be his own person and control certain things from his armchair. He walked through to the kitchen and straight over to the fridge. Pulling out a bottle of chilled white wine, a Pinot Grigio, he poured himself a large glass, one that took over half a bottle and wouldn't need refilled too often.

He walked straight back through to the living room where his furnishings were all dark colours, nothing cheery and colourful, no sign of a partner and nothing feminine anywhere. He sat in his custom-built soft leather office chair and pulled himself closer to the large screen of a top of the range computer with webcam set up. His soft-skinned, chubby finger, that had never seen a physical days work, hit the keyboard. He entered a series of complex encrypted passwords with his hand skilfully using the mouse to navigate through screen after screen of false topics and smoke screens, until he visibly tensed with excitement at opening his favourite interactive site and screen of choice. On the screen was a young boy sitting on a double bed in a bleak bedroom. He was in his underwear and a young girl stood near to a window. She was also semi-naked. There was no one else there, just two lonely wee souls totally unaware of what was to come next. Fat fingers gripped his credit card, his white furred tongue licked his lips and scraped it off of his teeth as he keyed in his number, his impatience and needy depraved anticipation, causing tiny sweat beads to pop out all over his forehead and round his receding hairline. A large sum of cash now withdrawn, he then tested the microphone. The two children in the room visibly jumped as they heard his voice over the speaker in the corner, not a kind voice, one filled with cruelty and a hint of desperation; not a comforting tone that scared children would hope for. Two men could be seen to enter the bleak room and both children scurried into the corner, desperately trying to get as far away from them. Both men were wearing see-through, face-altering creepy masks, which concealed their identities and terrified the children.

"Take the girl first and strip her, make sure the boy joins in and gets his fair share." He rattled off several sadistic and intrusive orders to the men to carry out on the children and finished the sentence by saying, "I've paid a heck of a lot of money for this and I'm damn sure I'll make it worth my while."

He stood up and undid his belt letting his suit trousers drop to the floor. Kicking off his shiny work shoes he settled back into the seat with his cock in his hand. He feverishly set about pleasuring himself even before the depravity began on the screen. Screams of fear rang out as his wicked demands were about to be played out and all controlled only by him.

He didn't hear it at first over the sounds of the computer but the second time he most certainly did. His head whipped round like a hunted animal, his senses fully alert. He felt vulnerable with his trousers at his ankles. He stood up from the chair, aware he had left his phone in the bedroom where he had heard the noise. He listened intently and craned his neck to try and hear it again but he heard nothing other than his computer. He quizzed himself whether he had left a window open or something that could give a logical explanation for the noise that had come from the bedroom.

Pulling up his trousers he slowly made his way through to the room, tentatively picking up an umbrella with a steel tip to use as a weapon if needed. He stood next to the door, his breathing rapid and his pulse feeling like it was going through the roof. He watched the door as it moved slightly and then back again and he felt a slight draught up against his face through the tiny gap. He felt himself relax a little at the thought that he had left a window open and then pulled the handle down forcefully with an air of new-found confidence. He swung the door open in a show of strength to whoever might be in there. He looked around the room with only the light from the hallway and noticed the window was slightly ajar. Explanation present and nothing obvious as he scanned the room, he felt more relaxed and put the umbrella down next to the door. He reached for the light and all he heard was a click, but no light came on.

"Fuck off, not now!" he muttered to himself and stepped further into the room, not yet fearful of anything more than a blown bulb and his money being wasted through in the other room. He took a couple of steps forward to put on the bedside lamp and stood on something that made him wince in pain and shout aloud. He reached down angrily to pick up the offending object from the floor. As he bent down, he saw a shadow move in the corner of the room, not close to him and small in stature. His hair stood up on end as fear raced through him and his animal instincts kicked in. Fight or flight? Being an arrogant bastard and quite a big man, he chose to fight and take on whoever was in the room. He moved quickly towards the shadow, expecting to send whoever it was flying onto their back with ease.

The spray came out of the dark and forced his eyelids upwards with the strength of its flow. His eyes began to burn intensely and all of the mucus glands in his face erupted into action, sending saliva and snot streaming down to the floor. The bottle smashed viciously over his head, instantly splitting his scalp wide open and causing blood to spray up the walls, the glass covering the floor and the remaining chilled white wine it had contained splashing onto the expensive carpet. *What a waste of good wine,* the attacker thought as a cut opened up like a zipper being pulled down in haste.

He tried to crawl away from the dark figure but the shards of glass cut deeply into the flesh of his knees. Suddenly he felt a clinical slicing, then an excruciating snapping sensation. The cut immobilised his trailing leg by completely severing his Achilles tendon. He screamed out loudly in agony and turned over onto his back in an attempt to get away from his pursuer using his only functioning foot for propulsion. He stared upwards and saw a face covered by a mask, he also saw his favourite cricket bat being raised up above him before it smashed down onto his unwounded foot, shattering his bones and causing even more excruciating pain. An evil cackle came from under the mask as distorted words were whispered out angrily from the mouth piece.

"You're turn now," was said in an emotionless tone, with vengeful purpose. "You're a fucking vile pig, how could you do that to them, you fucking sick bastard! They are innocents, just babies in this depraved world. Why would you? How fucking could you, you twisted fucker."

The words were rasped at him as he felt the blow hit full force on the side of his head, a second tear to his scalp now spewing more blood onto his precious carpet. Stunned and drowsy from the two massive blows to his head and the agonising effects from the CS gas still incapacitating him, he felt his wrist being gripped and pulled harshly over to meet his other one and he felt a thick hard plastic tie being pulled viciously tight, cutting into his skin. He then felt his genitals being pulled forcefully out of his zip with a gloved hand and another plastic tie was pulled tightly round them, this one much thinner. He could hear the locking grips pulling tighter, securing it. They clicked over and over as his tormentor pulled tighter and tighter, the pain becoming unbearable. He screamed loudly as his balls began to pulse like a racing heart. He looked down at them as their colour changed before his eyes and they swelled up grotesquely. His eyes watered as he gulped in short and desperate breaths, fearful of any movement that would intensify the pain or make them burst, they were now so deformed. His tethered hands, which tried to reach down in an attempt to try and free himself, were kicked away with force and determination.

The attacker slowly stood up and went to the computer where the sexual assaults had begun.

A forced deep voice boomed out to the men in the room, "Enough, that's enough, I've got to go out now, something has come up". The two men did as they were instructed. They were only doing what they were doing for the money being paid to them and if that's all they wanted for their money, it was no skin off their noses. Both stopped without hesitation, neither wanting to continue with the abuse.

The attacker walked back through to the bedroom and watched the man's futile attempts to free the now totally discoloured and deformed genitals.

"That should do," was muttered. A final sharp kick in that area and two full force stamps down onto his belly were enough to send a clear message to him and many others, regarding their poor choice of recreational activity.

Walking casually through to the living room, a calling card was placed on the coffee table. It was slightly crushed as the man had trodden on it through in the bedroom after it was dropped by the attacker by mistake.

Using the phone in the bedroom, the attacker had already dialled 999. Timing was important. A long enough time had elapsed to ensure the man's genitalia were now suitably unusable, the living tissue in his balls beginning to die, but the emergency services should arrive before the man died from his injuries and blood loss.

Chapter 6
Broken

Kay rolled over to face Taylor, who reached out her hand and stroked Kay's beautiful face. She winced in pain. Her body still ached from the damage caused by John Brennan's assault. As she recoiled, her heart also ached at the way she felt. She had been feeling this way for over a month now and although Taylor was there 100% for her, loving her, caring for her, she just couldn't seem to let go of the deep and painful memories of that fateful evening and how close she was to dying that night. Her physical scars were now the least of her problems - she was clearly mentally scarred as well from the harrowing events and unable to get back to functioning normally. She was fearful every day. Tears welled up in her eyes as she looked at the woman she loved, but who she hadn't let touch her since the night that had changed her world. Taylor hadn't faltered though. Normally sexually motivated, she had never expected anything from Kay and was well aware of how damaged her lover was. Taylor felt the tender touch of Kay's soft hand upon her face and looked up at her with tenderness, love and affection. She saw her sadness straight away, and quickly pulled herself closer to comfort her. Taylor sat up and nestled Kay in front of her, wrapping herself around her to try and make her feel safe. Kay whispered in Taylor's ear, "I love you, I genuinely love you. You've made me feel emotions, desire and many more things I would never have dreamt possible".

"I can feel a but coming on," Taylor said quietly.

"I can't do this anymore. I've tried, I've tried so hard and I just can't switch back on. I can't feel anymore, I'm numb. All I think about is him, not you, not us, not the future, no desire, no lust, no sensations at all, nothing, just nothing. I'm not coping and I don't want to hold you back, tie you down. I just need to be on my own. I need to get over this myself without feeling that I am burdening you with all of my issues. I know you were there and he hurt you too but he's still there morning, noon and night. I can smell him, hear him, see his face in my dreams. I feel him follow my every move and I can't escape him. I can't eat, I can't sleep. I need help, I'm losing my mind, I'm losing me."

Kay started shaking uncontrollably. At first Taylor didn't realise what was going on until her eyes rolled back into her head and only the whites were now visible, the convulsions violent and uncontrolled. Taylor held her head to prevent it banging on anything and waited what seemed like an age until Kay's body began to relax from the coiled, tight foetal position she was stuck. Taylor reached for her phone and dialled 999 for an ambulance. She knew Kay didn't have epilepsy and what she'd just seen appeared pretty serious. She observed Kay as she lay there, breathing heavily and unresponsive to her voice. She monitored her vital signs and was prepared to act if necessary. Taylor's heart felt heavy with Kay's words. Kay was a straight talker who spoke from the heart. She had meant it when she said she wanted to be alone. This hurt, it was something Taylor hadn't felt before. She had never been truly in love with someone and she still felt guilty for her infidelity. She knew Kay deserved better but for the first time ever she was in love and ready to give this relationship a go.

The paramedics arrived quickly and got to work straightaway. Kay was put swiftly into the ambulance and Taylor jumped in with her. She held on to Kay's limp hand as they sped to hospital. Kay remained unconscious all the way. The doctors met her on arrival and rushed her to the resuscitation room. Taylor could not believe what she was seeing, the words she had heard and the devastation that one man had caused for so many.

Taylor opened Kay's phone and thumbed down until she found her mum's number and dialled it. Her mother answered as Taylor spoke, "Who's this, is that you Kay?"

"No, no, it's a friend of hers, it's Taylor, I work with her."

"Oh, how can I help you, is it Kay, is she all right?"

"I'm at the Edinburgh Royal Infirmary, Kay's been admitted. She's had some sort of seizure and she's been taken through to immediate care at the moment. Can you come to the hospital to be with her?"

"Yes, yes, of course. I'll come up straight away. Who found her, where was she when she fell ill, was she at work?"

"No, she was at home. She hasn't been at work for some time now, I'm afraid."

"Really? She told me she was back at work and that things were getting better and that she was getting back to her normal self."

"Oh, is that what she told you?"

"Why? Do you know differently?" her mother quizzed.

"Yes, yes I do. She's not doing very well at all. Unfortunately, she is still suffering badly and I think she needs help, professional help, psychiatric help."

"Oh, okay, I'll speak to her. How did you say you found her again, were you visiting her?"

"Yeh, yes, just visiting when she took a bad turn. How quickly can you get here? She needs you."

The phone clicked off and Taylor went over to the desk to ask about Kay. She was told tests were being carried out and that Kay was sedated and wouldn't be awake for a while. Her life wasn't in danger and they would keep Taylor updated.

Taylor hated hospitals. She spent many of her working hours here and not many visits were pleasant, or had a happy ending.

She turned on her heels and was about to sit down and wait with Kay when her phone rang.

"Hello," she said abruptly and with audible annoyance.

"We've got another one!" Marcus's voice boomed down the phone, clearly a little excited that something big was now on the horizon, or so it seemed.

"Can you get here, when can you get here?" he asked with unbridled enthusiasm.

With sadness in her heart, and aware that Kay's mother was going to be there soon, she replied reluctantly, "20 minutes, I'll be there in about 20 minutes, don't leave without me, Marcus," knowing he was anxious get on with the investigation, walk the crime scene and see what all the buzz was about.

Chapter 7
Saviours

Going back 22 years

"POLICE, POLICE, open the door! POLICE, open the door or we will break it down. We have a warrant, we have power to enter your premises, and we will. Open the door."

There were sounds of scurrying around and a chilling squeal from a child inside. Megan had barged past Amy with such force it sent the little girl flying off her feet and into the wall, striking it with force. Nathan kept back out of the way, until he could get to his sister safely and help her. He shouted to the police outside, "Help us, help us, please get in here quickly". Amy was struggling to breathe, the air had been pushed so violently from her lungs and pain seared through her. Megan's bottom wriggled and wobbled in comedic manner, as her overweight frame tried to squeeze into the void under the sink, which appeared impossible at first glance. Seconds later the door was hammered by the huge public order officer, sending it crashing up against the wall.

"POLICE, POLICE," was again shouted loudly as they entered the disgusting house.

"Hey, watch out guys, there are a couple of kids up the hall. Get the medic up here too. Right now!"

The first two pairs of public order officers rushed past the children and into the rooms beyond, and a further two pairs rushed up the stairs to cover the remaining rooms and negate any danger that could come from within them. Next in were the public protection officers, who quickly knelt down beside the children to take care of them. Nathan rose up from his kneeling position and faced up to them, eyes wild and feral, animal instincts kicking in to protect his injured sister from these unknown strangers, his mistrust of adults ingrained in him since birth. He lunged violently at the first female officer, not trusting anyone. He tried to scratch at her face and got hold of her hair, pulling it as hard as he could. The officer winced as her head was jerked to the side. A reaction like this was unfortunately not that uncommon. She gripped his hand and pushed it down on her head with enough force to spread his fingers out like a cat claw, making him release his grip. She kept hold of his hand and ducked to avoid the other that came swinging round balled in a fist to try and punch her straight in the face. She took hold of both his little arms and wrapped them round the front of his body and held him with enough force to control him but with the minimum force necessary to contain him and attempted to comfort him. The other officer knelt down beside the little girl lying there, still gasping for breath on the floor. Both children were clearly emaciated and unwashed for months, possibly years.

The female officer holding Nathan spoke to him in a calm, gentle and caring voice and said, "Relax young man, we're here to help you. We're here to help you both. We need you to help us now, we need to help your sister, help us help your sister. What's her name?"

He screamed out and struggled so violently he nearly broke free. "Leave her alone, leave Amy. Don't you fucking touch her you fucking bitch. I'll look after her, let me go, let me fucking go you fucking fat slag, you fucking ugly cow, fuck off, fuck off, let me fucking go or I'll hurt you so fucking bad."

Although his speech was still childlike, and some words weren't pronounced correctly, the tirade of abuse, with the venom and level of aggression shown was a shock even for them. She pulled him closer once again. Tears were rolling down his young cheeks now and his anger was changing to sadness, highlighting the vulnerable little five-year-old boy that he was. The tension in his skeletal frame began to release and his sobs were audible and getting louder. The officer holding him changed her grip to more of a hug and she spoke softly to him.

"We're here, we're here now, to help you, help you and your little sister. It is your sister, isn't it?"

He twisted his head round to look at her, his big sad eyes stared at her as he nodded to her.

"That's Amy, I look after her, she needs me. Is she alright, will she be alright?"

The paramedic came through the door and had to squeeze in beside everyone, getting close enough to take a look at Amy, who was lying in pain on the floor. The officer shuffled backwards still holding Nathan in her arms on her lap.

"SUPPORT," was shouted out by the public order officers in the kitchen, "SUPPORT".

Officers came rushing through from the other rooms that had already been cleared within the two-storey flat. The officers in the kitchen had pulled out a very overweight woman from a cupboard under the sink and she had turned quickly towards them holding a knife. Lashing out at them violently, her teeth gritted together, she rasped obscenities, saliva spraying out of her disgusting mouth filled with decaying teeth.

"Get the fuck away from me or I'll fucking stab you, ya cunts, and ye better no touch ma fucking bairns. What are you fuckers doin' in ma fucking hoose anyway, fucking scummy wankers, cunts, fucking bastards."

She lunged forward stabbing out at the officers. The knife cut through the boiler suit of one and sliced into the pads beneath. She was manhandled to the floor by the front two officers with a combined weight of at least 50 stone, and was forced to release her grip on the knife. Handcuffs were jammed on to her wrists, her stubby arms stretching to meet one another behind her back as she still tried with all her might to fight the police.

"You are detained under Section 14 of the Criminal Procedures Scotland Act 1995 for suspicion of abduction. You are not obliged to say anything but anything you do say will be noted and may be used in evidence. Do you understand this caution, do you want to make any reply to this caution?" The officer that stood in front of her carried on to read more of the procedure to Megan, who was now in a sitting position.

"Fucking reply, I'll fucking kick your bollocks off, you fucking prick. Let me fucking go, I know ma rights, ya fucking arsehole, and how the fuck can I abduct ma own fucking kids, ya stupid wee prick?" The words rattled out from her depraved mouth like bullets from a machine gun.

"Lovely," the officer said as he smiled at his colleague, unaffected by the tirade of abuse that hadn't stopped since she was discovered jammed under the sink. Both raised their eyebrows at each other at the choice words they heard frequently, a total lack of respect regularly shown by the worthies of the area, through indoctrinated hatred of authority of any kind taught from birth. The dark humour that the cops shared always allowed them the release from reality required to prevent anything affecting them.

The paramedics provided medical care for Amy, the day's injury being the least of her problems.

The children were taken out of the house, Amy on a trolley chair and Nathan carried by the officer who he had tried to attack initially but was now clinging to and not wanting to let go. He allowed her to hold him like a mother would hold a child. He could feel her kindness and warmth and for the first time in his short little life he became sadly aware of how things should have been for him and his sister.

The detaining officers left holding on tightly to their prisoner, with another two for back up just in case. The others remained to search the remainder of the house, a house that displayed a severe lack of hygiene and signs of obvious cruelty. What appeared to be the children's room sent shivers down the spines of the most hardened officers. Blood, semen, vomit, rotten food, a couple of baby teeth, urine and faecal matter soiled the floor. A thin mattress with clothing for pillows and unrecognisable bedding, stained dark brown, had not been washed for years if at all. The mother's room was no better, a vision of a chaotic and depraved life. The children had never been out of the house by the looks of it, it was a miracle that they were still alive. The tip-off had come to the police from a family who lived nearby. The child had been given a telescope for his birthday and had used it regularly to watch through all of the windows in the houses and flats nearby. One day he had spotted Nathan in the afternoon and could see that he was bleeding from his face. He had run to tell his mum and she looked through the lens, giving her son a row at the time for being nosey, only to see, even at a distance, a man come up behind the little boy and take hold of his hair and yank him back away from the window with obvious force. She called the police immediately and further enquiry into the address pointed out by the boy and his mother, revealed enough concern to carry out an immediate raid on the premises as there was no record of any children living or registered there.

As the cops were ready to escort Amy and Nathan, and Megan Thomson, Natt Spears had waddled round the corner lethargically and breathless from the bookies. He stopped dead in his tracks when he saw the large presence of police vehicles outside his block of flats. He turned round immediately and walked as briskly as his fat, slob-like frame would allow.

Nathan wanted to travel in the ambulance with his sister but she was still not responding well and they didn't want him to see what the paramedics were doing in case he thought they were hurting her. The police officer and Nathan sat up front, the little boy blinking hard in the bright sunlight. He was excited to be traveling in the front of the ambulance but he was also distracted by the separation from his sister.

The ambulance bounced gently over the speed bumps down towards Niddrie Mains Road, the main road into the centre of town and off towards the Sick Kids Hospital. Nathan was staring out to the front, gripping the seat, leaning forward as much as the seatbelt would allow waggling his feet back and forward like a normal little boy. Suddenly, he froze, eyes focussed on the rotund male on the pavement moving away from where they had been. He was wearing a stained vest and soiled trousers hung heavily on the damaged belt below his grotesquely sagging gut. The officer moved up off the seat as she felt a warm wet sensation seeping through her jeans. Immediately she asked the little boy what was wrong. The boy pointed at the man on the opposite pavement and started shaking uncontrollably as tears flowed down his dirty cheeks.

"That's my stepdad," was whispered tearfully from his lips as he laid himself as flat as he could into the officer's lap. "Don't let him get us, please keep him away, please, he hurts us, he really hurts us!"

The officer's radio crackled and her words were clear and concise, "Outstanding male, south pavement, heading east on Niddrie Mains Road, filthy vest, brown trousers, overweight, late twenties, dark greasy hair, this is a hurry up, there are plenty of buses coming, don't let this one go, I think it's the outstanding suspect."

Within seconds three squad cars screeched to a halt beside the man and took hold of him. He tried to act casual and completely unaware of why he had been stopped. Without hesitation, he was detained and taken into custody for questioning. He did not fight. He was a coward and did not want to be hurt. He was cruel and evil but, unlike Megan, would avoid any reciprocated pain.

Medical examinations revealed both children were badly malnourished. Numerous old and new injuries, untreated fractures and sexual trauma were found. These had been painfully obvious to the medical examiner even before a full internal exploration was carried out.

Both accused were given substantial custodial sentences for their part in the systematic torture, sexual abuse, neglect and imprisonment of Megan's two young children, and Amy and Nathan were placed into the care system.

Chapter 8
Unfinished Business

Months had passed at work and there were no leads coming from their enquiries into the two brutal assaults barely a week apart. Kay had not contacted Taylor at all and, as she had said, she was true to her word that she wanted to be alone. She was now receiving in-patient care at an appropriate hospital. Days went by, hard days at work, all a little disappointing for all involved, full of frustration and false leads.

Fran Andrews was packing her bag to head for the gym. She was one of Taylor's team that had hunted the serial killer Brennan and was also unfortunate enough to have been seriously assaulted and sexually violated by him too. She had had an elicit highly charged sexual encounter with Taylor, her boss, whilst on that enquiry, and couldn't get it out of her head. It spun with thoughts of the pleasure and excitement shared with Taylor that night, and then moments later, the opposite, the pain and degradation forced upon her, the vile torture she endured at the hands of that monster Brennan and the recurring nightmares she faced daily since that fateful night. There was also the longing for Taylor, a constant temptation for her.

Taylor pounded the treadmill at the gym near to Newhaven harbour, her toned body laced with beaded sweat, her heart heavy and her head going over and over that night when Kay was assaulted and abused, her infidelity with Fran and renewed pressure at work with this new case. She gritted her teeth and ran even faster, her wavy dark hair held in a ponytail wet with sweat swishing back and forth slapping off her back. She also felt the burden of true loss. Kay was withdrawing from her, closing the door on her and society. She was finding it hard to accept and adjust to what she had endured and barely survived. Taylor knew Kay had meant what she had said and that she really did want to be alone. Her frame rippled with toned slender muscles, her taut abs visible beneath her cropped top. Many within the gym glanced over at her, some for how she looked, but more because of the speed she was now running and the sheer focus etched on her face as she hurtled forward on and on without pausing for breath. Her steps grew heavier and heavier and the gym instructor started to move towards her as he sensed something wasn't quite right. Taylor's vision began to blur and she blinked hard as if to snap out of a trance like state. She could barely breathe because she'd pushed herself so hard without realising it. She quickly leaned forward to push the button to reduce the speed of the running machine and her finger was met with that of the instructor's who was also taking steps to slow her down and stop her passing out. Her legs wobbled and as the belt slowed down the instructor put his arm round her waist to steady her as her legs buckled beneath her. He lowered her to her knees. She heaved in air, her diaphragm nearly popping as she gasped to get enough. She fought hard not to faint and could not believe she had got herself into this state in the first place. Once her head stopped spinning, she quickly stood up and tried to reduce the attention that the other gym users were giving her. She moved to a seat in the corner and was brought a cup of water, which she gulped down so quickly she was nearly sick.

"I'm fine, I'm fine, please leave me, I'll be okay, I just over did it a bit, I don't know what I was thinking."

She put her head in her hands and shut her eyes, trying to hide that she was holding back tears, trying her hardest not to break down and cry, not publicly anyway.

When Taylor eventually lifted her head and looked around, she saw Fran entering the gym. Fran was still off work with stress as she tried to fully recover from her ordeal at the hands of Brennan. Her toned figure, covered in tight fitting gym wear, glided into the gym, long dark hair down her back, with a small towel over her shoulder. Gleaming eyes and perfect pearly white teeth obvious, she politely acknowledged other regulars in the gym, not yet noticing Taylor's eyes watching her every move. Taylor hadn't seen Fran since the night of the incident, mostly due to the guilt she felt for her infidelity and the severity of Kay's injuries, as well as the unexplored feelings she may or may not have for Fran, who had made it clear what she felt for Taylor.

Fran climbed onto the treadmill and started to walk. Only then did she feel the sensation of being watched. She turned her head expecting to find some musclebound male checking her out, only to find Taylor's beautiful brown eyes totally focussed on her with a predator's stare, but also with longing and desire. Their eyes met and a mutual affection was obvious as they offered each other polite gestures of hello. Taylor rose from her seat and walked over to Fran who continued to walk trying to keep looking forward. She knew how she felt about Taylor and she had felt that their encounter had been more than just sexual. There had been definite emotion and feeling but she didn't think that anything else would ever happen.

She felt a presence and almost jumped as Taylor appeared beside her. She stopped the treadmill and said, "Hi, long time no see stranger?"

"I know, I'm really sorry, I couldn't with Kay being so ill," Taylor replied sheepishly.

"You could have. You chose not to but that's okay, I do understand you know. It would have been nice though," Fran replied with a hint of resentment.

"How are you, how have you been? I did think about you, you know. I can't believe he got us all, that savage prick."

"I'm fine. How are you? How's Kay doing? She's still in a really bad way, I heard?" Fran asked with genuine concern.

"Not good. She's not coping at all, she's been taken in to hospital." Taylor explained with sadness in her eyes. "She's had a nervous breakdown and she's really ill. She's so very broken," Taylor was now losing it a little herself. She cut the conversation off abruptly, afraid she would start to cry and walked off towards the changing rooms.

Taylor was still upset and sweating profusely as she stuffed her things into her bag. She swung it carelessly over her shoulder. Luckily, she was the only one in the open plan changing area and was on her way out of the double doors when Fran came in the other door from the gym.

Taylor stopped dead in her tracks and turned and stared straight into Fran's beautiful eyes, which were filled with sadness, confusion and true affection. Fran moved over to where she stood and reached for Taylor's hand, slipping it into hers and gently moving it hoping Taylor would respond. Taylor's hand stayed motionless and Fran's heart sank a little until she felt a subtle and caring squeeze, then her hand was gently held by Taylor's strong firm hands in return. There were now tears in Taylor's eyes as she finally gave into the strain she too had been under over these last months. Her shoulders started to heave up and down and her sobs were obvious, Fran pulled her round close to her and held her, held her tight and watched as the strongest woman she had ever known broke down in tears, weeping in her arms. Taylor allowed herself to be held long enough to get herself together and then declared that she'd have to go, a self-preservation mechanism inbuilt in her. Taylor was unsettled, unsure of everything. She still wanted Kay, she loved Kay, but Kay was clearly not in the right place and couldn't cope with life at the moment. She had made it clear that Taylor was not in her recovery plan.

"I've got to go, I really do Fran. Thanks though. I'm sorry, really sorry for everything. Take care of yourself," Taylor moved off, back towards the door as their hands slipped apart. Taylor's heart was sore with indecision and guilt. The door closed behind her and Fran stared at the empty space as she left.

Chapter 9
The New Boss,
DCI Sommerville

Brooke Sommerville strode into the building, head held high, uniform pristine, shoes highly polished, the three pips on her shoulders shining brightly as she walked up to reception and greeted the security officers, before making her way up the stairs to her new office. She had been sent to take charge of the Major Investigation team to take the lead on their current investigation, as it wasn't deemed to being going too well and there was a lot of public interest. She was a strong woman, tall, attractive, her mere presence and aura of control commanding respect. She had been in the police many years, gaining a vast amount of experience, and was well thought of by her colleagues.

She pushed open the door that lead into the open plan office and everything seemed to stop. Heads turned towards her and the gentle hum of conversation died. All eyes were on her as she gestured a respectful hello to everyone in the office.

Findlay came waddling out of his room, scratching his belly, to see why the place had gone so quiet. He was dishevelled and slovenly-looking as always, sugar on his top lip from eating yet another doughnut. His eyes nearly popped out of his head when he saw DCI Sommerville. He hadn't been told about this new move. His department had always been remotely supervised and they had never had a Chief Inspector work alongside them before. She approached him and held out her hand. Becoming instantly aware of the pudgy clamminess and general uncleanliness of his, she just managed to stop herself showing the revulsion she felt by abruptly ending the handshake.

"I'm Chief Inspector Brooke Sommerville. I've been moved here on a temporary basis to oversee the current investigation in relation to the revenge attacks. It's drawing a lot of public attention and it's all over the press so I'm here to offer a little more direction, control and advice when needed, that's all," she said. She was not power hungry and there to make her mark, she was there to review everything that had been done and see if there were any more openings that may have been missed that could be investigated more thoroughly.

Findlay closed his mouth, which was still hanging open, its internal contents still visible and simply stared at her. "They never told me that you were coming. Do you have an office to move into?" he asked, a little nervous that he would be sharing with her, his worst nightmare, which he knew would reveal his obvious failings.

"Apparently we're to share yours Martin, for the time being that is. You don't mind do you?" she said with a hint of enjoyment. It was well known and clear that he was the issue because the rest of the team beneath him had a good reputation.

"Where's Sergeant Nicks, I'd like to meet her. Is she here?" she said questioningly.

"Eh, no, eh, oh I don't actually know. Marcus, Marcus, come here a minute, where's Taylor today, is she out on a call?" .

"No, I don't think so. I don't think she's been in today boss, I've not seen her," Marcus said with a wry smile because he had been caught out. He hadn't even checked who was in, not that it was his job to do so. "This isn't like her, she would normally call if there was an issue". This wasn't normal for her, she wasn't usually late, and today of all days.

Findlay squirmed in his shoes. He just turned up for work and Taylor would normally sort everything out for him, although it was really his duty. Taylor was the one who made sure everything was taken care of.

Sommerville looked at him. Her eyes said everything. She had come there aware of why she was being transferred. It was clear Findlay wasn't pulling his weight and she was going to change that. She was also aware of Taylor's ability and her good reputation. Taylor was well known in the force and very popular amongst her peers. She was beautiful, strong and funny, and liked for many reasons.

"I'll need a chair Martin and I'll take the extra desk in the corner if you don't mind," the DCI requested. Findlay shrugged his shoulders, lamely floating his arm out as if to say on you go, knowing he didn't have a choice, and shuffled off to requisition a chair. Once back Findlay put down the chair and Sommerville moved over to take the best chair of the two, wheeling it through to her new temporary office. Everyone watched, a little apprehensive but also secretly pleased that their incompetent boss was going to get found out, get his comeuppance and have to answer for his failings. At the very least, they would be seen for how effective they were as a team.

Chapter 10
Just Let It Happen.

The doorbell rang out loudly into the still and silent night. Her hand was shaking as her finger dropped down from the door, a little worried she had got the wrong address. The night was cold and her presence was hidden from the street by shrubbery and trees. She made a mental note to mention that this house would be easy to break into without being seen.

Her heart jumped and started to pound through her chest when she realised how late it was as she moved to answer the door. *What the fuck? Who would be coming to the door at this time of night?* She thought about just ignoring it and had stopped moving but her police head was curious to see who it was and what they wanted. Slightly irked at the inconsideration of this uninvited visitor, she hesitated again as she got closer to the door. Her breathing changed as she had a flash back to the attack at the hands of the sadistic and evil Brennan. Hairs on her body stood to attention at the hideous sensation of being gripped with fear in her own home, all because a late caller had rung her doorbell, fear she never even considered could be possible, to her anyway. *"Fuck you, I'm not scared of you, not everything in this world can be that messed up."*

Fran grabbed the handle of the door and the lock simultaneously and then stopped, standing still as a stone. She felt sick and almost unable to move. Fumbling with the chain, she slid it on and spoke quietly as she asked, trying to sound confident, "Who is it, who's there?"

Silence. The visitor stood there and swallowed hard, totally unaware of the terror that they were causing to the person just inside the door. The visitor was also shaking for a totally different reason. They were fighting their own demons and emotions, avoiding what they thought was right or wrong, trying to block out what they had wanted since a shared encounter on a night that was so wrong on many levels, but too exciting to ignore.

The door opened a little, just enough to see a tall woman with her back turned. Fran's heart remained at a heightened speed but this was no longer with fear. She recognised the broad shoulders and the long brown wavy hair cascading down. Taylor heard the door close again and she turned quickly to stop it but it reopened, once the chain had been removed. Fran stood in the doorway in her nightwear, dressing gown tied. Taylor's hand landed on her stomach accidentally, as she reached for the door.

"Oh shit, sorry," Fran didn't speak or acknowledge that Taylor had pushed her a little. She just took hold of the back of Taylor's head and kissed her, her mouth open and desperately needing Taylor's kiss, tiptoeing up to the same height. A moment ago she was terrified, almost to the point of insane fear, now she was kissing the woman she had wanted for months. Taylor responded with equal desire, all her questions of whether she should have come here were answered in the kiss. The lust-filled encounter she had shared with Fran had clearly meant a little more than that to both of them. Their kiss lit them up inside. Fran's kisses were deep and sensual, her mouth open and needy, telling Taylor how much she wanted her, how much she had thought about her since the night they had shared a mutual appreciation for each other. Taylor pushed Fran with gentle pressure back through the door into the warm house, backwards all the way through to what she hoped would be the living room, making sure she didn't fall over. The fire was on and the room was lit with a warm and inviting glow as she lowered Fran onto the sofa. Taylor lay softly on top of her as their kiss continued, their mouths had never left each other since they stood at the doorway. Fran's breath was coming in short and lust filled gasps. She had desired Taylor for some time now and just wanted her to make love to her again. She took hold of Taylor's hand and pushed it down into her pyjama bottoms. Taylor stopped to undo the ties to allow her hand a little more freedom to get to where she needed to go and to do what she wanted to please Fran. Fran pushed Taylor's hand further down, impatient at the pause and only when Taylor's fingers reached Fran's wet pussy did she realise just how much Fran wanted her. Her fingers slid easily over her and deep into her; she was soaking wet with her lust for Taylor and her sex was very obvious to feel. Taylor moaned in time with Fran as her knees curled up with the sensation of touch, the tingling sensation already there, total arousal at the intrusion of Taylor's long strong fingers inside her, her fear, her desire spilling over. Taylor now aware of how aroused Fran was used this to plunge deep into her with her fingers, to avoid a desperate quick orgasm, spoiling what could be even better. She pleasured her deep and steadily allowing the tingling sensation to abate and Fran a little time to gain some composure to build this into the most deep and sensual, lust-filled orgasm she had ever felt. Her pussy pulsed around Taylor's fingers, gripping her with its power. The delight of the pulsing sensation made Fran laugh out loud as she gripped Taylor's shoulders tightly and kissed her face all over.

"God I want you. How do you know how to do that? That was fucking intense, I thought I was going to explode, I've never felt anything that good, ever!"

Taylor gently pulled Fran up until she was sitting on her tummy. Fran smiled at her and got on her knees, positioning herself so she was fully exposed, just above Taylor's face. Taylor licked her gently and then slowly over her clitoris. Fran nearly jumped through the roof with the sensation that was still throbbing from the last orgasm, too sensitive to go there yet. She had to push her hand down on Taylor's forehead to stop her licking her, but Taylor knew exactly what she was doing and what it felt like and she wanted Fran to feel that way. She moved off a little and stroked over Fran's sexy little bottom, stroking and gripping her pert cheeks. Her hands moved up Fran's back continuing their sensual trail. Fran moved with Taylor's hands enjoying her firm touch. She positioned herself over Taylor's mouth once again, this time raising herself up to invite her hands as well. Taylor lifted her head and stroked Fran's needy pussy with her tongue. This time the sensation was wonderful, a beautiful swirling and tempting feeling. Taylor lapped over her firmly from back to front, her tongue gently delving into her as she moved back and forward. She gripped Fran's bottom hard and pulled her down onto her face, moving her forward to push her fingers right inside her. Taylor's hand moved to the front and pulled down on a nipple sharply enough for Fran to whimper a little, causing her to push down hard onto Taylor's fingers, which went so deep that Fran moaned with pure pleasure, leaning her head forward onto the pillow above Taylor's head, her hair flowing over her face. Taylor's fingers worked inside her, pushing in time with her well-practised tongue. Fran's body moved up and down with them, pushing down hard every so often when the sensitivity became unbearable. Fran couldn't hold on any longer. Taylor continued to fuck her deeply, now sucking hard on her stiff nipples as Fran came hard, Taylor's mouth savouring the taste of Fran's sweet pleasure. Fran lowered herself down on top of Taylor, their soft silky skin touching, Fran's taught nipples brushing Taylor's. Their kiss was intense. Fran kept kissing Taylor and their eyes met. Fran smiled at her.

"I want to touch you, I want to taste you, god I just want you, every little bit of you," she whispered to Taylor.

Fran gazed upon Taylor's almost perfect body, her tanned, toned physique totally exposed right in front of her. She had dreamt of this moment many times since their last encounter in the lift. She kissed her naval, kissed and licked her breasts focussing on her nipples. She kissed Taylor's mouth tenderly, her tongue subtle and arousing. Fran touched Taylor tentatively at first, but when her fingers slipped into her, she knew how excited Taylor was, her need just as raw as Fran's. Fran was not inexperienced but was a little nervous at making love to someone like Taylor, who was so strong and confident and utterly stunning. Taylor licked her lips as Fran's hand stroked over her, her touch firm and tender. She definitely knew what she was doing. She kept moving with Taylor who lifted up to Fran's fingers. Fran pushed into her and kept on stroking until she came, her orgasm quick and powerful, something Taylor hadn't realised she had needed so much for so long. The second time was more luxurious, less tense and very tender and loving, Fran taking her into her mouth savouring every second of making love to Taylor. They both sighed, lying back on the pillows. Fran rose up onto one elbow and stared at Taylor with a big smile on her face. "God, you're one hot lady", she said.

"Fancy a glass of wine?" Fran smiled at Taylor.

"Yes, that would be really nice," her smile was broad and adoring as she watched Fran's nimble little body slip out of the room.

"Wow," Taylor exclaimed and lay back on the pillow her heart still pounding.

Chapter 11
Amy

The razor blade cut through her skin like a knife through butter, again and again and again, thin stripes of crimson red blood oozed from each slender incision. She winced every time the blade sliced her but each cut seemed to ease her pain, just a little though, never enough to take her inner pain away, so she cut more and more until the tension was gone, for now anyway.

She tried so desperately to enjoy Kerr's loving touch but no matter how caring and tender he was with her, every nerve deep inside her body recoiled against his touch, every touch like a flame against her skin. She knew he truly loved her and she did feel something for him, because all he had ever shown her was kindness, tenderness and genuine affection. Unfortunately, he still wanted to touch her and make love to her and this made her insides twist into a sickening knot, every vile memory of the abuse she suffered at the hands of those monsters stabbed violently into her. His masculine scent invaded her senses, not unclean, but still infiltrating her system like poisonous gas.

She had already scrubbed and scrubbed herself in the shower, her skin red and sore with weeping abrasions, and when she looked down at the sea of red covering her feet she got angry at what she could do to herself, the cuts reacting to the heat of the water and bleeding even more. Tears rolled down her cheeks as she begged to be set free, released from the constant reminder of her tortured childhood. She was frightened to leave Kerr and she was frightened to stay with him in case her emotions ran too high to be able to sort herself out. Kerr tried his hardest to help. She had been with him for nearly two years. He had pursued her relentlessly and treated her like a lady at all times but he was totally unaware of the true nature and reasons for her inner torture that she had to endure every single day. He had never seen her bare arms. He respected her so he never pushed the issue that she wore long sleeves even in bed and she never showered in front of him either.

She pulled the bandage tightly round her forearms, a routine she had become an expert at. She had smothered the cuts with antiseptic cream hoping to avoid any infection because the last one had to be treated with antibiotics.

"Are you okay Amy, you've been in there for ages, is everything alright?"

"I'm fine, fine, really, I'll be out in a minute!" Amy replied calmly, avoiding any alarm in Kerr as she didn't want him to feel he needed to come in.

When she finally came out, Kerr kissed her tenderly on the mouth. She nearly vomited. She had only just managed to erase their lovemaking from before, only for him to still want her.

She held down whatever had wanted to come up and gently pushed him away and said, "Come on Kerr, not now, I'm really tired, please."

He did as he was asked, a little sad at the constant rejection he felt. He didn't really understand and did not realise that every time he made love to her, she had a very intense and thorough cleaning ritual afterwards. He got mixed messages from her all the time. They had just made love and Amy was wild throughout, with what he thought was passion but in reality she responded irrationally as every demon within her resisted any pleasure and what he thought was passion was twisted fear and aggression masked in animated love making.

"I need to go out for a bit, I need some fresh air, you don't mind do you? You know I don't like being cooped up too long," she said in her usual meek and convincing manner. Kerr just stepped aside as Amy put on her coat and left the house.

"Be careful out there, it's dark," but he wasn't really worried about her because she did this regularly and he understood that she needed her space.

Chapter 12
Nathan

Nathan lifted her up into his arms, his gorgeous little two-year-old daughter Millie, who smiled and giggled as he threw her carefully into the air. He adored every bit of her and treated her like a glass princess, the exact opposite of his upbringing. His life was good now and he had managed to put the past into a box, at least he thought he had!

Now there were all these recent assaults taking place in the city. He had watched the news with heightened, almost obsessive interest, as the newsreader left out the specifics but gave enough information to read between the lines as to why the victims may have been assaulted, facts that he knew. He smiled when he heard the assaults had been extremely vicious and physically damaging to the victims.

"Sounds like they got what they deserved to me!" he had said so that Jen could see he had an opinion on the crimes, rather than to appear to be saying nothing about them.

His wife Jen came out from the house and smiled at them both as she watched them play lovingly in the garden. Nathan was a slight man, not overly tall, but strong and very capable. He cuddled wee Millie as they walked towards Jen, hugging her tightly and with deep affection, wanting to protect every hair on her innocent little head.

"You two look very happy, what have you been up to?" she quizzed them with a loving smile.

"Tell mummy what we've been doing then, tell her," he said nudging Millie and giggling along with her as she pulled out her cuddly toy from behind her back, wiggled it in front of her mummy and hid it again but didn't speak.

"Cutie, it's time for bed," Jen tickled Millie until she wriggled and giggled again and then sat down in the garden and continued to watch them play, her heart filled with happiness at their perfect lives.

Nathan smiled back at Jen. He loved her with all his heart. He turned away again to play with Millie, his eyes narrowing as his mind hurtled back to the thoughts of those brutal assaults, such cruel and personal crimes, degrading and vicious. He smiled to himself.

Nathan winced. It was like a sharp steely rod piercing through his heart. Tingling sensations filled his body in a hideous way, as his mind flashed vividly back to his childhood. The box he had kept tightly shut had spilled open like lava freed from a volcano, burning him deep inside. Memories of the pain he had suffered at the hands of his mother and her partner when he was so very young, came rushing back to him. He remembered all of the fear and cruelty once again and the depraved brutality that he had suffered time and time again at the hands of those two deviants, those who were supposed to protect him and his twin sister.

Suddenly, his mind flashed back violently to the dank, stale, filthy room where he had once lived. *A sister. Sister, sister, sister. My sister, I had a sister. Amy. Amy. Where is she, why have I never thought of her before now, why?* He had been so traumatised as a boy and had failed to adjust after the authorities felt that they had no option other than to separate the siblings, not realising the bond they shared, one of kindness and affection, nothing more sinister than that. Due to the nature of their abuse, social services feared this may affect their relationship negatively and feared further abuse, so they felt separation was the only option. They didn't realise the detrimental effect it would have on one or both of them, forever.

"Are you okay Nathan, you look like you've seen a ghost?" Jen came up to him and put her arm around his neck. Even Millie had taken hold of his cheeks and was trying to get him to focus back on her and their little game.

"What is it Daddy, what's wrong Daddy?" He hugged her again and tried to shake off the feeling of helpless terror. *I'm a man now, they can't harm me now, they can't. I need to find Amy. Where is she, what have they done to her, what's happened to her, where is she?*

"I'm fine Jen, I just need to go for a walk, I need to clear my head." Nathan pulled away gently from her and handed little Millie over. "Night, night sweetheart," he kissed them tenderly before he left.

Jen held his hand tightly. "Whatever this is, Nathan, we need talk about it. I'm a good listener. We love you and we need you here. We can sort it whatever it is, as a family, d'you hear me?" Her eyes pleaded with him, her face filled with concern for him. This was not normal behaviour for him.

"Don't keep disappearing on me Nathan. It keeps happening lately, don't shut me out. Stay! Please don't go, I don't even know where you go. Where do you go?"

"I just need a walk, I need time to think, and I'm sorry, really sorry but I don't think you could sort this."

Chapter 13
Out Into the Darkness

Footsteps moved gently on the pavement and an overcoat was pulled tightly at the waist. The figure moved slowly up the road, heart pounding, walking briskly and silently up the quiet street. This wasn't meant to happen quite so soon. The usual research to make sure it was going to be safe hadn't been done, but the burn tonight was too fierce to ignore and much worse than it had ever been before. A little fear crept into their thoughts, because, this was the first time they had acted on impulse, emotion and anger. There was a lack of control in relation to this visit, rage and torment twisting in their gut, an insatiable desire to punish the next victim for their unpunished crimes.

The night was still and you could hear a pin drop, breath was visible in the air as the figure moved briskly through the dark and quiet streets. There was very little traffic about, just a lone figure with a head full of thoughts of revenge and retribution. The night seemed to consume the person, swallowing them in their dark thoughts. They moved faster and faster, heading down into the Blackford area of Edinburgh, wealth and social status oozing from the many gated properties standing grandly in the street lights. They moved directly to the chosen address, that of a high powered pillar of the community. Their heart pounded and the sweat became visible on their palms, every instinct alive, hair bristling at the danger ahead, senses heightened as they stopped at the gate. The pathway was long and luxurious, you could almost smell the money. Three luxury cars adorned the crescent-shaped driveway, all matching in colour, a different one for each occasion and all top of the range. They moved quickly and quietly into the garden, careful not to walk on the gravel. Not a sound was made, the only evidence their footsteps in the dew. Their hand gripped their tools tightly through fear and for security, all the tricks of the trade they had learnt in children's homes had come in very handy lately.

The intruder was so busy trying to secrete themselves within the garden in order to get the upper hand, to allow them to break in, that they were totally unaware that they were being watched from the moment they had entered the garden. The home owner had been outside about to light a cigar and had watched the slight figure move stealthily over the grass. The man had almost laughed out loud at the audacity of the intruder, before he moved off out of sight. He was a twisted individual with an overrated opinion of himself and reckoned he could handle this little problem in his garden himself. He was also reluctant to invite the police anywhere near to his house given his background and current recreational activity.

The intruder reached the back door and looked through the window to see if there was movement inside, silent and professional.

Suddenly their head rocked forward with brute force, whipping back again as it hit off the window. The punch had slammed onto the back of their head, knocking them straight to the ground. The man reached down, grabbed a fistful of hair and dragged the intruder backwards into the house, feet barely touching the floor. The door was slammed behind them, sending terror spiralling through the intruder. The roles were now completely reversed. This wasn't part of the plan.

The night's events were not panning out quite as expected and regret now filled the intruder's mind at the stupidity of the spontaneous visit, real fear rising for the first time since their reign of terror had begun, a terror that they believed was their right.

The man stared down at what he thought was a pathetic individual and said loudly "What the fuck do you think you're doing on my fucking property, you thieving little git? Did you think I'd let you fucking get away with it, you sorry little freak? You're going to fucking regret this!"

He leant over and slammed another punch into their face and reached his hand down into their top, trying to establish who had tried to break into his property.

"Who the fuck are you? Take that fucking scarf off your face before I fucking tear it off."

His hands groped around and sickness filled the intruder's stomach, adrenaline flooding every inch of their body. The terror once endured lay bare faced in front of them once again, only this time the intruder was no longer a child. Emotions and sensations filled their body with an unbelievable will to survive, attack, and avenge the demons of their childhood.

"I don't give a fuck what you are anyway. You come into my home uninvited, you will get everything there is on offer," the man said as he licked his lips.

His hand reached down to his crotch gripping his already erect penis. He took off his belt and undid his zip in an intimidating manner and smiled sleazily down at what he thought was a weak and defenceless individual, an incapacitated weakling, ready to be abused.

Rage boiled up, this time so out of control that it overflowed and the hatred inside could not be restrained any longer. The intruder tensed up and gritted their teeth together so hard that they winced with the excruciatingly uncomfortable sound that screeched from between their lips. The sound was enough for the man to hesitate for just a second, his toes curling as he recoiled at the hideous noise.

The CS spray burned like fire in his eyes and the upward blow straight to his genitals rocked him and sent him reeling backwards, the spray continuing until he was choking. His nose filled with heavy mucus, his eyes red and streaming unable to see as he coughed uncontrollably. The intruder jumped up from the ground so quickly, that the man didn't stand a chance. His hair was pulled so hard it was torn out at the roots. The belt was pulled viciously tight round his throat stopping his breathing which was already curtailed with the spray. Kicks and punches rained down on him mercilessly, with more vengeful force than ever before. The restraint that was usually abided by was long gone, the fear of being sexually assaulted once again had ignited even deeper feelings and emotions, memories that they never wanted to relive again. This fear and hatred kept the assault going and going, no planning or sexual torture this time, just the desire to stop this person, and stop him for good. The belt was pulled so tightly that the man's neck was now visibly deformed and his face had turned a deep purple to black. His life was fading away fast. This was the last chance to let him go, let him live, and the intruder knew it but there was nothing within them now that made them want to stop. Tighter and tighter the belt was pulled until the man was no more.

His body lay limp. He was clearly dead as the belt was slowly dropped onto his bloated, terror filled, deformed face, eyes wide open and staring blankly. There was no sympathy, no remorse, just relief that this monster could no longer hurt them or any other innocent children. The man lying slumped on the ground was believed to be heavily involved in child pornography, regularly taken in by the police for questioning, but nothing would ever stick due to clever lawyers, loopholes in the law and other people willing to be paid to take the fall. He was the reason why so many children were continually abused, tortured and filmed for the pleasure of those who used the flesh of innocents to achieve their sexual desires and satisfaction.

The intruder leant heavily against the wall, realising that this time they had gone too far. The police wouldn't drop this one; murder was a completely different level to assault, even the hideous assaults they had already committed and unfortunately the police were pretty successful in relation to murder.

No time to tidy up. I need to get home before I'm missed and can't explain it away. "Shit, shit, fuck, my face!" It felt obviously swollen where the second punch had landed, "What am I going to say happened, shit?" Another huge lump was developing on the back of their head but luckily it was concealed by hair.

The door was closed carefully behind them and they hurried away carefully down the road, trying not to draw any attention as they made their way home.

"Hi Amy, how was your walk, you took your time. Everything okay?" Kerr asked her caringly. "Wow, what happened to your face?"

"Nathan, is that you. Millie's awake and wants you to give her a cuddle or she won't go back to sleep," Jen called out lovingly to him as the door closed quietly behind him and he stared in the mirror at the bruising on his face.

Chapter 14
Welcome Back

Taylor gave herself a shake before she got to Fettes, headquarters of Police Scotland, situated in the Stockbridge area of Edinburgh. She tried to dust off all of her unwanted feelings in relation to her work. She felt jaded, less enthusiastic about being there than she had ever felt before. Her emotions were all over the place. Brennan although dead, still haunted her every move. She had never thought anything or anyone would ever affect her like this. She still loved Kay, who didn't want her or wasn't capable of that just now. She wanted Fran because she excited her and she was good to be around. Her work, which used to be her stability in life, was now a very negative force, making her professionalism falter a little. She had been absent for three days without contacting anyone, which was totally out of character for her. She was usually the dependable one, totally reliable and rarely off work.

Taylor stopped at the main door into the open plan office, adjusted her clothing, held her head up high and waited for Findlay's rude and unprofessional outburst, his usual tirade of incoherent babble, which she had seen and heard many times before, directed at her or any other members of the team he thought made his fat lazy ass look bad. Taylor felt that she was above anything he could throw at her. She was very good at her job, she had just not been able to face another massive investigation, right on the back of that last one. She had just needed to cut lose for a few days, escape from reality.

She braced herself for the familiar onslaught of her ineffective Inspector, only to stop dead in her tracks. It wasn't Findlay that stood there. Taylor's mouth opened involuntarily, gaping at the woman that stood before her. Detective Chief Inspector Sommerville was well known, a formidable force and a highly respected detective. She did not suffer fools gladly. She was staring at Taylor and she didn't look very happy at all.

"Detective Sergeant Nicks, can I see you in my office please?" she said in a firm and authoritative tone. She tapped the door frame twice as she swivelled round on one shoe back into her office. Taylor felt like a naughty child being scolded. She hesitated and then entered Findlay's office, only to see Inspector Findlay was still sitting slumped with poor posture behind his desk, which appeared to have been shoved into the corner as an afterthought. Taylor smiled at this. She couldn't help it, her dislike of the man was so strong. Taylor thought his new position was well deserved and pretty funny.

"Something amusing you, Sergeant?" DCI Sommerville said with a subtle hint of amusement in her own tone but Taylor caught it. Sommerville must feel the same about Findlay. He was a liability, lazy and a waste of a uniform, a wage stealer. The smile, of course, went totally over his head. He didn't notice at all and continued to push papers round his desk looking busy, but not doing a lot, as usual. He barely looked up at Taylor, quietly wishing Sommerville would go through her like she had done to him. There was no love lost between them, his failings had become apparent after the last case whereas Taylor's strength and ability had been highly commended.

"Take a seat please Taylor. Is everything alright at home?"

"Everything's fine, well it is now anyway!"

"Where have you been for the last three days? There are protocols for absence and you didn't follow them, why was that?" she said with her eyebrows raised, awaiting the answer.

Taylor hesitated for a moment because she didn't actually have an answer or a valid reason. There was no excuse for not phoning in, other than pure defiance and the feeling of self-preservation, and a hint of stubbornness.

"I don't actually know Ma'am. I was feeling really low and couldn't face coming in, and that's all, no other reason," she lowered her head as she felt a little guilty.

"So low that you couldn't pick up the phone? That is not acceptable Sergeant Nicks. If you can't follow simple rules and procedures, then how can we expect your team to do it," she said with a stern tone.

"I'm sorry, really sorry. I just wasn't thinking straight. It won't happen again, I can assure you," Taylor said rather sheepishly, although she resented this lecture after all of the shit she had been through.

"I do realise that things have been hard for you lately but I need you back on board with this new case. We need your skills, your mind and your full commitment. Do I have it, or do you need taken off this case, Sergeant Nicks, because I can get a replacement?"

Taylor couldn't believe what she was hearing. *Fuck me, I only took a few days off, you'd think I'd been away forever.*

"Trust me, it won't happen again!" her words were said with attitude and resentment as this type of situation just made her want to prove a point. Her posture bristled with annoyance.

"Good, I'm glad to hear it, glad you're back on board. That's all!" she practically dismissed Taylor. "Oh and you'd better get up to speed with this enquiry. There are a lot of things going on in relation to the last two assaults." DCI Sommerville stared right into her, her gaze fixed and strangely appealing and, in Taylor's experienced mind, very deliberate.

Taylor wasn't sure what to do. She was never one to drop her eyes or her stare for anyone, so she kept it going. DCI Sommerville's stare was more than that of a scolding boss. She smiled slightly, a faint smirk and then dropped her eyes, her point now made, releasing Taylor back to her duties.

Taylor's stomach fluttered a little after this strange encounter, from rage to curiosity and faint attraction to this dominant but attractive woman. *That's all I need! I thought she was straight, I thought she had a partner. Hmmmm, might be bi, who knows, we'll see.*

Taylor walked over to her desk and Marcus looked up at her, sorry she had been reprimanded.

"Where the fuck have you been anyway? She's been going off her tits about you, since she's been here. She's obviously been sent to sort out Findlay and all of a sudden you do a no show, you crazy mare," Marcus asked with curiosity. He'd never known Taylor to do anything like this, not to the detriment of her work anyway. "How's Kay doing?"

Taylor's face crumpled in front of him, tears teetering at the edge of her eyes.

"Don't ask, not now, I can't go there, certainly not here anyway, everything is totally fucked up. I'm not coping in that department," she said taking deep breaths to stop herself losing it. "Look, things aren't good and the last thing I want to do is go off the rails again!" Taylor looked at him almost pleading with him to drop it for now.

Taylor sat staring at her desk as DCI Sommerville came up next to her and dropped some case notes down in front of her. "See what you can find in these, make some decisions as to what to do and where to go first before anything else happens. We have to act fast and nip this in the bud. This vigilante shit is really bad press. We're here to protect these people." Taylor felt Sommerville's hip brush against her shoulder, in her mind a very deliberate act, which could easily have been avoided. *What's she playing at, surely I'm reading this wrong?*

"Sure, I'll get right onto it Ma'am. I'll just try and sort this load out first and get on it," as she gestured to the ever-growing pile of papers on her desk that never seemed to let up.

Taylor looked up as the DCI started to walk away. She was tall, athletic and attractive and she knew it. As Taylor gazed at her, it was as if she could feel it. Sommerville slowed down and turned round to catch Taylor looking at her and smiled back, triumphant that she had caught Taylor out. She had heard all about Taylor and her lifestyle and had been very keen to meet her. Taylor's face flushed but she didn't regret it. Her own predatory nature was obviously still very much intact and open to further persuasion. *This could be interesting.*

Chapter 15
A Step Too Far.

A lone figure sat on the edge of the bed, the realisation of the previous night's events hitting home full force. *Oh my god, what have I done, what am I going to do, how can I go back from this? They'll catch me now, I have to stop. What the fuck should I do now?*

Amy showed her pass at reception at Fettes. She had worked for the social work department for over five years and regularly worked alongside the police in connection with child protection cases. Her makeup was thicker than usual today although nobody passed comment, but several noticed, attuned to the covert behaviour of those who suffered at the hands of domestic abuse.

An officer walked up to the front desk to escort Amy into the building. Many officers followed protocol to the letter when it came to other departments having access to police buildings. Items were known to wander although cops were over trusting when it came to their personal protective equipment, including utility belts and CS spray because things like that rarely went missing.

Nathan felt the bruise on his head when he rubbed the sweat off his brow as he tightened the screws on the panel in the refurbished toilets. Many stations were being transformed into open plan offices and the need for more facilities was apparent. Since the creation of a single force in Scotland it had certainly provided Nathan and many other contractors with pretty steady work. He twisted his Fettes visitors' pass round to stop it getting in the way as he stood up onto the ladder and leant over to reach a couple of awkward screws. His hand shook as he tried to insert the screwdriver. He had done this a million times before and had never had a problem. He felt a little sick and wondered if he should go to the hospital for his head. He wondered if he might be a little concussed. He climbed down from the ladder and went out into the hallway, bending over to try and clear the fuzz from his head. He lurched forward and nearly lost his balance just as the officer and Amy were passing. Amy rushed forward to take hold of him round the shoulders and steady him. "Hey steady there. Are you alright?" she asked as she helped him sit down.

"I'm fine, I'll be okay. Don't worry, I just feel a little dizzy!"

"Wow, what happened to your face," Amy asked quizzically.

"Nothing, I fell that's all. I feel a bit rough though," he replied trying to avoid the questions being directed at him.

"Have you had that checked, it looks a sore one?"

"No, not yet, I will though. I feel pretty crap but thanks for the concern and I do feel better than I did." He stood back up and started to move off to the canteen to get some water and turned and said, "Have I met you somewhere before. You look really familiar?"

"No, no I don't think so," Amy said staring at him.

She was about to drop her eyes when she took a closer look back at him.

"Nope, I don't think so, not that I can recall anyway," she said almost apologetically.

Amy began to walk away but her heart started to flutter, her hair stood on end at the roots and an incredible unexplained sense of nausea came over her. She did not know who he was but her senses knew otherwise, remembering everything they had been through together.

Chapter 16
Watching

Marcus walked briskly up the road as little David skipped along behind, trying to keep up with his dad as they were late for nursery. They chatted constantly as they walked happily together. Neither of them noticed the man sitting in a car reading a newspaper in the street leading up to the school. He was not too close to be overly obvious. There were other cars parked in the street and his didn't look out of place. He could have been another parent waiting to pick up their child. He stared as Marcus and David passed by. Peering over the paper, he watched and thought that the little boy would be perfect for his buyer, perfect. This was worth £50,000 for him on transference of the goods.

Marcus picked wee Davie up and cuddled him tightly, kissing him and munching his little boy's neck, whilst pretending to growl. Putting him down, he ruffled his hair affectionately.

"I love you, wee man."

"Love you, daddy. Are you coming to get me later?" little David asked sweetly.

"No, I'm going to work but mummy will be there for you," Marcus said back

to the most precious thing he'd ever had.

Marcus left the school and walked back the way he came.

This time he did notice the car and the man inside. His instinct made him look. There was no sign of any child seats or toys or the usual mess relating to a child. Marcus's senses bristled a little and he took a mental note of the number plate.

He shrugged his shoulders and thought that he would check it out later when he got to work. He paused, and then took out his phone to call it in; he just wanted to be sure. Leaving details, he made his way home quickly as it wasn't often that he and Maria were off together with no child to look after. He almost skipped down the road knowing that she was waiting for him, forgetting that his phone was still on silent from the night before.

Marcus turned the key in the lock and Maria raised her head up from the pillow. Throwing his jacket over the banister, Marcus took the stairs in threes, unbuttoning his shirt as he went. He still adored his wife, and his son, and sometimes couldn't believe how lucky he was. He knew he would do anything for them both.

He almost ran into the room, stopping dead in his tracks as he saw Maria stretched out in front of him. She wore white silk lace panties and a matching bra, which set off her lightly tanned skin beautifully. Her hair was wavy and lay over her shoulders, soft and silky. Her perfume was subtle but alluring and Marcus inhaled deeply to get the full essence of her enticing scent. She knew this perfume was his favourite and she enjoyed the way he would nuzzle into her when making love to her to get a deeper scent. It clearly turned him on. He came closer to the bed now, kneeling beside her and cupping her face in his hands to kiss her. He pushed his lightly stubbled face towards hers and his soft lips met hers. Their kiss was familiar and loving. She knew he wanted her, he always did. He never stopped telling her and showing her how special she was to him and their mutual appreciation certainly showed when they made love. He kissed her again and again, passionately delving his tongue into her mouth. Their well versed kisses grew as she pulled him close, her fingers gripping lightly at the back of his head.

"I am one very lucky lady, very lucky indeed," she said as she stroked down his impressive chest with her petite, well-manicured hand. She stroked over his nipples, knowing what he liked. She also knew he didn't need any extra stimulation, his jeans were already showing he was aroused. He gently pushed her back down onto the bed and pulled her legs round to him until her toes were on the floor. He brushed his fingers over her body. Her nipples were pert and alert with arousal and anticipation of what was coming. His strong hands slipped into her silk panties, one stroking low enough for Maria to raise up to his touch, silently inviting him, his other hand stroking up her inner thigh right to the top, his fingers deliberately stopping directly over her clitoris which pulsed and sent wonderfully exciting sensations up into her tummy, her face flushing at her need for him. He did this again, the hand under the silky material meeting the other and pushing down this time over her pulsing button and slipping into her a little bit. He could feel his excitement pushing against his jeans but chose to ignore his needs and take care of Maria's. He pulled her underwear to the side. She felt completely exposed as he looked at her, waiting, wanting. She liked this, it turned her on. He inhaled her intoxicating intimate scent and stroked his finger down into her silky cream. She moaned loudly and curled her knees up at the sensitivity of his touch. He pushed two fingers just inside her and moved his mouth to take her into it, kissing her firmly, knowing that her toes would be curling with the tingle of desire. She had explained to him once how good this felt and the waiting enhanced every nerve in her body. His tongue delved into her, tasting her, licking into her to stop her exploding with over arousal, knowing she would if he went straight for her clitoris. His tongue licked over his own fingers as they met. She pushed down onto them, wanting him, needing him. His tongue finally licked over her, this time hitting the spot, his fingers pushed deep into her powerfully, making her take a sharp intake of breath, not with pain, just pure unadulterated pleasure.

"Oh god, Marcus, Marcus," she moaned again, sending heated arousal rushing through both of them.

His tongue worked over her in time with his well-placed fingers, each complementing the other with their smooth rhythm and awareness of what they were doing to her. Her body rocked with them and pushed him deeper into her, over and over he pleasured her with his fingers and licked her until he felt her let go. She took enough time to make sure that every pulsing swirl had subsided within her, before she pulled him up onto her and fought to open his jeans to expose his rock hard cock, which was visible at the top of his white cotton shorts. She pulled his jeans down to his thighs and his pants just enough to free him. She put him where she wanted him before he pushed firmly into her, his cock filled her already wet and needy pussy. She curled her legs up and slightly round him, her panties still pulled to the side and his jeans against her legs. He filled her with his size and she moaned as he pushed into her again and again, her need still obvious and clearly ready for more. He made love to her knowing she was still up there and his pubic bone rubbed her throbbing clit as he thrust into her, his hand stroked round her, under her buttocks as he rocked her up against the headboard, his fingers gripping her cheeks and pulling her to him. She cried out as her orgasm climbed higher and higher, as his fingers gripped close to her ass, turning her on even more, the sensation of extra touch totally thrilling, almost invasive and slightly naughty, but totally wanted. She bucked her back up higher as he kept everything going in time, she was almost whimpering as his finger pushed lightly into her ass, just enough to send a heightened pleasure filled sensation swirling round inside her, tipping her over the edge and her release was amazing. He kept going as her pussy swirled and gripped him tightly. He thrust into her several more times to come himself, but kept on until they were both completely spent. He kissed her tenderly, both knowing that there was an inseparable bond between them, and a well-tuned ability to love each other both physically and mentally. She kissed him back, her tongue more subtle and more feminine, their mutual dance the finishing touch to the mind blowing sex. Sweat beads glistened over both of them as they lay back, Marcus still tied into his jeans, which were now wrapped round his feet. She gripped his pert bum as she pulled him over beside her and kicked them off for him.

She smiled and said, "It's a bit late for that now don't you think". They both laughed and he just looked at her, his body quickly recovering, and not unnoticed by Maria. Marcus was a fit athletic man, and once was never usually enough for him. Maria had a certain stamina too when it came to sex. She stroked her hand down over his taut torso and took hold of him, worked him with her hand. She then kissed his chest, going down and onto him, his erection full and ready once more. She sucked him until he was clearly on his way before straddling him. He took hold of her as she moved up and down, kissing him, breasts leaning down onto his chest and face, allowing his hands to touch her, stroke her, and pull down on her nipples with his mouth. He loved this, visually and physically. He moaned this time and came hard and Maria knew it. He kept going for as long as he could for her and used his fingers to make sure she came again too.

They were both smiling as they flopped to the side, cuddling and fooling around and enjoying each other's company, a couple truly happy for what they had.

Their lovemaking had been so intense Marcus had not heard his phone vibrate in his jacket pocket.

Chapter 17
Gruesome Discovery

Taylor's mobile went off when she was down in the canteen. She had only just picked up a well filled baguette and was almost salivating as she waited to pay for it. She looked at the phone. The DCI's number beamed up at her, making her feel like standing to attention. *Fuck me, what now, am I not allowed to eat?* That was the third time that morning the DCI had contacted her, the first two times were just to keep her on her toes. A little checking up on her, to make sure she didn't suffer another blip and to let her know who was in charge. Taylor grabbed her baguette and went somewhere quieter to call back. She didn't really mind the intrusion. She liked it better that the person getting the higher wage actually knew what they were doing, unlike Findlay.

"Ma'am," Taylor said in a slightly jokey but equally respectful manner.

"I need you and Marcus to head down to the Blackford area, take another couple of the team with you and meet up with the Scenes Examination Branch (SEB). They'll give you the full address on the way". Ms Sommerville's voice was curt and very matter of fact.

"No problem. What's happened? It sounds ominous," she said in a questioning tone.

"Just a murder, that's all," the DCI replied sarcastically.

"And?" Taylor paused, as there was nothing really special for her in that. Their team dealt with all the murders in Edinburgh.

The DCI went on to explain the seriousness of it. "There may be a connection with this crime and the other assaults under investigation. I think this one may have gone a little bit too far though."

"I take it the victim was or has been under investigation for something in connection with the child porn ring, is that what you mean?"

"Something like that but we'll need you down there as soon as possible," the DCI's tone was a conversation ender. She had decided there was no more to say.

Taylor got the hint, made a face at the phone and muttered, "Right then, that'll be that".

"Marcus, get the car and meet me at the front will you, we're heading out to a call," Taylor said in her usual chirpy upbeat voice a she took a large and savage bite of her sandwich.

They travelled quickly up to the Dean Bridge, through the area known as the Meadows and towards the locus. Once there, they donned full forensic suits, overshoes and masks. They were careful not to disturb the gravel, which had footprints and signs of a scuffle near to the door. They then moved forward slowly, noticing the slight spray of blood on the door where it looked like the assault had begun. The SEB team were already there and had marked various items of note on the way into the living room - scuff marks on the floor, like someone had been dragged, a vase smashed near to the door and other things out of place. There were also tiny droplets of blood on the floor. They were barely visible but someone had been injured outside and it looked like they had been taken or dragged back into the house. The door of the living room was ajar and as always Taylor and Marcus did not know what to expect. The cleaner that had found the deceased was now on her way to the station to give her statement, but she hadn't been at work for a couple of days so they could only guess the time frame at the moment.

Marcus and Taylor peered in and saw a middle-aged male lying on his back, his face severely discoloured, a belt pulled tightly round his neck. It looked like his scalp had been slightly split and a large clump of hair lay askew on his head. His trousers were undone and his penis was visible at the top of his pants. It did not look completely flaccid and was bruised.

Taylor sniffed the air. "Can you smell that Marcus? That's CS, see, look at his eyes, they are totally bloodshot, and look at his top. There's dried snot everywhere and CS crystals."

"Yeh, I can. Once sniffed, never forgotten, eh?" They both laughed because they had once accidentally sprayed each other in the face whilst dealing with an uncontrollable assailant, and the incident continued to be a source of childish amusement between them.

Marcus poked her in the ribs as he still believed she had done it deliberately. Taylor grunted and gave a 'what me?' expression, denying it as usual.

"Come on! Switch on and stop pissing around you immature twat. We've got a job to do." Taylor straightened herself up and put her work face on just in time to see Fran and DC Carlo walk in.

Taylor's face flushed, not unnoticed by Marcus and Fran, and by un unexpected visitor, DCI Sommerville who walked in seconds behind them.

"Fuck me, what's she doing here?" Taylor whispered to Marcus.

Fran mouthed to Taylor, "Sorry," for bringing her with them and moved swiftly into the room and closer to Taylor and Marcus. A sheepish looking DC Carlo followed her as he too could sense the undertones floating around.

"Have you found it yet?" the DCI said questioningly.

"What," Taylor said, genuinely not knowing what she was asking about, which made her look and feel a little stupid.

"The porcelain doll of course!" she almost snapped at them. "It's usually placed somewhere in the locus of the assault."

"Not yet. This looks different though, this looks like things may not have gone to plan and we'll still need to do some lab tests to see whose blood is on the door and floor. It looks like more than one person might have been injured in some way?"

The DCI paced up and down, frustrated at the lack of evidence that would link all three crimes together. Taylor raised her eyes at her and the DCI stopped, realising suddenly that her pacing was taking place in the crime scene. Luckily, where she was had already been examined and samples taken. She shook her head and realised that her frustration had clouded her mind for a second, secretly glad her faux pas hadn't interfered with the enquiry. She was normally spot on when it came to procedures and protocol.

SEB were still working the living room, plotting all of their finds and taking samples from the walls, floors and furniture. There was blood spatter all over the place.

The specialist support unit pulled up outside the driveway in a van with safety cage to the front and a long wheel based unit to hold nine officers and kit. The public order officers, were all very big and well-built and climbed down awkwardly from the van, pulling their kit behind them under instruction from their Sergeant. The usual cruel banter passed between them as they made fun of some unsuspecting victim. The biggest cop had to squeeze himself into one of the ill-fitting white paper suits. As he bent down to pull it over his size 14 boot all that was heard was an almighty ripping sound. The tear was massive, his trousers beneath visible and his teammates belly laughed at his expense, their twisted sense of humour overflowing as they shoved him playfully against the van nearly making him fall over.

"Fuck off ya baw bags, get me a bigger suit will ye," said the muscular big lad.

"They don't do XXXLs these days, just don't bend over ya fat bastard. I'll help you with the next one, you don't want to bankrupt the force!"

Once ready, they were given their search tasks, parameters, limit of exploitation and their brief outlining the items to be seized and why.

The second SEB team had finished photographing the

outside of the building and the gardens and the search teams moved off on a line search, systematically looking over every inch of the garden with fingertip searches in specific areas. They were thorough as they pulled thick bushes apart and pulled themselves through impossible spaces to avoid breaking their line.

"FIND," was shouted out with a little excitement in one of the search team's voices. There was a tiny white porcelain face staring up from beneath the rose bush near to the doorway of the house. Its dark eyes projecting the ice cold stare that two defenceless children had had to endure throughout their painful youth. The doll had the creepiest face, enough to send shivers down anyone's spine.

"Why the fuck would anyone have an ugly piece of shit like this, ever?" the cop looked up at his peers, who just made faces and shrugged their shoulders.

The Sergeant called Taylor on her personal radio. "We've found the doll. It's not very bonnie," he said with mirth in his voice. Taylor came out of the house from the back and bounded through the gardens to the search team, who were about to bag the doll, as it had already been photographed in situ.

"Where was it?" Taylor asked.

"Just at the front door there, under a bush. Might have been dropped by mistake."

"Assaulted out of their possession more like," she replied. "Good work though guys, the DCI has been going her dinger over this little beauty".

"Speak of the devil," as he nodded towards her boss, who was striding over to where they were all standing. The search lads gave a nudge as she got there, none daring to make their usual sarcastic remarks.

DCI Sommerville smiled as she took hold of the bag and stared at Taylor who stared right back at her, not sure if her eyes were gleaming because of the find or because of the incredibly sexy set of hazel eyes looking right back at her. Both dropped their eyes simultaneously as Fran and DC Carlo came out of the front door.

Chapter 18
Snatched

Little David skipped down the road holding onto his mummy's hand. He was giggling and talking about what a nice day he had had. They walked their normal route home, passing neatly trimmed and well-kept gardens, saying polite hellos to those who passed. Everything seemed normal, cars parked, people within, waiting for their children to appear from school. Maria wasn't as streetwise as Marcus and she didn't notice the car near to the end of the street with a man sitting inside it. He turned away as she passed, nothing obvious, but enough to hide his face from her. He moved off as they got to the end of the street and turned out of sight, following them at a safe distance. As he turned the corner he slammed his fist against the steering wheel. They had disappeared; they must have got to their house before he could see which one it was. *Mind you it must be pretty close by, as they didn't have time to get too far. I'll wait around for a bit,* he thought to himself.

He took a long drag of his roll-up, his haggard and unshaven face staring back at him from the rear-view mirror. He felt as if he had been there for ages. He muttered obscenities to himself as his phoned chimed.

"HAVE YOU GOT HIM YET? THIS GUY'S NOT GOING TO FUCKING WAIT FOREVER," an impatient voice rasped at the end of the phone.

He replied in an exasperated, tense tone, "I'm fucking trying. I've been here for ages fucking ages and they just vanished!"

His eyes squinted as he heard a youthful commotion behind him. He twisted round quickly to look back and saw a group of youngsters running out from a house nearby,. The boy was with them, the perfect little blond boy. He didn't care a jot about the children he took, he just wanted the money for delivering them. He didn't ask why but he did have an idea, although he was completely unaware of the grave danger this little one was in.

The children ran in and out of the bushes playing tig and hide and seek; they jumped around and screamed, laughing and frolicking in the sunny afternoon. Maria sat in the garden watching over them, giving the odd word of advice when the kids got a little too boisterous. From the last wrestling bout, one of the little boys stood up with a bloody nose and came running over, crying to Maria who stood up and took him straight inside to clean him up.

The man watched as she went up the steps. He knew he only had moments to act. He got out of his car casually, not drawing any attention to himself, and walked quickly up the path holding a pink diamond effect lead and a pack of dog treats. He started to call pleasantly, "Pepper, Pepper, where are you?" his voice calm and non-threatening. Wee David looked round straight away. He loved dogs and was the type of lad who always wanted to help, just like his dad Marcus. Most of the other kids, except one, had followed Maria into the house to stare at the blood and reassure their friend. The man went up to them and knelt down beside them. They were completely unperturbed by his scruffy and dodgy appearance, one that would have sent shivers down the spine of any parent, their innocence and trusting nature making them totally unaware of the obvious danger they were in.

"Have you seen my puppy kids? It's black and white and very, very cute. He's been naughty and run away? Can you guys try and help me find him?" he said in a friendly tone.

Cleverly he asked the little girl to go and get the mummy

to come out and help look for the puppy and to let her know what was happening, making her feel that everything was okay with their search for the dog, which also made David trust him too. It didn't matter how many times his parents had told him not to talk to strangers, his will to help and love of puppies superseded any lectures of 'stranger danger' and stories of bad people. David just wanted to help and he wanted to see the puppy.

The little girl skipped off into the house. The man knew he only had seconds. He turned to David and said, "There he is just down there at the bush, come on quickly, you go that way and I'll go this way and we'll catch him there just behind the bush".

The man ran off first and David chased happily after him, hoping to get to hold the puppy and give it a cuddle. He ran full speed to the other side of the bush and the man went the other way. Once behind the bush, which obscured them from the house, the man suddenly scooped David off his feet, lifting him round the waist, and moved swiftly towards his car. David kicked out his legs and tried to scream but a rough hand squeezed harshly over his mouth and evil eyes gave him a warning stare, which terrified David into silence. The man popped the boot, and shoved the frightened boy carelessly down into the darkened hatchback of his rental car. He was mean but not unnecessarily cruel, unlike the twisted vile man that had offered a large sum of money for him to abduct a child.

He stared into David's innocent eyes and snarled, "Make another sound and I'll come back and make you be quiet and you won't be able to make a noise again. Got it?"

Tears rolled down David's sweet face, fear etched all over it, his little heart pounding. His mummy's words now rushed round inside his trusting head. *Now remember David, don't go away with strangers, not everyone is as nice as they might seem!* He lowered his head and stared at his feet, sniffing, too scared to call out and force the hand of the monster in front of him.

The man's breath was foul, his expression equally hideous, frightening and sinister. Wee David knew he meant what he had said. He wanted to scream out as loud as he could and was just about to when the boot slammed down over him, muffling his cries. The man moved quickly and jumped into the car, turning it over and revving the engine loudly into action as he floored it and sped off away from the house just as Maria came racing out of her front door, motherly instincts bristling. She had only been away a couple of minutes, when the little girl ran in to tell her about the man and the puppy. A total cliché but when she heard the words come out of her mouth, Maria's heart sank. She felt physically sick as her heart plummeted into her stomach, every nerve in her body becoming electric, filling her with dread. She dropped everything to rush to check on David and was just in time to see the back of a silver car racing away at speed. She screamed from the pit of her stomach, a wild and feral wail.

"DAVID, Daaavvviiiid, where are you, you come here right now," she screamed helplessly, hoping he'd answer, "I need to see that you're alright, you're not in any trouble, just come here please, now!"

Her heart was beating out of her chest, she didn't want to believe what she was starting to think. Tears welled up in her eyes, her stomach twisting into knots as the most painful and sickening feeling increased within her. She pulled out her phone and called Marcus directly, all the time running around totally bewildered and shocked, shouting repeatedly for David, ever hopeful that he would pop out from behind a tree and this nightmare would end. But something sinister gnawed away deep inside her, something that was telling her that David wouldn't be coming out. Something evil had happened to the most precious person in the world and she was helpless. She ran up the road in the direction of the car that had sped off screaming and crying maniacally. Her neighbour managed to stop her and ask if she was okay but she was incoherent and just kept babbling David's name over and over. Then she snapped out of it. "Shit, shit, shit, the other kids!" and she turned and ran back to make sure the others were all right. "Phone the police, get them here, get them all here, please, please. David's been taken; he's been stolen, abducted. He's gone. Help me, help me, god help me find him!"

Marcus hadn't answered his phone straight away and now returned Maria's call. All he could hear was a tearful scream down the phone, "David's been taken, he's gone, he's gone, someone has taken him. There was a man, a man in a silver car, get some police here now, get all of them Marcus, we need to save him, a frigging silver shitty car, puppy, help me, help me, please, Marcus, save him, save him, please Marcus, he's got our baby, our baby, save our baby!"

Marcus felt sick too, right to the pit of his stomach as he thought back to the silver car the other day. He clapped his hands loudly together in the office to get the team's attention. Once alerted, he gave instructions to all the detectives to head to his address and surrounding areas, to get road blocks in place in the city and put calls out over all channels city wide. "Get local sets to flood the area, get door to door started, let's see who's seen what, check CCTV, all of it, ANPR everything." Once he had stopped talking his red face went sheet white and he dropped to his knees and yelled out like a wounded animal. He threw up on the floor, an involuntary reaction to the desperation of his situation. He could not believe what he had heard and knew that these type of cases did not end well. Many children that were abducted were raped, violated and even murdered, or damaged mentally and physically forever. He shook his head abruptly, his facial expression changing from wounded to hunter. He stood straight back up, just as the others were coming to help him. His face meant business, rage now taking over from fear.

Taylor came running into the office. "What the fuck's going on? What's wrong with Marcus?"

Marcus stood in front of her, tears rolling down his cheeks. His mind had already gone through every scenario possible for his son and none of them had a happy ending. He couldn't comprehend why anyone would take his gorgeous little boy. Rage burned within him, his teeth ground together hideously as his thoughts turned to violent aggression, something his team had never seen in Marcus before. The animal instincts inside him bristled ferociously as he longed to protect his son, any way he could, by any means, lawful or not.

Fran briefed Taylor as the others were finishing getting their kit together. Taylor gripped Marcus by the shoulder, pulled him close to her and held him tightly, as she couldn't begin to imagine how he was feeling. She would also stop at nothing to get his boy back.

"Come on Marcus. We need you, we need to go right now! We need to get there and see what's what. We need to get to Maria; she needs you, David needs you. We'll get him back, I promise you. Come on let's do this!"

The team headed out to the scene and the main routes out of Edinburgh were sealed off within minutes; this would only be effective if someone had plans to leave the city. Unfortunately, David's abductor had no intention of leaving town. He just had to make it to a secluded house near to the airport, unnoticed and unchallenged and his job would be done.

Marcus sat in the passenger seat visibly stunned, silent and ashen faced. His eyes were red as he had to keep rubbing them to wipe away the tears that flowed involuntarily. There were no words of comfort that Taylor could offer to help ease Marcus's pain. He just stared ahead squinting painfully as his mind slipped into thoughts of his precious child in the hands of an uncaring, cruel and depraved beast.

They spun round the roads fast and efficiently until they pulled into his street and parked. Maria came running up to the car, running straight to Marcus, almost knocking him over, wailing now, not caring who could see her. His embrace stopped her from falling to the ground as her knees buckled and her emotions took over, control of her muscles gone completely.

"We'll find him Maria, we will. He's a clever little boy, he'll be okay, he has to be okay," Marcus whispered into her ear.

"He wasn't that clever was he, he went with that man, he

bloody well went with him Marcus. What was he thinking? I've told him a thousand times. Why would he do that? Why would he, why, why?"

She curled up on the pavement at Marcus's feet, banging her hands off the ground.

"What happened Maria, how did he get hold of him?" Taylor asked calmly, trying to get some sense out of her, saving her partner asking that question of his wife.

A question he didn't want to hear the answer to. He didn't want to know she had done something that would have led to any danger coming to David.

"One minute, one goddamn minute Marcus. I went into the house with one of the kids to wipe the blood off of his face and David and little Maive stayed out the front playing,. One minute, one goddamn minute, one tiny little fucking minute. That was all. He must have been right there the whole time. He had to be, he had so little time to get him. He's been watching us, he must have been fucking watching us Marcus! That car, that car last week Marcus. What colour was it? It was silver wasn't it? God, what have I done, what have I done, our baby, our baby, he's gone, my baby's gone."

Marcus rocked back a little at the realisation, that he hadn't followed up on the results of the car he had seen the other day.

Taylor reached down and held her hands out, helping Maria to her feet. She pulled her close and held her tight, Maria was a complete mess. She was sick to the stomach, helpless and terrified that she might not see her son again.

"Maria, listen to me. We'll get your boy back, we'll get him back, by whatever means it takes, I promise you," Taylor said sincerely, hoping that these words would be true and they would find David alive.

Maria allowed herself to be held. She needed to be held. She was broken, total devastation engulfing her. It felt like every feeling within her was shutting down and she couldn't feel anything anymore, numbness was taking over, filling her from head to toe.

Marcus just stood there fixed to the spot, frozen in suspended animation as he watched his wife crumble before his eyes. A tiny part of him wanted to blame her for not being there for every second but nobody should have to be like that, and he knew that he too would have gone to the aid of the injured child. Nobody could have guessed that this was going to happen, children should be safe to play anywhere they want.

The officers were like ants busily going from door to door, hurriedly searching for clues, any information they could get. Cordons were set in place preventing any destruction of vital trace evidence, hairs, fibres, footprints, DNA, anything that could help find who had been there.

Marcus's radio crackled as one of the officers stated excitedly that a neighbour had remembered the make and model of the vehicle and noted the registration. The man had done so because he had been irked that the car had been parked in front of his house for so long. He was very protective of his neighbourhood and his parking place. Taylor quickly had the details circulated city wide and wider, not knowing that they were already too late.

Marcus heard the details of the vehicle and his blood ran cold. It was the same car!

Chapter 19
Rich and Powerful.

The sound of tyres seemed amplified as they crunched over the gravel, loud and terrifying for little David, who now cowered in the darkness and pushed himself as far back into the boot as he could in a childlike attempt to escape the reach of what he was afraid would come to get him. He lurched forward as the car came to an abrupt standstill, his tiny little heart fluttering wildly inside his ribcage, his immature innocent mind realising the danger he was in.

The boot swung open and light flooded in, blinding David momentarily, but as he blinked to try and focus all he saw was his abductor's haggard and ugly face peering into the boot. A rough hand reached in and grabbed for David's foot. David thrashed his legs up and down trying to stop him but a powerful grip pulled him from the safety of the darkness. He wet himself in terror as he was dragged close enough to the man to be picked up and lifted unceremoniously out of the boot. Despite his young age, David had the insight to look around him, trying to take in his surroundings, something his dad had always told him to do, more for the enjoyment of it, not for the situation he now found himself in.

The man strode purposefully to a luxurious front door, marble pillars, gold fittings and a comprehensive security system. There were high-spiked walls surrounding a large sprawling garden, with security cameras all the way round the perimeter. This was a house nobody was meant to get in or out.

The doorbell rang grandly as David gave up trying to hold himself up to look and flopped down, staring at the marble flooring beneath him. He shut his eyes in an attempt to hide from everything, a childlike thought process to escape from a nightmare, like the one he was now trapped in.

The door opened only after the camera had scanned them, moving up and down to check out who was there. A man came out. He was thin and balding and wore a tight fitting suit, expensive with silky fabric. He had a fairly pleasant face to look at, which was able to cleverly hide his true self - a vile and monstrous demon. He had to blend in and live in a way that his neighbours and work colleagues believed to be a normal, but secluded lonely life. Little did they know that he was the ringleader of a highly sophisticated paedophile ring, dealing children like playing cards. They used children like toys, slaves for their depraved acts, passing them round like they weren't human, like the children's emotions and pain didn't count. They had no concern for the fear, suffering and perpetual terror that they put the children in, at their hands.

The man lived a gifted and wealthy life, his money affording him anonymity from any prying eyes and unwanted attention from the law. His well-polished and practised lawyers could find loopholes in any charges he had ever had to face, so he had never suffered any real consequences, only inconvenience, for his alleged actions.

He reached out with his manicured hand to beckon in David and his abductor, his eyes alight with depraved excitement at the sight of the perfect little boy, the acquisition for a meeting planned for the next evening. He had heard from the courier, that he had seen a boy that fitted his desired request perfectly. Unfortunately, it had taken several days to get the chance to snatch him, and he had almost given up.

He gently stroked the side of David's cheek with his fingers, his tongue gliding over his top lip at the thought of him. The courier recoiled in disgust at this and almost felt a pang of emotion and remorse towards the boy he held in his arms but £50,000 was too much money to ignore. He comforted himself with the thought that David wouldn't really be hurt and that they would let him go after, that's what he told himself anyway. He moved past the man at the door and into the luxurious hallway, through the house towards the back area.

"Where do you want him?" he asked impatiently, wanting to leave as quickly as he could to avoid any change of mind. He wanted and needed that money.

The slight man pointed towards a door. It seemed to blend in with the wall and had a hidden looped handle. The courier only noticed this when it was pointed out to him, otherwise he would not have seen it. He pulled the door open and it revealed padding within, sound proofing of some sort, sending a twist into his stomach. He noticed a movement towards the back of the room, then another, but could not focus properly. His heart sank a little when he realised David wasn't the only one there for the occasion.

"Just put him down and shut the door,» the man barked sharply. "The rest has nothing to do with you! I'll get your money and you can leave, and I promise you, if you utter a word of this, you will not be able to walk in this city ever again or walk for that matter, do you understand that?"

He was well spoken. His was a soft voice with a sinister tone, one that made the courier's skin crawl.

"I won't say a word. Clearly I'd be in as much shite as you if I did." he replied impatiently with his hand out.

He gripped the proffered envelope tightly, looking inside at the neatly bundled notes before turning and making his escape. He knew he had to dump the car quickly and leave the city. As he strode towards the vehicle, he was already regretting what he'd done but with the money in his hand, he was in too deep already to quit now.

Chapter 20
Hidden memories.

Nathan was thinking as he played with his little girl Millie. He watched as she stumbled towards him, falling clumsily down over his legs. He loved her with everything he had to give. He started to drift back to his tragic childhood and his sister, his twin sister Amy. He remembered bumping into the woman at Fettes, the sensation he felt, when he had looked at her face. *Who was she? Why do I feel something for her? She looked about the same age as me. She stared back at me. Why would she do that? Maybe she felt something too.*

He remembered the dark room they shared, the stench and cold damp bedding. He had held Amy tightly as she had cried in pain and fear. She was quivering at the thought of either of them coming back into the room to finish off their sordid evening, and because of the rags she wore that were never enough to afford comfort and warmth against the cold. She loved her brother. He had tried to protect her. He just hadn't been able to. He had also suffered at their sadistic hands, probably more so than Amy as he would stand his ground so they would choose him over her. He would almost taunt them away from his sister, which often led to a more brutal beating and a prolonged session of depraved acts carried out upon him. He loved his sister. She had been the only nice thing in his life then. She had made him feel loved and cared for. In the hours alone they had played games and chatted with each other, pretending to act out the few movies they had seen when the vile creatures they knew as parents had let them go into the living room. If they were really lucky there would be something nice and child friendly on the television. They would laugh and giggle with each other, always quietly as they had learned from the cruel sting of a hand when they made too much noise and were drawing unwanted attention to themselves. Their bond was strong and committed, and the only good thing in their pitiful little lives. He felt pain as he remembered Amy's screams and her cries in the police station as she was taken away from him. That was the last time he had seen her. *Why would they do that? Together we at least had each other, something to cling to, hope and true unaffected warmth and love.*

No, no, no! Surely they couldn't think that I would harm her too, maybe re-enact what they did to us. Did they think we were too damaged to stay together? Did they really think we could even dream of carrying out the warped and twisted acts that we had suffered at our so-called parents hands? Never, never! She was my sister, and I had to save her, I had to protect her from them.

Tears ran down his face as he remembered his heart aching, night after night in his foster home alone, wondering where his sister was, hoping they would let him see her again, even just to let her know that she would be alright, but that day never came. Never came until now. He realised the feeling he had felt was instinct, remembering who she was, without his mind cottoning on. *Amy! That was Amy today. I need to find her, I must. I need to let her know that I'm her brother and that I remember.*

"Nathan, Nathan! What's wrong? You look like you've seen a ghost." Jen said as she gently took hold of his shoulder. He nearly hit the roof as he was thrown out of his trance-like state. He felt like he was travelling at lightning speed back from his past. The sweat was clear to see on his brow, his face was flushed and he hadn't realised that he had been shaking uncontrollably as he painfully recollected a past that he had fought so hard to blank completely from his memory, until now.

"Shit, Jen, you scared the life out of me," Nathan rasped.

"No way Nathan. Something else was scaring you, not me. What the hell is it? Tell me, please Nathan, tell me, you have to tell me. Let me in. Try and share what it is that you are hiding, that thing you seem to carry around with you. What can be so bad that you can't tell me? What happened to you? You've never talked about your past before we met. What happened? Please try and share what it is that you're thinking about!"

Nathan stood up abruptly, wiped a tear from his eye and was about to walk out of the room but Jen took hold of his hand, firmly at first to stop him leaving before releasing it to a soft affectionate grip, enough to make him turn round and look into her warm and loving eyes, eyes that he trusted and knew loved him unconditionally. She took hold of him and held him, embracing him with every bit of affection and support she could show him. He tried weakly to pull away, but he knew he wanted to stay in the comfort of her arms, a comfort he had longed for as a child.

"I love you Nathan, I'm here for you. I always have been, always will be. Please talk to me, share whatever it is that haunts you. Let me help you. What is it that is clinging to you like death's cape."

Nathan's shoulders heaved up and down as he started to sob, tears that had been hidden away for 22 years, tears of his lost childhood, tears for a sister that he had loved and lost, tears of sadness, pain, and untold terror. He folded to the floor and leant against the wall and cried and cried as Jen watched the man she loved overflow with sadness. He was transformed into the innocent young boy who had been abused and tortured relentlessly and abandoned into care, taken away from the only family he cared about, his twin sister, Amy.

He told Jen everything as it came rushing back to him, the words spilling from his mouth as he recollected his buried memories, his life as a small boy, a prisoner and slave to his vile mother and her depraved partner. How he and his sister had had a pact to look after each other forever, an inseparable bond, they thought. This had been severed unfairly and had scarred him deeply. He could feel the weight slowly lifting off his shoulders as he recounted tales of brutality, torture, rape, sodomy, relentless cruelty and the enjoyment his parents had displayed as they stole their childhood, and the squalor, hunger, fear and worthlessness they were forced to feel. Jen felt physically sick as she listened in disbelief at his tortured childhood. She could not believe that people could act like this and her heart was breaking as he talked, her thoughts floating to their own beautiful little girl, ages with Nathan and his sister when they had been living at the hands of these monsters.

"God Nathan, why have you never said anything?"

"Would you? I spent many years trying to erase it from my mind and thought that I had done until I met that woman at work today. I felt something, something that brought me right back to this. I thought I saw her. It *was* her. I felt it in my heart, I really did see her."

"Who did you see?"

"Amy, I saw Amy, my sister. I felt a strange familiarity, that bond, enough to bring all of this shit racing back to me - terror rippling through my guts, electricity zipping through my veins, sadness, loss, fear nausea, everything and it felt like it was real. I was actually there again, just because of a woman I met today. She asked if I was alright when I felt unwell."

"Are you sure? How do you know, did she tell you her name?"

"No, she just looked at me and held her stare. I think she felt it too but like me couldn't quite place what it was. I had put this all so far behind me so that I could start to believe it hadn't actually happened to me. She didn't really exist anymore. It made it easier because the pain of losing her was too hard to bear. It was worse than any pain I ever suffered at their hands. I had to stop the pain from hurting me again and again in my mind, in my dreams, every breath I took. They poisoned my life so I blanked the pain from their torture and the torture of losing my sister Amy, all of it. Poor, sweet little Amy. It was her Jen! I felt it and I need to find her, I need to let her know that I'm her brother."

"Okay Nathan, I'll help you. Don't worry, we'll find her!"

Chapter 21
Inner Dread

A fingertip search was ongoing where David had last been seen and further field, a large row of search trained officers crawling slowly along the pavement, stopping at every little thing that may be of some significance. Items were plotted, measured, marked, photographed and bagged carefully to prevent cross-contamination. The search team officers' shoulders rubbed together as the bigger members of the team squeezed out their lighter colleagues, sometimes deliberately to their amusement, which in turn created a little light-hearted humour in a dreadful situation. The smallest female officer who was well liked in the unit was always teased as they deliberately reached over across her area, blocking her face out with their arms so she couldn't see the ground in front of her.

"Piss off you big ape, keep to your own bit," Nicky elbowed her 25-stone musclebound workmate in the ribs.

He just chuckled again to himself and smiled at the cop at the other side of her, winking at their success and their silent and mutual agreement to squish her again when the opportunity arose. This time she swiped him full force in the ribs, smiling as she did so forcing a dull grunt from his mouth.

"Fuck off, you prick, just look at the ground, you'll miss something." Nicky was laughing as she deliberately leant her weight down on his fingers, crunching a couple of his knuckles.

Doug pulled his hand away quickly, the pain of having his fingers crushed into the concrete putting a halt to him doing anything else to her.

"Ow, ow, that hurt, ya wee bag," he said as he shook his fingers.

"Stop being such a childish knob then! Serves you right, ya big dafty."

Doug was still grinning from ear to ear, not noticing that the Seargent had been watching their escapades.

The Seargent wasn't a bad sort but fully aware of the perception of police actions and behaviour.

"Oi, you three, cut out the shit! I know it's been a long day but stay focussed. Save this shit for your own time".

He knew they did a great job day after day and he had been watching. They hadn't moved forwards at all when they were having a laugh and nothing had been missed. He too appreciated the banter and the humour the team shared and knew it was a necessary survival tool of the job. No one could comprehend what Marcus was going through and those with kids didn't even try.

"Sorry boss, just trying to lighten the mood, either that or we'll all be crawling along here greeting!"

"Just calm it down and move on. This is crucial to try and ID him".

"Sorry Searg," Nicky also said, a little embarrassed that her immature teammate had got them into trouble.

Once the Sergeant turned his back and walked away, she rasped humorously to Doug, "Dickhead, you're such a fucking big twat sometimes. Come on let's do this, Marcus needs us".

Marcus was at Fettes in the squad room staring at his desk. Maria was having a formal statement taken, along with the other children that had been at the house. Their distraught parents felt guiltily relieved it wasn't their child that had been taken. They were broken hearted for Marcus and Maria, their own near miss twisting theirs hearts viciously, realising how close they had come to their own total devastation.

Maria crossed her legs and uncrossed them over and over, her discomfort at every word she said clear. Thoughts of her sweet innocent little boy seared into her mind, cutting her like a scalpel through flesh, deep through her nerves and feelings, slicing cruelly into her senses, guiltily beating her invisibly as she went over and over what happened. She couldn't keep still as she tried to fight off the pain of the loss, wounding her deep within, tears soaking her face. She recounted every second of what had happened that afternoon. She had only been inside the house for one minute when the little girl that David had been playing with had come running in saying that there was a man looking for a puppy. She had sprinted out instantly to see the silver car speeding off down the road. Her face was soaked with tears and she was shaking uncontrollably. The female officer stopped the interview and knelt down beside her, hugging her tightly as Maria wailed out loudly, total despair taking over again. The officer summoned Marcus on the radio and he rushed through the building to get to his wife. He too couldn't think straight. He was also being torn apart thinking about his little boy, helplessness engulfing him while his precious boy was out there somewhere afraid and alone, wishing his parents would come to save him.

Taylor and the others in the office watched as he rushed out of the room. They could see tears in his eyes and pain etched on grey face, something none of them had witnessed before. The DCI also watched as he left the office. She got up and came into the open plan office and spoke to everyone there.

"We need to work fast on this, we need to work with the clues we have, work the evidence. There really is no time to waste here. I think this is a life or death situation. He was taken for a reason, something specific. This was well planned, painstakingly so. Someone was watching him. The time frame it was too tight for a random snatch. What about the car, the car is too hot to keep, where is it? Find the bloody car, then we'll work on that, if there is anything left of it. How many burnt out cars have we had today, how many? Any silver ones, any that have anything left to work on. Find the bloody car and we'll have a start. Come on let's get out there. That boy is still alive, I know it and we need to get him back before something more happens to him."

She spun on her heels and marched back to her office, slamming the door behind her. They watched her slump down on her chair and put her head in her hands, her shoulders visibly rising and falling as she heaved a sigh.

Moments passed and Taylor gently tapped the door and waited to be told to come in. It took a while for the DCI to speak. She was clearly gathering herself together, hiding her emotions, which she did not like to show.

"Come in."

Taylor walked slowly into the room, a cup of coffee in hand.

"Are you alright, Ma'am? We're all feeling it, you know?" Taylor said in a low and sincere voice. "We're all human! I can't stand seeing Marcus so broken".

"Find that car, the car is the key to the whereabouts of the boy! These people never get their hands dirty. This is a paid abduction and if we get him, he'll burst and turn Queen's evidence on whoever is behind this."

"We've spoken to all the officers in charge of the fire stations telling them to treat any car alight as a high priority for the foreseeable and to get there before it becomes a burnt-out shell! They said they are on it. Most of them have kids and a lot of them know Marcus."

They stared at each other, eyes locked, as they shared a moment of grief and despair, fear that they may not get the vital clues they needed. They may not be able to save his boy and that made everyone feel physically sick.

Taylor said, "We will find David, no ifs or buts. Failure on this one is not an option. We have to save Marcus and Maria's boy or I won't be able to live with myself or keep doing this bloody job. It would be too much".

"Work the car when it appears, and it will. It hasn't left the city so it will be dumped somewhere today."

Taylor walked over and squeezed Brooke's shoulder, nothing sexual or intrusive, just enough to show support for her boss. Brooke put her hand up and squeezed Taylor's back, tightly.

"Thank you. Have you got that list of suspects? How many are there that could pull off shit like this?"

Taylor was just leaving the office as Fran stood bolt upright, grabbed her coat and gestured to Taylor to get her attention.

"They've got a car alight down at the old gas works at Granton. Come on let's get there, take the fire extinguishers, the big fuckers, just in case we're off there first. Move it! C'mon, c'mon, let's go!" Fran said in a loud strong voice and with a tone of control and commitment. She had changed over the months, her naivety totally gone after the assault at the hands of Brennan. She was now a more confident and motivated person that did not take any shit from anyone.

Taylor moved through the office, picking up two industrial fire extinguishers, shouting back to the office staff left to get them replaced. Everyone left the office and others went to find other extinguishers before they left. They had to save the car and it was only minutes away from Fettes.

"Seal off the roads, someone had to put it there, let's get there, let's catch the little fuckers," Taylor commanded.

The car was well ablaze when they arrived. They were first at the scene. They jumped out of their car and started spraying it, concentrating on the interior, but they had to go close and the heat was oppressive. They could feel it singeing their eyebrows. Fire service sirens were audible in the distance. The car's tyres hissed loudly, a warning for all who had heard the sound before to get further away, as the tyres were about to explode. Nobody wanted to move back but nobody wanted to die either. The fire crews were quick out of their units, hoses ready and spraying within moments. Three engines for a single vehicle, not the usual protocol. There were numerous reels out, foam and water directed at the silver car. The seat of the fire was within the interior of the vehicle and they could all see that the boot was still shut, and not yet burnt.

"Come on, don't let the heat get to the fuel tank, come on, come on," Taylor said aloud.

The radio crackled. "Sergeant Nicks, we've got two males stopped running up through the pathway towards Morrison's supermarket. They're sweaty, out of breath and they are stinking of petrol. They claim they were out for a jog."

"Aye right! Detain them for suspicion of fire raising. Find out who paid them and how much, get descriptions of who paid them. Take all their clothes, get them processed and interviewed asap. They are just pawns, they have no idea what this car was used for. Offer them immunity, a reward, anything, little shits. Oh and well done, great capture guys. Well done uniform, quickest response ever. Good local knowledge pays dividends."

Steam was now pouring out of the car and the boot had not yet exploded open but the shell was still melting hot. Everyone there was aware that their timing may have preserved some crucial evidence, which could give them their first clues or DNA hits. All of them stood there hoping.

Chapter 22
Untouchable

Computer connections and contacts were triple coded and dressed up like normal sites for children's entertainment, masking the dark secret beneath. Password after password revealed even deeper secrets, a sinister indescribable hell for those that were forced to provide these pleasures for those with unnatural uncontrolled desires. A coded message was displayed boldly on the screen, the planned event was tonight, "2 x 5 guaranteed for complete satisfaction, in for a 100 G, make sure you bring the snuff box on this cold night, invite only". Ten pairs of eyes lit up at varying times of the day as the reflection of the computer screen shone in their eyes, sweat beads appearing on their foreheads with anticipation of the ultimate sexual prize.

A twirl of the dial, a familiar clicking sound as it spun round, the cold hard murderous cash sealed inside the safe, waiting for the planned event, sinister and sickening purpose untold.

"What are you doing darling, it's late?" he nearly jumped out of his silk shirt as he turned to face his wife.

"I'm just checking the safe is locked and everything is all where it should be, darling."

"Why, what are you worried about?"

"Nothing, just with all the break ins going on it the city dear! You know how it is."

"I know, there are quite a few it seems".

"Are you still going out to your gentleman's club?"

His face flushed a little as he now had confirmation of the night ahead, most probably repeated sexual assault, rape, sodomy, unnecessary cruelty and ultimately murder. All present would be guilty of if traced and caught and thereafter proven to have taken part.

"Yes, I am. Arnold is hosting it tonight. I'll be late back, he's put on some special entertainment, so don't wait up dear," he said as casually as he could.

His wife had no reason to mistrust him or think they were doing anything else other than smoking expensive cigars, drinking brandy and playing a game or two of high stakes poker. That's what she thought the money was for. She never bothered, his absence gave her some peace.

She turned away and carried on with organising her next big event. They were very wealthy, both in their own right. He was a successful businessman and she was an event organiser with very high ratings and highly sought after. A very busy woman who was not aware of her husband's dark secret, she was more than happy for him to leave her alone and not have to suffer anyone who was overly needy and time intensive. The more time he spent away away made her busy life a whole lot easier.

He turned back to the safe, his stomach now twisting with unremorseful excitement at the evening ahead. He was aware of the boy missing in the city and why, and this just added to the risk and thrill. What they were doing or going to do was bad, horrific in the eyes of the majority and he knew they would be hated for it, but this would not stop them. He had got away with many things before and he didn't think the police would ever have the skill or ability to trace him or any of the others. He truly believed that they were untouchable, and the police were stupid and behind the times. Anyway, they wouldn't be leaving any witnesses alive to tell any tales. That in itself made the whole thing even more terrifyingly tantalising. Some of the things he'd been involved in would hold a hefty custodial sentence but he'd never been caught and this simply added to his falsely confident sense of invincibility and belief that he was untouchable.

Chapter 23
Perfect Coincidence

The laptop was closed abruptly after keying out of screen after screen. They knew this elusive monster was up to something tonight and they had been following him, along with many others, for months. They knew that he had evaded the law on several occasions in relation to a significant child pornography ring but the police had failed to prove any links connecting him and could not convict him of anything, nothing at all. They knew, reading between the lines, that he was guilty of so much and they believed him to be the ring leader. *Luckily enough I won't have to prove it in a court of law, I make my own rules of justice.*

"I've got to go out for a bit, I'm taking the car and I should be back in less than two hours or so, is that okay?"

"Where are you going?"

"Out, just need to clear my head, I need some head space, I can't just sit in. I'll be back in a bit, don't worry about me." Keys rattled in the door and then it slammed shut.

The key turned in the ignition and breath steamed up the windscreen. "Brrr, it's friggin cold tonight," the words rattled between their teeth as they shuddered to try and keep warm.

David sat on the mattress crying, tears covering his sweet little face. The room was poorly lit, a hint of red, a bit like a brothel. He sat with his arms wrapped round his legs with his face buried in his knees, trying with all his might not to look at anything in the room. He was terrified, shaking like a leaf and had no concept of time and how long he had been there. He had not moved an inch since he was put there, not daring to peep up. His hair suddenly stood on end as he heard a scuffling sound coming from the corner of the room. His thoughts were filled with monsters from Scooby Doo and other cartoon baddies who could be in the room with him. Why would he think of anything worse? He was just a wee lad, full of naive innocence. He had no idea how evil these people were or how twisted and depraved their need for him was. The sound came again and he tightened his grip round his legs. Whatever it was was coming closer to him, until he could feel its presence right beside him. Something touched his shoulder. David nearly jumped out of his skin in terror and scurried backwards crawling away from whatever it was that he thought was coming to get him. All of his childish nightmares exploded in his head, until a soft voice spoke to him. It was a child's voice and David's fluttering heart started to calm a little as he raised up to see who was beside him. It was another little boy, similar in age to David but the exact opposite of him. The boy had dark hair, sallow skin, brown eyes and was beautiful to look at. He too had been handpicked but there was no report of him being missing.

"Hiya, what's your name? Have you been taken away from your mummy too?" the little boy asked inquisitively.

David just looked back at him, his mind racing back to the man that started off as nice and changed into something really scary. He started to cry for his mum. She would be getting angry that he wasn't home and upset that she couldn't find him and he was late for tea.

The early evenings were still dark and held a secretive ability to make one feel more uneasy. Climbing into their car, they drove off slowly, taking time to check their pockets to feel for the implements inside. These would be needed for the evening ahead.

They had driven by this address many times before, watched the cameras move, where and what they covered and had sussed where to park and how to get to the cameras without being seen. They parked close by, heart racing, blood pulsing forcefully round their body, fear creeping in as they contemplated what all the security was protecting within. They had no idea of the vile acts planned for the evening.

Millie came running up to her mummy in the kitchen and tugged at her jeans, "Mummy, mummy, where's daddy, where is he? He said he would play with me tonight, I've got all of my dollies ready for our picnic?"

"He's gone out sweetie, not sure when he'll be back darling, sorry. I'll play with you instead. Which one of the dollies will I play with." Millie took Jen's hand and skipped through to the living room with her mummy, no longer disappointed at her daddy's absence.

Several cars passed lighting up the road and then back to darkness once again. For the first time they feared for their safety. This man was mega-rich and very much in control so they did not know what to expect. They had seen the man before and he was nothing to look at but he was powerful in many other ways.

Is he alone just now? Will the others be here? What were the cryptic messages online meant to mean? What was happening here tonight? It seemed like it could be a full house.

He walked through from the living room slowly, carrying two sets of pristine white underwear, age four to five years. He did not have his face covered as there would be no one talking after tonight, no witnesses. He stood at the doorway, his pause deliberate as he attempted to control himself. He knew what he wanted to do but the night was planned and the goods could not be damaged or interfered with. All those attending had paid a premium price up front. He unlocked the door and the two boys scurried to the back of the room together, holding onto each other, both helping the other to get away from the what was coming through the door. The man seemed to slither into the room. He stood there and stared at the boys, smiling unpleasantly, his eyes fixed on their soft skin and perfect little features.

"Pop these on boys. I take it you can do that yourselves because your mummies aren't here to do it for you," He was not bothered that they were clearly distressed and frightened. The boys didn't move and he held out his hand and dropped the small white garments onto the floor.

"Come here and pick them up and put them on, right now, or so help me," he rasped.

The little boys were terrified of him. He was different, not nice like other adults would usually be to them. They moved swiftly to get the pants and vests on as quickly as they could. They didn't want to annoy him anymore than he already seemed to be. He was aroused as he watched them take of their clothes and was shaking as he turned and locked the door behind him. His eyes narrowed. He knew there was no turning back from tonight and the consequences they faced if caught. He had to be sure everything went to plan and that all loose ends were covered up, a watertight conclusion and contingencies for others to take the fall if necessary.

Sweat beads glistened as they balanced and stretched to reach the cladding that covered the wires. These were state of the art for their coverage but, fortunately for them, not impossible to disable.

"Shit, shit, shit," they wobbled as another camera swung round to where they were on the wall, just beneath the canopy of a tree. They reached over and used their snippers to cut the plastic, then grips to rip and pull off the casing, exposing the wires beneath. The other camera was still stationary and appeared to be focussed on where they were or was that just their imagination. Little did they know that there were no security staff monitoring the cameras tonight. They had been given a paid day off and did not question it. The expected visitors insisted on no CCTV, no evidence and no witnesses to them coming and going.

SNIP, SNIP, the noise seemed excruciatingly loud, an illogical thought that the camera 20 metres away would pick up on the sound. The monitor within the house went blank, then another, then another, before they moved quickly round to the other cameras that covered the rear door, making sure their presence was not noticed. The recorder had been switched off as promised by the host but the intruder was not to know this.

The host sat waiting in the bedroom. He had changed into what he classed as suitable clothes for the evening ahead, tight fitting and a tad grotesque on a man of that age and physique. He teased and fingered at his hair. It was very bouffant. He was so narcissistic and engrossed in his own appearance, he didn't feel the wisp of air that pulled into the house as the back door opened and shut, opened just enough to get in and no more, care taken to close it silently again.

The host's laptop was still open, and he was curious as to what news there was surrounding the disappearance of his special little blond Edinburgh boy that he had described paid a high price for. He revelled in the hysteria and notoriety he commanded. He didn't care about the torment the parents would be feeling now or forever more. The cruelty, fear and pain the children would have to endure didn't even register as an issue in his twisted mind. In his mind, what they did to them was only wrong in the eyes of the law.

Now where the fuck are you, you untouchable little prick? Tonight you'll get justice for all of those little kids that have been abused at your sweaty little rich hands.

There were lights on all through the house. Its layout was elaborate, wealth oozing out from every corner. The rugs on the floors, the ornaments, fixtures and fittings and artwork were all unaffordable for most. The labyrinth of pain and suffering of the innocent had a cold and unloved aura about it. It was filled with grotesque displays of power and symbols of success, which people like him, believed to be what matters in life.

The intruder's head whipped round like a hunting leopard as they heard their prey. The sound of footsteps above were loud on the highly polished flooring in the host's immaculate dressing room. He was up there and they were coming to get him. The stairs were thickly carpeted, silencing every step, pure luxury and perfect for an unexpected guest.

The host's hair bristled as he felt a presence, senses already on overdrive for the crimes about to be committed that night, excitement and anticipation, abruptly stalled, an instant switch to fear, fear of who might be in his house. He stood up and stared at the doorway. The intruder had stopped just short of it and waited, sensing they may have been heard, their gulp almost audible, adrenaline suppressing any fear. The host stood listening, not moving and couldn't hear a thing. He started to calm a little and wondered if he was just on edge because of what was happening later. Maybe he had imagined it.

He shook his head, abruptly shaking off the crawling feeling in his spine and sat back down, decision made, he looked in his mirror and returned to his favourite view. He was full of self love, arrogance and misplaced confidence. He carried on preening himself. Nails manicured, hair immaculate and face clean shaven and moisturised, he turned his head from side to side admiring himself in the mirror, and that's when he caught a glimpse of the shadow moving outside the bedroom door. He was quick to stand, but the intruder was quicker and ran straight at him, swinging a baton at his face, nearly overbalancing in the process and missing completely. The host had pulled back with the agility of a boxer, which was an unfortunate surprise for the intruder. The host grabbed at a hand and managed to swing his attacker round onto the floor, throwing the closest thing he could find, a bottle of champagne, straight down onto their chest, winding them, and leaving them breathless on the floor. He kicked out at the prone figure's head intending on smashing their face in, only to have his foot ensnared by a well-practised arm lock, vice like and firm. The man twisted like a crocodile with its prey. Still gasping for breath, the intruder managed to unbalance him and brought him down heavily. They now wrestled for their lives but the host fought harder and got on top, gaining the upper hand, trying to squeeze his thumbs forcefully into the intruder's eyes. Bucking their hips up with all their might, the intruder managed to reach into a pocket and take out the CS spray, emptying the whole can straight into the host's eyes, nearly dislodging his eyeball. They were so close together that the intruder was also exposed to the effects, although nowhere near to the same degree. The intruder stood, trying not to rub their eyes, snot hanging down from their nose, tears streaming as they picked up the baton again. The host was also getting to his knees. He appeared to reach up for help, as if the intruder would actually oblige. *Not a chance*, they thought to themselves. They had other plans and they certainly weren't there to help him.

The baton broke every finger on the host's outstretched hand, the next strike hitting the other hand that reopened to protect the injured one. Bones crunched loudly as they twisted at the force of being stuck. The intruder kicked him back over onto his back and then walked round him stamping on anything that they could, kicking slapping, punching, gouging at him, deliberately degrading this untouchable character. A man that had nearly caught the intruder out. They thought of this as they wrapped his jewelled belt round his arms and body to prevent escape or defence. Their intention was not to kill him, it was to get him to face justice for the vile acts he had committed and helped others orchestrate and never been punished for. The host was now begging for forgiveness and for the pain to stop, a weak and pitiful sight, relished by the now dominant intruder.

The only reply was, "Why should I show you any compassion for what you have done to others? Did you show them compassion, mercy, sympathy? No, you did not, so you will not see mine!"

The next kick struck him beneath the jaw and rendered him unconscious. The next three or four blows were aimed to prevent any further sexual torture of anybody, or anything for that matter. The intruder stood over him breathing hard and trying to gather themselves together.

Phew, that was hard, too close for comfort! Too bloody risky. Shit! I've got to go, the party will be starting soon and I'm not invited.

A hideous porcelain doll was pulled from a pocket, and they stood and stared down at it, sadness gripping and twisting at their heart, painful tears reopening inside them, a pain so harsh that it would never leave their tortured soul. They pulled the hair back from the doll's hideous face, it's soulless eyes and piercing stare sending shivers down their spine. The calling card was set up in full view on the vanity mirror, a note to the police saying «me again». The intruder located the host's laptop, which luckily lay in the bedroom, and put it beside the doll. To their delight it was still logged on, much easier for the police to interrogate.

The intruder knew they would eventually get caught but they were going to make sure they took as many others with them when they fell. Only those that had escaped the law, those they believed had committed serious crimes, and were getting away with it. They hoped they'd serve some serious time after recovering from their injuries.

The dressing table was immaculate and everything was in its place, except a set of big mortice keys, which didn't seem to belong there.

What are these for then Mr? The intruder looked towards the motionless and bleeding victim on the floor, feeling slightly sick that they were capable of carrying out such violence on somebody, but an inner sense of sacrifice to save others appeased the guilt, because of the abuse they had suffered at the hands of people like this monster.

They skipped down the stairs in twos, their fear of getting caught now very real. At least eight others had responded to the encrypted web chat and the law of averages to escape were becoming greatly reduced the longer they stayed. The intruder stood in the hallway unsure of which way they had come in, but looking both ways they realised which way was front and headed off towards the back.

The house was silent now as they walked past several doors, all of which were perfect with pristine paintwork, no marks, not even a hint of dirt, all the same. They came to what appeared to be a blank wall, which seemed a little out of place, the area too long a stretch of hallway without another door. The intruder stopped and hesitated, listening, but their fear of being caught was more powerful than their curiosity and they kept moving. Once at the back door, their thoughts flipped back to the words used on-line. The phrase «bring your snuff box» stabbed through their heart as they realised its connotations - brutality and sexual torture that ended with murder. *But who was the intended victim?* The intruder's blood ran cold, horror searing into them.

What if the victims are already here? Is there enough time to look? Those keys, those fucking keys, what are they for?

They ran back to the wall, running their hands over it, finding the loop, then the outline of the door. It rattled as fists pummelled furiously to get a response. The intruder needed to see if anyone was in there to justify the risk of going back up the stairs to get the keys. There was no sign of life behind the door with its cleverly disguised keyhole, not a sound.

Fuck, fuck, maybe I'm wrong, there's nobody there! I've got to get out of here now or I'm fucked.

The two boys were crouched in the corner of the room, terrified of the loud banging, neither daring to make a sound. But even David's young mind wondered why no one came in. *Could it be a goodie at the door?*

The intruder was halfway along the corridor about to leave when they heard a child-like shout. Their heart skipped a beat and the implications made them throw up on the spot. They had nearly left someone behind.

My god, they've got a kid here!

They couldn't run fast enough back to the door. "Is there anyone in there? Please, I won't hurt you, please don't be afraid. What's your name? Are you alone?

"I'm David and I'm five and there is another boy here too, like me".

You sick bastard, you were going to kill these little boys. Christ, what if I'd left?

The intruder was now in a fit of rage, an uncontrolled monster themselves, as they made their way back to the bedroom to get the keys they had seen earlier, praying that they were for the solid door downstairs. All they mercy they had shown earlier was now erased and murder was on their mind. The punishment should fit the crime. They took off their own belt this time as they entered the room. The host was still unconscious, a pitiful specimen but they couldn't stop themselves. The belt was pushed roughly round his neck as his head flopped to the side. Slipping the end through the buckle, the intruder pulled, and pulled and pulled, so tightly the colour change on the host's face told its own story. The intruder did not let go until they were sure he was dead. Then they ran back to the children.

The keys rattled outside the door and the boys inside cowered. They hoped someone nice was coming.

The door swung open and both little boys stood there in their matching sets of underwear, their innocent trusting faces gazing up at the masked visitor. Both of them started to cry.

"God no, don't cry, please don't cry. I'm a friend, I'm your friend, I won't hurt you, I promise. Come on, come here." The intruder spread their arms wide open and invited them in.

The boys hesitated until the intruder pulled the balaclava off and knelt down, continuing to beckon them reassuringly to come to forward.

"You're safe with me, please come, please. I need you to come with me. We can't stay here. Bad men are coming and we can't be here. I didn't mean to frighten you and I know I'm a stranger but you have to trust me. Come with me, please. We are all in danger and we must go now."

The boys were mesmerised by the intruder, unsure whether to be naughty and go with them, especially after the last time they had trusted a stranger.

The intruder knew it would be impossible to physically carry both boys away. The only option was to persuade them to run with them and not from them.

They held out their hands one last time, a kind expression

on their face. Although desperate to flee, there was no way the kids were being left behind.

That's when the crunch of gravel echoed loudly at the end of the driveway outside the front door. The boys looked at the intruder and recognised the terror etched on their face.

"Please, please, come now or it will be too late. The bad men are coming and we can't stay here, please."

"Are they bad like the man that took me?" David asked sweetly.

"Yes, worse, really, really bad!" they said deliberately trying to frighten the boys into leaving.

Both boys reached out and took a hand each. They felt the intruder's grip tighten on them, not oppressively but just enough to get purchase on their little hands to pull them away from the danger. The trio sprinted across the grass, dewy prints left behind them.

"Shit, shit, the wall." It loomed up in front of them.

The intruder looked around desperately trying to find something to help the little ones get up onto the high perimeter wall and over it safely.

There were small gaps and protrusions in the stonework and the climbing game began. With a shove from behind, they managed to get both boys up, straddling the wall like a horse as they waited excitedly for the intruder to climb up beside them.

Vehicles could be heard arriving at the front of the house as the intruder jumped down on the opposite side of the wall, reaching up to help the boys down one at a time. They all ran to the car parked close by. The boys were helped into the back and buckled up. The intruder drove off, speeding at first to get far enough away before slowing to a less conspicuous pace.

As they drove off, the enormity of their find struck them. These kids had been destined to be murdered that evening, and now they faced the biggest dilemma on earth. What to do with these children without getting caught!

Chapter 24
Vital Evidence

There were numerous officers off working near to the scene, the door to door team working tirelessly to get any scrap of evidence available. CCTV was being checked for the whole city taking up hundreds of man hours, painstakingly trailing every silver car in the area and their movements.

The hair samples salvaged from the boot of the burning car were being rushed through as a priority for analysis for DNA. The lab pushing them to the front and working on them within an hour of collection.

Taylor strutted through to the office, where she handed out everyone's tasks like Christmas cards, flipping the notes like an American paper boy, the job sheets landing nowhere near their intended destinations. This lightened the mood as some flapped into faces and others landed on the floor. It almost became a game in the office full of somber people and it was refreshing see a smile on their faces.

Marcus had gone home to be with Maria. She had phoned in tears, sobbing her heart out unable to function, thinking the worst, unaware of the fateful twist of the evening before and just how close her feelings were to being the truth.

Fran looked up at Taylor, trying hard to hold her gaze. Taylor's eyes were sad and isolated, not wanting to feel anything for Fran, because it just felt wrong. Everyone was feeling it, none more than her, the twist of emptiness was physically cutting deep into her soul. The edge of her lips curled slightly but the last thing on her mind was her own emotions and needs.

The phone rang in the CI's office; everyone stopped what they were doing and listened. You could hear a pin drop as the CI came into the room to address the team.

"DNA confirmed - one is that of little David and the other is Ivan Wolski, a Polish national with numerous convictions in his two years here in Britain - extortion, theft, assault, breach of the peace and fire raising, with three possible addresses on the system."

Taylor took over, "Fran and DC Carlo, you're on the first address and take a full PSU for entry and arrests.» She went through the orders for the other teams and secured resources, and had an all points bulletin put out, to stop Wolski getting on any form of transport out of the country.

Door after door was smashed in, the red ram crushing the structures and their frames as it pounded against them, "POLICE! IT'S THE POLICE," rang out at three addresses in the city simultaneously, one in Leith, one in Southhouse and the other in Clovenstone. The doors crumbled and the loud thudding of police boots thumped through each dwelling. Every room was searched as all the occupants were gathered together. Everyone checked and then taken off to the local police stations for interview as their houses were ripped apart piece by piece in a search for the small boy.

Everyone involved hoped that wee David would be found but there was nothing to suggest he had been in any of the houses and there was no sign of Ivan. Every personal item was raked through but there was no sign of a passport anywhere. The heightened risk of Wolski leaving the country was now of highest priority.

Photographs were circulated in high definition and full briefs sent to every possible outlet from the UK. Manifests were checked for all flights from every airport. Harbours, the Eurotunnel; all known exit points were scrutinised.

Marcus was now back at work and bristling with anticipation, tension and a temper barely under control. He had been at the main address, the one believed to hold out the best possibility of Wolski being there. Marcus banged his fists violently against the hall wall when the search for the suspect came back negative. Taylor went straight to him, she taking hold of his wrists before he could do it again.

"Calm the fuck down Marcus. We knew this might happen, you can't go breaking the rules and getting yourself into bother when things don't go your way. Sort it out or you'll have to go home. I can't have you screw up anything and give the defence any reason to side with the accused. I know you're hurting, I know, and we are all with you on this. We just need to do our jobs and do them properly." She clasped his shoulder reassuringly but with a hidden warning.

Her grip was firm but kind, trying to understand what he was going through.

"Stay focussed Marcus. We need to do this right. Please! For David."

His eyes squinted at her at the mention of David's name. A hint of aggression flickered over them because she had dared to use his name to get him to toe the line. His name was enough to send fury through his heart, and then it was quashed by deep sorrow, a sadness that tore away at his guts, a wound that was affecting his judgement and fundamental principles as a person. He was losing it and he knew it. All he could think about was revenge.

Taylor's phone rang and Sommerville relayed that one of the witnesses had burst. They said that officers had only just missed Wolski when they got to the flat. They gave details of the car he was driving and that he was heading for Edinburgh Airport.

Airport sets were put to work searching the car parks, vast and filled with vehicles similar to the one they were looking for. Row after row, they drove past slowly until at last they found it. Radios crackled as the information was relayed and further officers filled the airport, most of them armed.

Airport security was on full alert, watching every face, every detail, making sure he couldn't slip by.

Ivan Wolski stood in the check-in queue for the flight to Poland, a little nervous but unaware of how much heat was on him at that moment as an ever-increasing number of officers filed in behind him.

Marcus and Taylor ran into the check-in area. There were dozens of queues and they only had the word of one dodgy witness to go on. Wolski could be anywhere.

Sweaty palms glistened as Ivan handed over his passport. The woman taking it looked at it casually, her facial expression changing as realisation hit. *Flipping heck, it's him! I hope he hasn't noticed that I've clocked him.* Her finger was shaking as it hit the personal attack alarm, silent but crucial to their safety.

Airport security let the police officers know that an alarm was sounding and where it was. The woman at the check in tried not to be too obvious with her deliberate stalling but Wolski was getting noticeably irritated. He leaned in close to her in a menacing way and spoke quietly and confidently.

"Any reason why this is taking so long?" he asked impatiently.

She answered politely, stating that check-ins take a lot longer these days with all the terrorist threat issues; she sounded convincing.

It was not enough to keep his impatience and fear under wraps, however, and his face contorted into an angry snarl. He only just managed to respond politely.

"If there isn't a problem, then it shouldn't take too long then," he said again, his eyes flashing angrily.

"Just another swipe and we're done sir," she said with a cautious smile, nervous at the man's demeanour, and how it was changing quickly.

His fist tightened and he became aware of what he now perceived to be a deliberate delay. He had seen numerous people before him get through in half the time. He had had enough and turned to leave, walking straight into the body armour of the firearms officer that had moved in right behind him. Wolski tried to run but was lifted off his feet as the officers stopped him. They walked him out of the queue in as low key a manner as possible. Wolski tried to struggle but his efforts were quickly stifled with the officers' superior strength.

Wolski was frog marched towards the exit. Marcus was standing five metres just inside the door and Taylor saw him move off towards his son's abductor, but she was too slow to stop him. He ran right up to Wolski and grabbed his face hard, his grip tight and oppressive, his own face just a couple of millimetres away as he screamed at him threateningly, spit flying from his mouth.

"Where the fuck did you take my boy, you vile little prick! If anything has happened to him, I promise you, I'll kill you, you fucking evil, twisted, insignificant, money-grabbing bastard. You better get talking or I will take the law into my own hands and I will hurt you. That's a fucking promise."

Taylor grabbed hold of Marcus's shoulders. He was about to push her off when he came to his senses, realising he had overstepped the mark.

She pulled him away. "Take it easy Marcus, we need him. We need to do this right and you are not going anywhere near him, I hope you understand that this is the only way!"

"Yes, yes I do. You're right, sorry. Clearly, I can't be near him. I want to hurt him, really hurt him. He's scum, total scum. I can't be trusted. I'm cool with just doing admin, I'm okay now, thank you Taylor."

They got back to St Leonard's police station and carried out the procedures in relation to legal representation, which as always took vital and precious time and everyone was frustrated at the deliberate delay in this process. Time was something they did not have.

Eventually, Wolski's lawyer arrived. He wasn't earning so all expenses were paid for him and the best available afforded to him. Of course he was told to give a no comment interview and not implicate himself in anything.

The case had gone all the way to the top and they needed to hear what this man had to say, anything he could give them.

They needed Wolski's help to find David. There were talks behind closed doors and deals and offers were put on the table, not a carte blanch let off but they needed him to become their witness.

The recording equipment was switched on and those present were introduced, cameras all focussed on the accused. He was clearly nervous and untrusting of the police and any offer made. He started off by answering no comment to the first ten questions.

He then asked Taylor a question, "Who was the guy in the airport? Is he the lad's dad?"

"David's dad, the lad's name is David, and yes that is his son. Does that change anything?" was the reply given abruptly by Taylor, humanising the commodity this man was referring too, trying to reach the human side of the mercenary being before them.

She continued, and repeated herself in a more civil professional tone, "Yes, that was that man's son. We believe you kidnapped and sold him on. In fact, we know you did it and now is the chance to save yourself from the many years and years in prison that you will get, because I'll personally make sure you do. Come on, give the boy a chance. Do the decent thing and save him, that's if he's not already dead. You'll be facing life for your part in his murder. Do you want that, because that's the way it's going?"

This time Wolski looked up, realisation dawning that they had enough evidence to crucify him. He didn't want to go to jail as a child killer, and he knew he deliberately hadn't asked any questions in relation to the boy he had kidnapped.

A minute later he burst, reeling off the address and the directions to where he had taken David and how much he had been paid. He went on and on, not giving them time to ask any questions in between. It was almost a relief for him to say it out loud, he had been kidding himself that the boy would be alright and returned unharmed. He didn't think he was a monster, he was just a guy that had been offered a huge sum of money, no questions asked and he couldn't see past that.

He had tried not to think of the human cost. He knew it now though and the realisation made him lose control. He vomited on the floor, his despicable act finally hitting home, his cruelty and disregard for the little lad and his family making him retch repeatedly.

"I'm sorry, I'm so sorry. Hurry, you've got to hurry. There was a deadline to get him there and I'm sure it was for last night, fuck!" He retched again at his stupidity in thinking that he could have got away with his crime; the police were not slouches.

Taylor slammed her hand down on the desk so hard it hurt, "That little fucking boy better be alive, you low life shit!" She lost it when she heard the deadline had been the previous night. What if they were too late?

"There are cops already on their way, DCI Sommerville, are you coming?" Taylor shouted.

"Yes, I'm not going to miss this one. Pray to god he's okay. Where's Marcus, do you think he should come?" DCI Sommerville asked Taylor.

"Try stopping me," came from Marcus as he swung his over-shoulder utility belt on.

Taylor looked at him with a worried expression.

"I'm okay Taylor. I promise I'll be cool. I need to be there. Whatever has happened, I need to be there. You have to understand that, please don't leave me out," Marcus was pleading with his eyes and voice.

Sommerville nodded to Taylor as she squeezed Marcus's shoulder, "Come on you, let's go and get your boy".

"I hope so," he replied with tears flooding his eyes and blood pulsed through his veins.

Blues flashed and sirens rang out in a grim chorus as they sped though the streets of Edinburgh in a desperate bid to get to David.

Chapter 25
House Guests

Nathan came home two hours after he had left and sneaked in the back door and crept through the house trying to keep them quiet. There was a room at the back of the house, the rarely used dining room, Millie still preferring a high chair in the living room with a Peppa Pig DVD on. The only problem was keeping them quiet, but he fed them and made up two beds and gave them some milk and they both appeared really sleepy and went to sleep without a peep. Jen was up the stairs with Millie and did not come down.

Amy arrived home and put the car in the garage, Kerr came to the back door of the house to meet her. She came rushing up to him and motioned for him to come inside with her.

"Where have you been, you've been away for ages? You look like you've been dragged through a hedge backwards, Amy you need to talk to me, let me in, let me know what goes on in that head of yours."

"I know, I know I'm hard to work out Kerr, but I'm trying to work through things just now. I can't help it and I certainly can't explain it, I don't want to, it hurts and there is a deep fear inside me if I let it out. I am sorry Kerr, I know I don't treat you very nicely a lot of the time and you always stay. I know you care for me and love me very much and will stand by me with everything that I put you through, you always have done and I really appreciate that. I really do. I hope I don't let you down Kerr, but I do love you, I do and I don't show you enough, and I'm sorry for that!"

Amy kissed him lovingly on the lips and Kerr responded, both for once sharing a loving moment, a first ever for Amy.

The boys cuddled up in their covers, food eaten and appreciated and had been told to use the potty if they needed the toilet again. One boy, his English understandable but broken with an Eastern European accent and little blond David snuggled up together, a mutual understanding between them that they knew they were safe with the person who had freed them. The stranger's had a kind voice, warm and caring, and they trusted them but longed to be with their mummies. Both of them were still frightened that it was dark and they were left with no adult close by but they still had each other and that was a great comfort as they fell asleep. They both had new clothes, thick warm Asda joggers and hoodies giving relief from the cold, light pumps and fuzzy socks. They had been told to play hide and seek in the car while the stranger had gone to the supermarket. The rules were not to be seen by anyone and they were excited that they had succeeded and were rewarded with some sweets, crisps and fruit juice.

Chapter 26
Broken

The screeching of tyres was a little too obvious as the police vehicles came hurtling into the leafy street, expensive cars shining out from every driveway two or three in each, Daimlers, Jaguars, and a Porsche Carrera 4 and Ferrari in the driveway where they stopped. Most of the houses were of individual designs, three-storey, minimum 20 rooms per unit, some old stone built and all extremely expensive, reserved for the mega-rich of the capital city.

Firearms officers spilled out of their four by fours, highly polished boots crunching on the ground as they got into position. Officers from the specialist support units jumped down from their protected vans with the grills visible on the front windows, the sliding doors rumbling on their runners, clanging as they slammed against the stopper. They arrived 20 metres shy of the driveway. From the lead van, six large men and one female exited and stood to the side, the males averaging 18 to 20 stone, and the only female PC, 5'6", slim, with long dark hair and feminine features. She was more than capable of holding her own. The MOE (mode of entry) team were at the front with the 26 kilo battering ram, or big red door key as it was known, the hooley bar for maintaining tension or to force the door like a giant crow bar, the hydraulic spreader and the rabbit - a manual spreader that could be inserted into the door and the frame. Even the most solid doors would crumble at the combined use of either or all of this equipment in the hands of its strong operators. All of the SSU officers wore protective body armour, including steel toe capped boots and NATO helmets, everything protected and flame proof, a very intimidating sight. Their Sergeant came down from the front seat of the van. She was petite and had long blonde hair tied up in a ponytail, not an ounce of body fat. She was very fit. She beckoned the officers towards her and gave clear and concise instructions. Raid teams were identified and arrest procedures clarified. There was no room for procedural errors here and no time to wait.

She clapped her hands and said "Let's do this, no mistakes, and remember your own safety, you don't know what's in there".

The officers moved forward as a unit, the dogs and their handlers still in the vans further down the street for the search of the mansion. The solid ornate wooden door stood proudly before them. It wouldn't be there for long. The hydraulic was put in place and the hugely muscular key holder moved forward to swipe ferociously at the door. With the pressure of the spreader, two wild ape like swings were made and the door splintered before giving way on the third strike. The units piled forward covering all of the rooms on the ground floor and systematically worked their way through this massive house.

Room after room, floor by floor, the shouts of "clear" rang out from booming voices. Shouts of "POLICE" could be heard too. Marcus and the other detectives stood just inside the front door, waiting until the protected officers had made the house safe. This was normal protocol. The detectives would only ever come forward to boost numbers if the initial units were outnumbered or in danger.

"Sergeant, sergeant! You need to come up to this room, and bring a detective or two with you."

Marcus went to push forward but the DCI pulled him back, "Taylor, you go up please, - alone".

"Yes, Ma'am," Taylor said respectfully, dreading what she was about to find.

Marcus was shaking from head to toe, "Please no, please don't let him be dead, please I pray, please spare him, my sweet little boy, please!" He dropped to his knees in front of everyone and started to cry helplessly. He could not hold his emotions back any longer, sick to the pit of his stomach at what they may find up there.

His imagination kept filling with nightmare visions of David. He blinked away the tears as he raised his head to watch Taylor stride up the stairs two at a time.

Taylor gulped hard as she braced herself for what she was about to see. She wanted to do this for Marcus but the last thing she wanted to see was his dead son.

The burly SSU officer stood aside to clear enough space to let her enter, her eyes half closed to limit the horror, only to see a man's body trussed up with a belt tied tightly round his neck. His face was discoloured and his neck deformed by the tightly pulled belt. The relief was unexplainable, delight at the sight of the dead man clearly murdered in front of her, delight that it wasn't little David.

"Ma'am, we have a body of a man here, no child present, thank god," she reported back, her voice quivering.

Room after room was called as clear until the whole house had been searched but no children were found within.

Marcus's stomach twisted with relief and bemused renewed distress. *Where is he?*

"Where the fuck is he? Where is he, who the fuck has got my wee boy now? God, please help me find him!"

One of the SSU officers came forward to speak to Taylor. Noticing the DCI, he turned to address her as the higher ranking officer but she nodded his attention back to Taylor, who was running the show. Sommerville was only there in case the situation escalated due to Marcus being there.

"There's a room down the corridor here, the one with the flush hidden doorway and there's a key in the door. There are kid's clothes inside. I remember the abduction brief, the top looks similar to the description of the missing boy, Searg ."

"You've not touched anything have you?" Taylor quizzed the giant man that stood before her.

He just looked at her incredulously - as if he would be that stupid.

"No Searg, the clothes are just lying on the floor."

"Shit, fuck, piss, what size?"

"Tiny, four to five maybe, no bigger!"

The DCI listened. She knew that the boy had been here but where was he now? What had happened here?

Taylor had a hunch and went back up to the murder scene for a snoop around, and there it was - a hideous evil faced porcelain doll on the dresser, lifeless cruel eyes staring straight at the exposed corpse as if judging him.

"Ma'am, there's a doll here. This could have been one of the most fortunate double bookings ever. What are the chances of our killer coming on the night of this party. It doesn't bare thinking about if he hadn't come here!"

Marcus was now listening intently, "What are you saying Taylor, that whoever killed this freak has now got my boy? And you think that is good!" he said, almost losing it.

Taylor responded quickly and defensively, "I do actually. I don't think the person that killed this man will harm your boy. There's a computer up there with the screen locked onto an open line into something pretty sinister and I think the last thing he would do is hurt a child!"

"That's comforting. We've not been able to trace them yet so how the fuck to you think we'll find them now?" Marcus said with uncharacteristic sarcastic aggression.

Taylor turned to him quickly, aware of his understandable mood. "Marcus, I think they will come to us if they have David. I think they came here with no intention of ending up with a kid, there is no way they knew he was here, if he was even here!"

The SSU officer butted in at that point, "Searg, there appears to be two separate sets of clothes in that room!"

"Eh, what do you mean?" she whined.

"Just as I said, there are more than just one set, two pairs of pants, socks trousers and tops, two sets and two pairs of shoes too!"

"Get forensics in that room asap, let's see how much DNA is in there and get confirmation as to who's been there. Now!" her voice was demanding and impatient.

No one had noticed Marcus moving towards the room where the clothes were found. It only took seconds for a him to confirm that the little top in the room belonged to his son, and for the first time since he went missing Marcus felt a tiny flutter of hope. It took him all of his strength to not grab it and bury his face in it to smell the familiar scent of his wee boy again.

"Fran, DC Carlo, you stay and work the scene and corroborate all of the samples they take. There should be hundreds, sorry," Taylor said sympathising.

A full venue cordon was put in place as the press were already on the pavement beside the vans taking photos of the riot police and firearms cops now back at their respective transport, taking off their kit, always a popular photo. A very dramatic scene would be described in the next print of the press.

Everyone else from the office headed back, leaving the search teams and SEB to gather evidence under the watchful eyes of the two detectives.

Chapter 27
Relief

"How are you two boys this morning?" The friendly voice woke them from their slumber, although it was still dark.

The decision was made that the boys were too hot to keep. They knew that the longer they had them there, the more pain their parents would be in, and they didn't want to do that to anyone. They had to find a way to get them back as soon as possible.

"Here's some brekkie. Sorry it's only toast and jam but it's all I have that little boys might like. Oh, and a glass of milk too, I hope that's okay." They smiled at the happy little faces, delighted with toast and jam.

The boys were starving and they were very grateful for the sugary treat and the milk. They ate every little bit, even the crusts.

"I need you to listen to me. I need you to make me a forever promise or I can't let you go home to your mummies. Now listen to me carefully, you can't say anything about me, nothing, nothing at all. Don't tell anyone anything. Pretend I was never here, that you don't know what I look like or I'll be in lots of trouble. Do you understand me?" The boys looked sheepish and wary of this secret. The stranger noticed and said, "Aaahh, I know what's wrong, you're not supposed to keep secrets from your parents are you, but this one is different and this is a special secret, a good one".

The two little heads nodded as they listened giving their full attention, fear now gone because this was a good stranger.

"You need to do exactly as I say now and we'll go and see your parents. Okay?" .

Agreement came from the wee boys once again with nods of their heads. They really wanted to see their mummies, whether they both would would be another matter.

The car pulled out of the drive and the boys were back under the cover in the footwell in the rear of the car, quite liking this game of hide and seek as they giggled with each other.

Still not sure how this would go down, or if it would even work without being caught, the stranger had to do this whatever the risk. They would never harm or upset children, that was against everything they stood for. They had to avoid the CCTV, but had to get close enough to make sure the kids got to the police station safely and were found quickly. They still had the victims phone. They had taken it on discovering the children for this very purpose, an untraceable call.

These were very young boys - would they do what they were told, safely? they thought to themselves.

They drove up to Tesco at Corstorphine. It was 6am, still dark and not too busy as they got out of the car, a scarf covering their face with only their eyes showing. There was no CCTV in the area of the carpark where they had parked. They found one of the deep trolleys and took it to the side of the car. The boys were lifted into it one by one and a blanket put round them. They sat with their little heads poking out of the top. They tried not to look suspicious, acting like a parent having fun with their kids, albeit it was a little early. They walked away from the store and parked the trolley right at the front door of the police station which was situated not far down the street.

"I know it's cold boys, and you've been really good, but this is the last game. You two must stay in this trolley. Don't try and get out. Stay here until the police find you, okay. Promise me. You'll be alright."

Both boys, their little eyes wide open and focussed, listened intently, nodding their heads, both scared of being left alone again.

"Are you going away?" David asked in a worried voice, afraid now that their protector was leaving them.

"You won't be alone for long, I promise you. Now remember our secret, please don't tell. You'll be safe until the police find you. I'll be watching until they arrive."

With a final smile, the stranger turned and left, a little sadness filling their heart, 999 already dialled.

"What is your emergency and what service do you require?" the voice asked.

"Police, quickly, it's urgent," their voice was forced and deep, trying to mask their normal tone.

Driving out of the store car park slowly, pausing to watch as promised, the stranger could see two cars had already stopped at the station, their occupants staring in disbelief at what they were seeing on their way to work.

The call taker could not believe what they were hearing and feared it could be a hoax call. They remembered the brief the previous night and called several sets to attend, none of which were at the station and had to return from or leave other jobs.

The stranger smiled as they saw a woman walk towards the boys in the trolley and lean down to talk to them and then look around herself to see where their mother was and why they were here on their own, looking a bit bewildered that this was possible.

They'll be safe now, I can't do any more for them. Good luck little ones! They left as police were beginning to arrive, blues flashing at their haste to get there. The officers were delighted to find a trolley with little boys in it, an unexpected happy ending.

Each boy was lifted from the trolley carefully and taken into the station, the passers by who had stayed with them taken in too to get statements and details from them.

The phone rang loudly in the office. It was answered casually by Fran. "Major Investigation team, " she said. The person at the other end of the phone enquired after DC Black and had an urgent tone to his voice.

Fran told them that he wasn't in yet. The person at the end of the phone wasn't put off and asked for Marcus's mobile phone number. Fran asked why this was so urgent, worrying that they had maybe found a body.

"There have been two little kids found, left in a trolley at Corstorphine station, a little Romanian boy who didn't give a name and the other said his name is David Black!"

Fran's mouth dropped open with astonishment and relief. Taylor was also in early and looked over as Fran mouthed the words, "They've found them, they've found them alive, two little boys and one is called David. Call Marcus and Maria now. The boys are at Corstorphine being checked over by paramedics as we speak".

"Come on, we need to get there. We'll call him on the way. Let's go Fran," Taylor beckoned her out of the office urgently, impatient to check out the story.

Marcus screeched his car to a halt to answer his phone. It had to be important if he was getting a call at 6.15am. His brow began to sweat at the thought it could be the bad news he had been worrying about.

He hesitated, and screwed his eyes shut, trying to avoid hearing the worst. "Hello!" he said quietly.

"Marcus, are you driving?" Taylor spoke desperately down the phone.

Marcus's heart started thumping through his chest, terror ripping through his body.

"Marcus, they've found him, he's alive, he's bloody alive!"

"Where is he, is he okay, has he been hurt?" he swallowed hard and his skin crawled at the thought of David being harmed in any way.

"He's being checked over at Corstorphine Station, and he seems fine," Taylor sounded relieved.

"Corstorphine? Why there?"

"He was left in a shopping trolley with another wee boy. Passers-by stopped to help and phoned it in apparently."

"You'd better go back and get Maria. Don't let her drive, or do you want us to send a set to get her?" Taylor asked.

"Is there a set free to do it. I don't trust myself to drive any further than I have to, and I need to see my boy, I need to hold him," Marcus expressed in earnest.

"I'll get one and I'll see you there, and drive carefully. I told you he'd be okay, didn't I?"

Taylor tapped the wheel impatiently as she waited for the security gate to open at the station, the ambulance was still there.

Her heart sank a little as her mind imagined little David being injured in any way.

She swiped her card, allowed Fran to enter first as she held the door open and they went in through the back entrance and asked where the Sergeant's office was but they were met by the Sergeant who led the way to the interview suite where the boys were being examined.

She pushed open the door gently and peeked her head round to look in.

The boys were on comfortable seats with their legs swinging back and forward as the paramedic played games with them while they checked them over. Their infectious giggles rang out through the station, a sound that everyone was glad to hear.

David looked up first and saw Taylor. He jumped up and ran towards her, a familiar face at last. She knelt down to greet him, hugging him tightly. Wee David wrapped his arms round her and asked where his mummy and daddy were. She squeezed him gently again and told him that they'd be there soon. She smiled at him and asked who his friend was.

"He's called Januk. He was in that horrible room with me, with that mean man. He doesn't speak the same as me though, but he's nice, he's my pal".

Marcus abandoned his car in front of the station, not prepared to wait for the car park gate to open. He swiped in and ran up the stairs in threes, an officer recognising him and pointing the way to the right floor.

He could hear Taylor and David chatting away quite the thing and tears flooded his eyes, love spilling over in his heart at the sound of the familiar little voice, something he was terrified that he'd never hear again.

His head appeared round the door and David didn't notice at first, but when he did he shrieked out in excitement "Daddy, daddy," as he came running over open armed and pounced onto him nearly knocking him over.

"Why are you crying, is something wrong?" David wiped the tears away from his dad's face, bewildered as to why his big strong daddy would be crying. He comforted him as best he could, repeatedly kissing Marcus's forehead.

"Where's mummy?"

"She's coming as quickly as she can. She'll be here soon, I promise. A police car is going to get her."

Just then Maria arrived at the station. She was visibly shaking, glad of the lift as there was no way she could have driven there safely. She could barely control her breath and her tears were clouding her eyes.

She was led up the stairs, her visitor pass clipped to her coat, apprehensive in case David was hurt or broken in other ways.

She hesitated, clasping her hands on her chest before she walked into the room, David looked up and his eyes lit up instantly, "MUMMY, MUMMY!"

He ran to her and she melted as she felt the warmth flow back into her soul, her child's smile still undamaged, unchanged from his ordeal. His sweet voice was music to her ears. She, like Marcus, had thought the worst, that they may never see their precious little boy again. His arms wrapped tightly round her neck.

Marcus moved over to join Maria and David and surrounded them both with his arms. The emotion in the room was overflowing. The officers present were clearly affected by the moment and they too were visibly relieved.

Marcus turned to the other little boy in the room and spoke to him slowly. The boy looked sad and when Marcus spoke it was clear he didn't understand very well. He held out his hand to the boy who took it in his. Marcus shook it, the boy shaking back, smiling a little.

Marcus turned and looked up at the cop in the room, "How are we getting on with little Januk? Any trace of where he might have come from?"

"Nothing so far but we think he may have been trafficked here and sold on for sex," he replied quietly to make sure the boys didn't hear.

Marcus's face went red with anger. He felt sick at the thought of these two boys being subject to anything like that, and more, knowing where they had found the murder victim, and what could have happened at the finale of the evening.

Once all the processes and requirements were completed, Marcus and Marie left happily with David to return home and to some semblance of normality. Little Januk was taken into care.

Chapter 28
Back to work

Nathan almost skipped up the steps to the second floor at Fettes; he felt much better, fighting fit and ready for a day's work. He felt rejuvenated by the last few days and was now on the lookout for the woman he thought was Amy and hoped he would see her again. He was met by a colleague, another joiner, who asked how he was, following his absence of a couple of days after his little episode the other day.

Amy also headed off to work, trying to maintain a semblance of normality. She too had had a hectic couple of days. She had also been feeling some warmth and true affection towards her partner Kerr, which for her was not normal. She usually treated him like a convenient companion, someone that was just there but who she didn't feel anything for. Her head allowed herself to think that she may actually be able to live a normal life, filled with love and affection, which is all that she had ever dreamt of.

Taylor and Fran were back at the office both relieved at the two boys being found, Marcus staying home with Maria and David for the day. Just as they were about head for a coffee, the DCI came out of her office, with a slightly stern look on her face.

"I don't want to burst anyone's bubble here but there is still a murderer out there that has killed two men and injured several more. We have a duty to trace that person and get the evidence to prosecute them for what they have done and hopefully stop them doing it again, because I think they've got a real taste for it now."

Taylor looked up, a little perplexed at the thought that they were slacking in any way, because they weren't, they were just enjoying the relief of yesterday.

Taylor held her stare towards the DCI, a little confrontational at first and then she saw a change in the DCI's gaze, very subtle, but it was there. She had deliberately held the look for longer than necessary. Sommerville felt it and so did Taylor, both of them not intentionally looking for anything.

Fran smiled at Taylor knowing fine well that this sort of pushy behaviour would get right up her goat and have the opposite response.

"Cheeky mare," she whispered under her breath, "I think she means well though." The last thing Taylor needed was an unhealthy relationship with her new boss. Fran smiled at her and giggled, she too not willing to get on the wrong side of Ms Sommerville.

Findlay poked his head round the door, a little smirk on his face at the fact that Taylor had just had her feathers clipped, or so he thought anyway.

She looked straight at him and shook her head. He just couldn't help himself although the presence of the DCI these days had certainly put his gas at a peep and he could not berate Taylor or anyone else openly anymore or he'd find himself in trouble and he didn't want to draw any more unwanted attention to himself.

Chapter 29
Nightmares

The room was dark, shadows crawling from the dim streetlight down below and from the moon that shone menacingly above. Her tiny frame shivered with the cold that crept into her underfed little body, her pyjamas filthy and in tatters affording no warmth to the cold winter night. The thin makeshift blanket was also ineffective and she tried to snuggle backwards into the body of little Nathan curled up beside her, fast asleep.

The noise was faint but audible, her ears pricked up to try and hear it again, but she didn't want to look. She hated this room, dank and inhospitable, and those dolls, she hated those porcelain dolls.

Her head shot up from the bare mattress as she heard it again, a scratching in the corner of the room, slightly louder, rat like and terrifying. She pulled the blanket was up in front of her eyes, peering over and straining to see what it was in the corner, buried in a sea of piercing blue eyes, all fixed on her.

The noise continued, Amy shook in terror, eyes now watering as she grabbed at Nathan to try and wake him up. She tugged and tugged at him, calling weakly to wake him, but she couldn't. The noise was getting louder and louder, which meant whatever it was that was making it was getting closer to her, closing in on her. She wet the bed, the warm liquid seeping into the mattress, crawling down her legs in its own treacherous route of degradation. This wasn't the time to worry about the punishment she would receive at the hands of her twisted parents, there was something more sinister in the room with her.

Scrabbly nails scraped against the ground as it clawed its way towards her bed. She felt the covers being tugged off her as it started to climb up the side of the bed. She lay there frozen unable to move or call as she saw the grubby sheet being pulled away from her face. She was now staring straight ahead too frightened to close her eyes, waiting to see what was climbing up to meet her. Her heart raced and pounded. She stared, never daring to close her eyes, as she saw it rising up into her line of sight.

Piercing blue eyes came peering over the edge of the bed, round and glassy on a grotesque porcelain face, white and circular, with bright red lips, its hands stiff and made of plastic. Amy nearly choked as she watched it climbing up towards her, hands moving and gripping at her. She tried to scream but no sound came from her mouth; she was frozen to the spot. The doll pulled itself up onto the bed and crawled closer to her, tilting its head slowly to the side. Its lips parted and revealed sharp peg like metal teeth bared demon like as it moved towards her face, Amy twisted round to Nathan. This time she heard herself screaming out loud as she pulled him round. His eyes too were piercing blue and his face cold, white and doll like. His mouth opened like that of a vampire, fangs sharp and terrifying.

Amy screamed and screamed and screamed until Kerr gently put his arm round her shoulders. He was used to this. Amy regularly suffered from severe and damaging nightmares. Terror ripped through her night after night as her childhood true life nightmare haunted her adult life. She was soaked through, the sheets wet with sweat and urine. Even in her adulthood she still wet the bed when reliving the horror of the abuse suffered at the hands of her parents.

Kerr was caring and kind to Amy, never judging her, never asking, but always willing to listen if she ever wanted to share her inner torment, torment which he could only wonder what it was that had happened to her, and what could have caused this much pain and fear in her adult life.

This time Amy leant into Kerr and allowed him to hold and comfort her, something she usually rebuked, as any physical contact ignited old scars and vivid painful memories of her brutal and tragic upbringing.

Kerr looked at her. Tonight felt different. Amy was wanting to be held and she started to talk to him. She was tearful, sadness pouring from her mouth, words of an abused child. She struggled hard to recount the details of her very early years but she persevered dredging up the painful memories that she had deliberately tried to bury deep inside her.

Amy longed to let go of the pain that had ruled her life every single day, unable to trust, to feel or to live. She had just existed, and now for the first time ever, there was a change, a twist of emotion, a glimmer of hope and the only thing she could think of that may have triggered this change was the chance meeting with the man, who she was now sure was her loving twin brother Nathan. Her twin that had been separated from her because social services believed that they were too damaged to remain together. Nathan had always tried to protect her. He would put himself in the way of a beating or further sexual assault to keep them away from her. He would rather feel his own pain than hear hers, her screams at the hands of their torture cut him deeper and hurt him more than the assaults carried out on him.

Amy talked to Kerr for hours and the relief she felt at finally being able to share the burden of her abuse was immense. It didn't take away her inner pain but it felt nice to have someone care about her and listen to her, someone she had finally let in and trusted. She realised she did actually love him.

Kerr listened and held her close at the end of her traumatic release.

That night she moved into his space and allowed him to hold her, comfort her and love her.

Chapter 30
Night Out

All of the early shift team were heading out after work for a well-earned drink at the Raeburn Hotel to celebrate the two boys being traced safe and well. There was still so much work to do with the perpetrator still out there but they were entitled to a little down time, to live, love and to forget for a few hours, finally away from the pressure and expectation that always hung over them. They trusted their colleagues that followed on the next shift and who took hold of the working reigns firmly. Taylor's team walked wearily away from a busy and traumatic day.

Each and every one of them had a smile on their face, however, for Marcus and Maria, and the return of their precious son David. There was a new enquiry into the identification of the other fortunate boy found with David. Everyone had worked 16 to 20 hours straight for the last couple of days, nobody wanting to leave the enquiry, but it had been worth it. The opposite result would have been catastrophic and heart breaking for all of them.

They smiled and chatted, laughter in the air, the relief obvious. If the outcome had been any different, life in the office would never have been the same again.

Taylor flicked her hair over her shoulder as she strode down the road. Fran walked quickly with the group in front, enjoying the pleasant change of mood. There was an excited buzz as little groups of detectives spoke of the events over the last few days and weeks, and of the future. DCI, Brooke Sommerville even joined them in going out for a drink. Findlay the Inspector, however, chose not to share a drink with his hard-working subordinates.

Once in the bar Fran sat next to Taylor, the boss also sitting close to them at the same large table. Everyone put £20 in the drinks kitty to start with. Tomorrow was a day off and everyone wanted to let loose a little, get a little drunk and chill. Glasses clinked together as they toasted the return of the children. More drink was had in their name and several hours went by.

Taylor's words began to slur a little as she talked and Fran mimicked her for her own amusement. Taylor turned and smiled fondly at her and squeezed her leg under the table, hoping that it would go unnoticed, but it didn't. Brooke had been watching Taylor too . She had wondered about those two prior to the night out.

There was an unwelcome pang of unexplained jealousy but she had no right or history with Taylor to feel that way. Taylor carried on talking to the group as Fran took her hand and stroked the length of her leg from knee to her inner thigh. Taylor felt herself flush with unexpected pleasure. She hadn't felt anything like that for a while and she dropped her hand down to meet Fran's. Their hands held together for a short moment before Fran gently broke free and stroked her a little more intimately, subtly and just enough to show Taylor her intention when they got home. Taylor managed to carry on her chain of conversation without even flinching, just a glance at Fran to acknowledge her naughtiness. DC Lomond chatted away, animated and entertaining, his sense of humour appreciated by the team. He looked at Taylor too as he had once thought that he had a chance with her before Marcus told him how it was. This didn't change the fact that he still admired the view, along with a few others.

Taylor excused herself as she walked a little unsteadily

towards the Ladies room, looking back laughing apologetically. Fran waited to avoid being too obvious. She wanted Taylor, her absence for the last couple of days had been a cold and uncomfortable experience, as Taylor had practically closed down and withdrawn any warmth to or from anyone. Her only focus had been Marcus and the search for his son.

Fran could see Taylor's boots underneath the door. She couldn't help but giggle quietly as she heard Taylor relieve herself of the over-consumption of alcohol and commented about some kind of race horse.

She waited and watched as a tipsy Taylor steadied herself rocking slightly against the cubicle. Taylor cursed a little at the fastening on her jeans and then straightened herself up before walking out, forgetting that Fran was there. She had only walked a couple of steps before Fran's arm wrapped round her middle. Her mouth pushed up against Taylor's, her kiss soft and needy. Taylor met hers with a far more forceful and dominant response, mouth open and desperate, but Fran just pulled Taylor back into the cubicle to avoid anyone walking in on their encounter. Fran wanted her, wanted to touch her and love her. She didn't want to be ignored. She stroked her hand over Taylor's breasts and then pushed her nimble fingers inside her blouse, softly rubbing over Taylor's taught nipple. She kissed her chest and opened up a couple of buttons to kiss her breasts, pulling Taylor's bra down to expose her and take her into her mouth. Taylor was taken aback; she was normally the one in control but she didn't mind. She was mellow and intoxicated and she wanted Fran's touch. She invited her with her powerful kisses that she stole as Fran came up to meet her mouth. Fran's hand slid over Taylor's trousers and she moaned loudly as she was already aroused. Her fingers pushed firmly over Taylor, sending a naughty pleasure right through her.

Taylor was aware that someone had joined them and was in the next cubicle. Taylor giggled quietly and pointed to the exit. They both knew this wasn't going any further. Taylor opened the door, quickly washed her hands and left.

Fran stayed to use the facilities and heard the door open in the next cubicle and the person move over to the sinks.

Brooke took her time washing her hands. She wasn't a fool, she knew that the two of them had been there and shook her head at their behaviour.

Fran came out of the cubicle, too nosey to let them leave without knowing who it was.

"Ma'am," she said respectfully with a flush in her cheeks and another on her neck from her little encounter.

"Brooke," Sommerville replied, "call me Brooke when we're out. I am a human being you know". She was smiling and her eyes floated down to Fran's neck and back up, letting Fran know she had seen how red it was.

"Are you too hot?" she said with mirth in her voice fully aware who had just left a minute before.

"Yeh, just a bit, it is a little warm through there," Fran lied badly.

"Yep, definitely hot in here too," she said with a smile on her face.

Fran now realised that her boss was joking with her, although she was blissfully unaware that there was a hint of jealousy there too.

Everyone was back at the table and Taylor looked up at her boss, just as Sommerville looked up too. Their eyes met and Taylor was aware that again, Brooke had held her stare, this time it seemed with more intensity. Taylor put this down to the booze.

She felt Fran squeeze her leg and gesture with her eyes and head that it was time to leave, the reason clear from their brief unfinished encounter in the toilets.

Taylor felt aroused and wanted to go home too, to allow Fran to continue with what she had planned for her. She wanted to offer her body to be taken for a change, she wanted to be wanted physically and wanted to feel desired after the feeling of complete inadequacy early in the week.

Taylor and Fran got up to leave at the same time and there was the quiet rumble of chatter and rumour mongering instantly, which was normal behaviour from their colleagues if there was a hint of an affair. Only Marcus knew that anything was going on between them, and now the DCI was in on their affair as well.

They gave their apologies independently and Taylor was quite obviously a little drunk. Fran saw this and said to the group "I'll make sure that she gets in a taxi safely".

DC Lomond quipped, "I bet she will," and the two beside him tittered to themselves.

Fran gave him a hard stare, aware that they would be the next topic of conversation.

Nonplussed by this, Fran took Taylor's arm to steady her as they made their way out of the door.

It wasn't too late and Stockbridge had a frequent supply of cabs coming to and from the town centre, being just down from Fredrick Street and leading to a major trunk road and many other areas of town.

Fran's hand shot up as the first taxi came into view, its inviting orange light glowing like a saviour in the night. It stopped just beside them and she opened the door and assisted Taylor inside. She was teetering on her heels and very obviously under the influence of alcohol. Fran gave her a little shove, which unfortunately sent her face first into the back seat.

The driver leaned over to look at them as they laughed and clowned around trying to get themselves upright and onto the seats. He said, "She better not spew in my cab or you'll be paying the 50 quid to clean it up, right".

Fran looked at him with a scowl. "Keep yer hair on, she's not that pissed, and if she does vomit, I will make sure it's paid for," she said cheekily to the grump behind the wheel.

She gave the address, hers, and they both sat back in the cab. Taylor began to dose off and Fran put her arm round her, holding her in a way that said she was more than just a caring friend. This was noticed by the cab driver and he rolled his eyes but he kept on watching them as Taylor turned round to snuggle into Fran. Taylor not even aware that she was drunk leant toward Fran and kissed her full on the mouth, a lingering passionate kiss. She fully aware of her faculties and nowhere near as drunk as the taxi driver had thought.

The kissing got a little more steamy as the journey went on, both of them not allowing it to go too far as they were aware they were being watched and they had already felt the taxi straighten up twice as his eyes were clearly not on the road at all times.

On arrival, Fran pushed the notes into his waiting hand and said, "Keep the change mate, and keep your eyes on the road next time or you'll cause an accident one day." Her tone was sarcastic and a little disgruntled because of the hostility he had shown when they first got in.

Taylor was first to walk up the pathway, far more steady on her feet this time as Fran steered her forward with her hands playfully on her hips. They were both relaxed for the first time in days. Taylor leant against the door as Fran stepped up to her and kissed her passionately, full of lust and desire for the warmth she knew she would get from Taylor. Fran turned the key and Taylor nearly fell through the door backwards as her weight shifted. She had to take a wide step so as not to fall.

"Easy Fran, do you want me on the floor," Taylor joked, as she smiled at her.

"Well actually," Fran was in fits at her boss, unsteady and looking a little dishevelled, which was totally out of character for her. Taylor was always in control and well groomed but tonight she had allowed herself to let her hair down and become a normal and vulnerable person, just like everyone else.

Fran thought this unusual display of vulnerability was endearing. It was nice to see a softer side to Taylor, one that was very rarely shown. This week had really got to Taylor. Her close friend and colleague Marcus had been a broken and helpless man. Only through a strange and unlikely twist of fate had his son been saved. The outcome could easily have been another murder enquiry, that of a child, an innocent and beautiful child.

Fran took Taylor's hand and steadied her. Smiling warmly, she led her to the bedroom, and turned on a couple of lamps that glowed softly and instantly warmed the room. She turned

Taylor round and gently pushed her backwards onto the bed, the soft bedclothes inviting and warm. Taylor was a little taken aback when Fran lay gently down on top of her and began kissing her again, slowly at first. Her kisses started to travel down her body, kisses light on top of her blouse, lingering where Fran knew would please her most, Fran's thigh pushed up firmly between Taylor's legs, Taylor enjoying the sensation through her thin dress trousers. Fran's hand joined her thigh and undid Taylor's buttons, helping her out of her trousers and underwear. Fran kissed down between the buttons of Taylor's blouse, gently caressing her breasts with her mouth. Taylor's nipples were exposed from beneath her pristine white bra, the licks from Fran tongue igniting Taylor's arousal. Fran's hand was now gently stroking between her legs and Taylor's pleasure was very noticeable. Her mouth followed her hands as Taylor's hands gripped the covers and she drew in a sharp breath. Fran pleasured her, her fingers and hands smoothly enhancing the orgasm that followed. It was a twisting and deep release of needy pent up emotion for Taylor. She had not realised how much she needed to be loved and wanted, and relished being able to lose control, rather than always being in control. Fran continued to kiss and hold her, unaware at just how stressed and out of sorts Taylor had been these last days.

Taylor had a head full of unfinished issues - Kay, the investigation, her lifestyle, her feelings for Fran, and the trauma of the abduction by Brennan and the overwhelming negative affect it had had on her personally, which she had never addressed or sought any counselling for.

Fran helped Taylor into bed and within seconds she was asleep, her body giving in to the fatigue that had grown over the days from the stress of the enquiry, the relentless amount of work and pressure upon all of them and the lack of sleep that had accumulated with no respite. It was a culmination of everything and at last a chance to let go, relax and take a mini break.

Fran lay close beside her, offering comfort and love that was no longer acknowledged as Taylor was now fast asleep. Fran too had had an incredibly busy day but unlike Taylor she had just had a single task to complete and had dealt with it until fruition. Taylor, on the other hand, had to juggle everyone's jobs and tasks, making sure they were all dealt with to a satisfactory conclusion and that nothing was missed. She also shouldered the responsibility that came with her role.

Fran lay awake, unable to shut off. Taylor had not committed to her, never saying anything that confirmed a relationship. She held her feelings close to her chest. The last couple of days had shown her that Taylor avoided looking for support or assistance when she needed it most. She had chosen to isolate herself and not seek support from Fran in any way. This worried Fran as her feelings and emotions for Taylor had grown. She was quite sure she was in love with her but was completely in the dark if there were any reciprocated feelings. Was Taylor still holding out for Kay and was she just an affair and nothing more? She knew that Taylor liked her and enjoyed their time together but was there more?

Fran thought about the case as well as her own personal life. She was certain that these kids were saved by the person the team were hunting. This in itself added an unnatural twist of emotion in the capture and reporting of someone who had clearly saved the lives of two young children. It was likely they were also the victims of sexual abuse. Unfortunately, they were suspected of brutally murdering and torturing several men, irrespective of the crimes these victims had committed. This superseded their lifesaving actions to risk their own capture to ensure the kids weren't harmed.

Chapter 31
Forensic Results

DNA and fibres had been found on the garden wall at the murder scene, the location where the children were now confirmed as being held. There were hair samples of both children that were held there and the clothing present was proved to have been worn by them. The property was being protected with tarpaulin and other evidence protecting devices to avoid any vital clues being lost.

The DNA and clothing fibres found on the wall would be far more difficult to attribute to the possible suspect and proved beyond reasonable doubt, as there could have been a legitimate reason for anyone to have been on an outer wall, no matter how farfetched the explanation.

The DCI was in early, as usual, and was very aware that Taylor and Fran were not. This bothered her a little. She knew that they would still be with each other from the other night and her thoughts wondered what sort of activities they may have shared. She was finding herself drawn to Taylor and her lifestyle, and her thoughts had led them to be together in her mind on more than a few occasions.

Marcus popped his head round the door and everyone who was in the office gasped in amazement. They all got up and embraced him warmly, the smile on his face warm and genuine, a smile many thought they would never see again. He was upbeat, back to his immaculate old self, back in control and ready to work. He wanted these crimes solved, like in any case he was ever involved in, full commitment in everything he did. In this particular case, he wanted it solved to allow him to meet the person that saved the boys, especially his David, even though, they were still a brutal criminal. He inwardly praised them, that they appeared not to have spared a thought for themselves when they took the boys out of that vile place, risking their own capture to save them.

Marcus went to his desk, his heart racing with anticipation at the day ahead. He had a new lease of life. He had been a little torn leaving home that morning, an unnatural fear that the same thing would happen again. He and Maria had talked and talked about David's safety, even though they had always been careful before. They didn't want to become prisoners in their own home and spoil his childhood. They were going to be sensible and safe but both would never stop looking over their shoulders, never wanting to feel that lost, with such a desperate and empty feeling, ever again. The sickness they felt to the pit of their stomachs at the thought of their little boy being so alone and in danger, helpless to save him. He shook his head to clear those thoughts from his mind and got down to work, bringing himself up to speed with what else had been going on in the last couple of days. The enquiry was ticking along and there was great news regarding the DNA found on the wall, although there were no hits on any of the databases, CHS or PNC.

His thoughts now turned to requesting permission to do a sweep for DNA recovery from a section of the Edinburgh public - males within a certain age group, most would come forward and offer it. Those on their lists that didn't provide it, naturally, would be asked why not, and some would be quizzed in regard to other crimes that came to light with this gift of their personal identification code. He went through to the DCI and politely mentioned his idea to her. Of course the thought had occurred to her too but there were logistics involved of getting the ball rolling, the ins and outs of the legality to require people to do this.

Taylor appeared next in the open plan office, bright and relaxed looking, her three-piece fitted suit figure hugging and elegant, her hair with a silky shine cascading down her back. She noticed Marcus at the desk and she gave him a beaming smile and skipped over to him to hug him as he sat, squeezing him as hard as she could, squishing a friendly kiss into his cheek.

"Steady on now," he joked as he turned to share the embrace.

"I didn't expect you to be back so soon, but hey, we need your skill here, I'm glad you're back!" Taylor squashed her face against him again, giving him another big kiss, with true affection and relief for this lovely man. Taylor loved him, she trusted him with her life and respected everything about him. He was simply a decent, genuine caring guy.

Taylor sat down opposite Marcus, and the last stragglers came into the office before the briefing. Taylor stood up and addressed the team going through all of the evidence they had to date, the leads to follow and the dead ends, which unfortunately were many.

"We have the disappearance of CS spray from here. This should be our most positive lead although CCTV does not cover everything and everywhere and there are numerous contractors here just now for the renovations, but we'll start there. These sprays hold the key, although the lowest number of people for in here on any day is in the hundreds so I appreciate it will take a while to check everyone out."

"What's the significance of the porcelain dolls then? Where do they come into it, because this is very significant to me, something personal? How are they choosing their victims,?Do they have access to our systems or are they surfing open sources to find out who and what their victims' past involved? Who is he, what is his past, why is he doing this?"

Fran piped up and said, "You're assuming that it is going to be a male?"

Taylor turned to her, the thought had crossed her mind and it wasn't an impossibility, but the type of crimes being committed and the brutality involved, was leading the majority of them to think male, rather than female.

"Good point, and this won't be ignored if the evidence ever points that way but regarding the DNA we will start with males 20 to 35 years, although remaining open to your suggestion Fran."

Once the briefing finished and everyone had their lines of enquiry to follow, they left the office leaving Marcus, Taylor and Sommerville. Findlay had phoned in sick that day.

They went through the logistics of the DNA, CCTV for Fettes and interrogation of all entry points into the building and what passes had been used.

"I think we just start here with the DNA, and I'm well aware some people won't be happy about it, but we need to do this."

Sommerville asked them to get the resources to facilitate the DNA collection and she would seek authority for this to get the ball rolling.

Chapter 32
The Meeting

Nathan walked into the front counter security area of Fettes, signed in and received his temporary security pass to go about his business within the building. All contractors are vetted and checked out to lower the chances of security breaches. He went on his way and through to the offices and facilities that were being refurbished and renovated. Walls of less than colourful paint and certainly not inviting. But brighter than before and unmarked by many visitors.

Amy was also on her way to work. She wasn't at the usual social work offices today. She had several meetings at Fettes and was full of anticipation at the possibility of meeting the man she believed to be her brother.

Amy parked her car in the street, fed the meter and ran up the walkway to the entrance, her haste due to the excitement at maybe seeing her brother again. Nathan used to be the only person she loved, the only one that had shown her kindness in her very early and most vulnerable years. She was a visitor to Fettes so had to sign in and get her temporary pass. The sheet was handed to her and she was just about to casually sign at the bottom, but decided to look up the list and read some of the other names. Her heart skipped a beat as she saw the name Nathan. The surname she didn't recognise but the first name Nathan made her pulse race. This was too much of a coincidence she thought. Even though there are thousands of Nathans in this world, she believed that this one was him. The reason for his visit was stated as refurbishment, and the man she had tried to help had been wearing a joinery belt. *It's him, I knew it. I was allowed to keep my first name when they took me into care so he must have kept his too.*

Amy asked the security guard where the workmen would have their breaks and who their supervisor was. She looked again at the sheet to see the time Nathan had come in. She had only missed him by ten minutes. She couldn't wait to find him, to talk to him and to tell him who she was.

As Amy made her way through the canteen, she was aware of a couple of detectives getting drinks at the coffee shop. She recognised Taylor as the tall woman that had read out a couple of the press releases about the brutal crimes that were being carried out in the city. Amy stood behind her in the queue and bought herself a coffee too.

Taylor was talking to Marcus, not guarded in any way as she talked about DNA. This was not a secret, it would soon be common knowledge. Amy was so nosey, she said excuse me and asked them how things were going with the inquiry. Taylor recognised her from the social work department but of course would not give anything away.

"We're getting there. Things like this always take time," Taylor said, always polite and understanding of other department's curiosity about cases like this one.

Amy was happy enough with the reply and wished them good luck and went on her way to find her brother. She climbed up to the second floor offices that were having the partition walls removed and being made open plan. As she walked in everyone turned and looked at her accept the chap hammering the skirting board in the corner. She looked round at all of the faces but his wasn't there. She couldn't help but feel the disappointment twist uncomfortably inside her, until the guy in the corner stopped hammering when his boss called his name.

"Nathan. Oi, Nathan! There's a lady here to see you," his boss shouted over the hammering.

He stopped and got up, saying "Who is it, who would want to see me in here?"

When he turned round he saw a woman he recognised as the lady that had helped him when he fell the other day. This time he looked at her longer. He looked straight at her face, which was smiling right at him, her eyes fixed on him in recognition of that long lost familiar face. She had already made up her mind it was him and even though he was years older, his eyes and face were still that of her brother's recognisable features. His kind and trustworthy eyes were still the same.

"Nathan, I'm Amy, and I think I'm your sister!" The words just came out of her mouth, an involuntary thing, her thoughts slipping out, anticipation and apprehension in her heart that he may not recognise or remember her.

Nathan looked at her and scratched his head in disbelief but had not taken his eyes off her. He smiled; he recognised her. She still had impish features and her eyes, too, were just the same as when she was a little girl.

He moved towards her and put his arms round her, hugging her instinctively and when he was close to her, he was absolutely sure it was her. Both had tears in their eyes, neither of them ever thinking that they would see each other again as all of their files had been fully restricted. Everyone in the office just stared at them wondering what this was all about but didn't say anything because there was obviously some deeply emotional story here.

Nathan explained to his boss what the score was and asked if he could have ten minutes to go for a quick chat, which of course he was permitted to do. His boss said to take longer, squeezing Nathan's arm as he went.

Once seated in the canteen, they sat silently at first and just stared at each other, painful emotions emerging from the enormity of their shared situation, the suffering endured by them and the forced separation many years ago, which was the most painful wound of all. The pain cut deep as the two children had relied on each other so much. Nathan had been her rock. Unfortunately, due to the level of abuse they had suffered and the possible permanent affect it would have on them, the decision had been made to separate them. The damage both physically and mentally may have changed one or both of them beyond repair and due to that they may have been a danger to each other. Social services couldn't take that risk keeping them together. Unaware of the strength of the bond that Amy and Nathan shared, they did not realise the damage they were doing by separating them. Both became insular and badly affected by this choice, and without each other the isolation had manifested within one or both of them causing untold permanent damage.

They shared their stories and Amy wanted to meet Millie, the niece she hadn't known existed until this moment. She started to cry again and Nathan instinctively put his arm round her shoulders, something he had always done when she was upset. This action alone caused deja vu, which stabbed straight through Nathan's heart, bringing back all of the tragic memories of his failed struggle to protect her. He held her, sobbing as he apologised to her. She told him not to be so silly and that it was not his fault. She went on to tell him that he had made her life back then bearable and had saved her from so much more torment because he had endured it for her. They talked like they were back in their childhood room, their closeness reignited, the bond instantly back and time apart irrelevant. It was something that could never be erased after what they had been through together.

Nathan invited Amy to visit his house the next day and stay for tea with Jen and little Millie. She quickly accepted. Nathan then apologised for his ignorance and asked if she had a partner and extended his welcome to them too.

"I do have a partner. He's lovely and his name is Kerr but I would rather visit on my own at first, if that is alright, so we can talk. He doesn't really know much about what happened to us back then and I don't think I want to share our time together, not for the first time anyway!"

"I totally understand and respect that. Millie will love to meet you. She's wonderful. You need to have kids Amy, it's the best thing in the world. You can make sure they have the start in life that they deserve, loving and safe, unlike ours." He paused before speaking again, "It really helps Amy, it helps you heal. It warms the freezing void that you never think will leave. You spend your days so happy making sure that they never ever feel the way we did. She's helped me live again."

"Who knows, maybe I will, but I still have nightmares nearly every night. I can't sleep, I still feel that ripping pain even now! The darkness, the fear, everything, I feel it every day."

"I'll help you Amy. I'll listen. You talk it out and we'll get help for you. You need to let it go," Nathan said truly hoping he could help her.

They walked back up the stairs and went their separate ways, both looking forward to the next day and spending time together at last. They had 22 years to make up for and many, many wounds to heal.

Amy walked into the office as she was attending a multi-agency meeting in relation to child protection. The social work team, the police offender management unit and other agencies were all in attendance to discuss another vile case, where there was proven sexual abuse of two young children, one five and the other six months old. There was physical evidence that both had been violated. The case had been heard in court and due to the age of the victims and the length of time before the crimes were reported, there was no DNA or forensic evidence available, the medical examination only proving the incidents had happened but nothing to prove who had carried out the assaults. Due to insufficient evidence, a conviction had not been secured and both children were now on the child protection register and the suspect was a free man. The mother of the children, however, believed her now ex-partner was guilty and had used her naivety and her desire for his affection to get to the children. She was now working in conjunction with the police to ensure the man would never have access to them every again, even though he had been released without charge. This was one of the fears of any police officer, to see someone that everyone believed to be guilty walk free, because they could not get a sufficiency of evidence to prove beyond reasonable doubt their guilt.

Amy listened to the harrowing details of the abuse of the five-year-old and the physical evidence on the baby. Her heart pulling painfully within her, the veins on her neck pulsing visibly as her inner torment made her feel physically sick, instantly washing away the safety and warmth she had just felt in the arms of her brother. *Why do I do this job, why, if I can't save them all, it is too painful to listen too, I can't bear it.* Her own personal torture now came rushing back to her with force and she had to excuse herself from the room. This was noticed by everyone there. They saw that her face was flushed and that she didn't look well at all, everyone thinking she was clearly ill.

Chapter 33
DNA trawl

Taylor and her team had sent out a press release appealing for males within a certain age group within Edinburgh to come forward and offer their DNA, all of which was guaranteed to be destroyed at the end of the investigation. There was a positive buzz about the office as the detectives were carrying out a minute by minute CCTV trawl around the area of Tesco on the day of the children being found. There were numerous cars that had left the area in that time and there was another car park outwith the CCTV coverage, which they presumed would have been where the suspect parked, clearly deliberately avoiding being filmed, which was unfortunate, because once out of this vicinity there would be thousands of vehicles.

They also had all of the dolls that had been left as calling cards, their age and where they could have been purchased. There was a connection to all of these brutal assaults but where was the perpetrator getting the information to base their choice of victim upon? What was their story? Was that significant? There was also the non-registered DNA left behind at the scene and, of course, what the two little boys had said, which unfortunately had been very little, almost like there was an allegiance between them and their saviour. No matter how much their parents and social workers tried to persuade them to speak, the boys wouldn't budge on the details of the kind person that had saved them, almost aware if they told it wouldn't be good for the stranger and they didn't want anything bad to happen to them.

Marcus tried to explain to Taylor just how much of a closed book David had been since his release in relation to the person that saved him. "God knows what's been said to these boys but neither of them is giving anything away."

Taylor was amazed by this. Normally you couldn't stop children speaking and spilling the beans but not this time. This was also a first for Sommerville, both children utterly tight-lipped and no matter what treats and promises were made, they still refused to say a word.

The DCI asked Taylor to come into her office for a one to one meeting. This wasn't something Taylor was used to with Findlay. He never showed an interest in her opinion. He also didn't like to admit he was a little intimidated by her presence.

Taylor didn't mind this meeting though. There was a lot to discuss and she didn't mind a little help and guidance. Fran, however, watched closely as Taylor walked into the office and closed the door behind her, a slight wave of jealousy brewing inside her. They sat at opposite sides of the desk. Taylor spread out some paper work in front of them and they got down to work, going over the plan and what they had and, clearly, what they didn't have. They also discussed the luck and timing of finding the boys and possible reasons why they wouldn't talk. They were both genuinely engrossed in the investigation, neither thinking about anything else until Taylor's foot knocked against Brooke's accidentally. It was totally unintentional but both paused in their conversation, Taylor apologised but there was a little embarrassment in both of them and an uncomfortable flush in Brooke's face, which Taylor noticed straight away. After the slightly embarrassing and enlightening moment of attraction, they carried on about their business professionally but Taylor was now certain that the DCI had a little twinkle in her eye for her and Taylor couldn't help but enjoy that thought and what may or may not happen. Taylor was very aware that she was deliberately holding back from showing any commitment to Fran and she could feel Fran was aware of that too but she hadn't said anything to her yet.

Taylor gathered up her things up as Brooke ended the meeting in her usual slightly abrupt and must get on manner but Brooke held her gaze, admiring Taylor's wonderful physique and her alluring and attractive smile.

Taylor said, "I'll get a team with the lists from the DNA trawl and get them started on them right away, even though I don't think for a minute he will come forward".

She turned and walked back to the office, aware of Fran looking up to try and catch her eye. She turned and smiled at her, shrugging her shoulders a bit in an innocent way as if to say 'it's not my fault', which Fran sort of accepted.

Chapter 34
Reunited

Amy was nervous walking up the path to Nathan's house. She had brought wine and flowers and a gift for little Millie, a cuddly dog with a stretchy pink lead. She couldn't wait to meet her niece.

She hesitated before pressing the bell and took a deep breath before ringing it. She waited and the door opened. The most beautiful little girl ran up behind Nathan and practically jumped into Amy's arms and said, "Hi Auntie Amy, I'm Millie, it's nice to meet you".

Amy thought this was wonderful. She clicked instantly with Millie and Amy couldn't wait to spend time with her. The only relation she had was Nathan and now suddenly she had this perfect little gift as well.

The feeling of love and protection she felt for the little girl put her head in a spin and she felt feelings that she didn't think were possible, pure love. She then met Jen and she too was lovely and very easy to talk to, very open and responsive to Amy and really glad that they had finally found each other and welcomed her into their family.

She loved Nathan and was well aware that there were still demons in his closet and genuinely felt for them both, unable to understand what they must have gone through and how they could have lived through it.

Amy sat on the floor with Millie and played with the new toy dog. They shared the lead and pretended to walk it and teach it tricks. They then had some food and at the dining table Amy helped feed Millie and they were both in their element as they giggled the evening away, Amy almost morphing back into a child as she played. The lost innocence from her own childhood came out and their play and bond was as natural as could be. Nathan watched them with tears in his eyes and it felt like a sword had been thrust through his heart as his mind flashed back to their own childhood. A loveless, cold and cruel time, their only affection came from each other, their only laughter was when they were alone and even then, they had to be quiet or their play would invite unwanted attention from their mother and her repulsive partner.

It was time for bed and Nathan asked Amy to help Millie get her ready and to read the bedtime story, something that they had never experienced, something that other children enjoyed night after night.

Nathan had no idea what Amy had been through in her adult life, how she had grown up, or anything about her, but he trusted her with his life and knew that Millie was safe with her. She was going to get her ready and into her fresh clean night dress, bright and pink, soft cotton, with a little princess on the front, a far cry from their bed time routine. Theirs was a dark room, you either kept your dirty clothes on for warmth or were left in whatever their parents decided to leave them after they had visited them. They remembered the hunger pains, the filth, the hideous body odour, the pain and then the struggle through the night to keep warm, innocently snuggled up together with sheets, clothes, pillows and paper, anything they could use to offer heat.

Millie stood there undressed ready to get her nightie on and Amy looked at Nathan to check if it was okay to dress her. He gestured with his head to carry on. Amy felt her stomach lurch with true affection and a feral instinct to protect this little girl, who stood so vulnerably in front of her, for the rest of her life. She quickly pulled the night dress over her head and asked Nathan to put the nappy on as she didn't know how to and would prefer him to do it anyway. She gave Millie a big hug and wished her sweet dreams and kissed her fondly on her forehead. She stood at the door and blew her another kiss and said night, night, before leaving Nathan to get her off to sleep.

Amy came back down into the living room and sat on the single chair near to the couch where Jen was already sitting. There was a coffee sitting there that Jen had ready for her coming down. They carried on their conversation from dinner and felt comfortable in each other's company. Jen was a teacher and Amy a social worker and there were several aspects of their jobs that crossed over, many areas overlapping. They talked about society, parenting, poverty, cinema, Millie and the news. The topic eventually came round to the violent offences and the two suspicious deaths that had taken place in the Edinburgh area. Amy looked up at her, quickly giving her opinion on the matter, explaining why this might happen to certain people. The police had not divulged any details in relation to any possible connections between the assaults and the murders.

Nathan came into the room just as the question of the link had been mentioned. He said without hesitation, "They were up to their necks in some illegal twisted stuff and they'd been caught out". He said this with vengeful venom, not holding back his emotions. He then said, "They were all well to do and very wealthy. I think they were all kiddy fiddlers, they looked like the sort that would anyway, from their pictures in the paper".

Jen gave his leg a slap as he walked past her and said "Nathan, you can't make sweeping judgements like that".

Nathan defended himself by saying, "I bet you when it all comes out in the wash there is definitely something to do with child porn or abuse, or something along those lines".

Amy looked up at him. She could see his anger. It was clear in his eyes, pain etched in them, sadness and rage brewing up visibly inside him. She too thought there may be this type of connection with these crimes and said it out loud. Jen was staring right at Nathan. She had never seen this side of him before, it was almost like the reunion with his sister had reopened old wounds and suppressed fear and brutal torment had escaped from a sealed container, freeing a hostile and aggressive reaction at the thought that crimes like this were still happening.

Jen tapped her knees with her open palms and said, "Right, this is meant to be a fun evening, you guys can revisit this some other time! I want to get back to some well needed girl chat and you can join in Nathan".

This was enough to snap him out of his spiral of resentment and he visibly transformed back into the kind gentle man she knew.

The evening went on and they talked for ages until Jen finally retreated to bed and the siblings carried on chatting for a while longer. They got onto Amy's work and it just went from there. She hadn't meant to but she got onto talking about her most recent case and how sad and helpless it made her feel. It wasn't normal for her to talk about her work and most definitely not her cases but she trusted Nathan with her life and didn't think there would be an issue. She mentioned the children's ages and a little detail about the sexual abuse they had suffered and the worst bit of all, that the suspect had been released without charge due to insufficient evidence. Nathan put his arm round her and said "That's the system, sometimes it doesn't seem fair, when you know they are guilty, but there is nothing you can do!"

They looked at each other, their childhood fondness there between them and a shared sense of resentment at the justice system when it appeared to fail to do the right thing.

Amy smiled and got up, thanking Nathan. She had already thanked Jen. "The taxi will be here soon, I ordered it before I arrived."

"Tonight was wonderful, Nathan, you are a very lucky man with all these precious things to look after. Hopefully, we can do this again".

Nathan said, "Of course, wee Millie would love to see you again and so would we".

They hugged each other and he watched as she trotted down the path pulling her coat against the biting wind. She turned back to wave before she got in the taxi, with her infectious smile beaming back at him, a newfound warmth rekindled and an open wound finally beginning to heal.

Amy arrived home, her head swirling with the fun she had had that night and wished that her childhood had been like that of Millie's. Her mind went over the anger shown by Nathan when talking about the linked incidents on the news and his deep interest in her recent case.

Nathan came to bed and just lay there beside Jen, his mind racing with emotion, vile hatred, revenge and torment, and it was several hours before he managed to get to sleep.

Chapter 35
Recovering

She sat at the window looking out over the sea view, she loved the sea. She had been there for a couple of months now and she was finally starting to feel normal again. She no longer saw the vile face of John Brennan every day, just once in a while. He was the depraved and violent predator that had violated and brutally assaulted her with the intention of murdering her. She had suffered a nervous breakdown because of the brutality of the assault, the injuries inflicted and the mental torment that had followed, and found herself unable to get on with normal life. She then chose to shut the door on anything that reminded her of that evening. His face would flash up in front of her night and day, a vivid image of oppression and hate. She could smell him and she was terrorised by this inability to banish these thoughts from her mind.

She thought of Taylor today, the first time in a long time and smiled at the good times they had shared together before that fateful night, one of unparalleled brutality and fear. She had barely allowed herself to think back, as every time she did the nightmare would take over her thoughts and bury anything nice, swapping it with evil and fear. Kay was a strong and vibrant young woman, naturally attractive and had a bubbly personality. She had fallen deeply in love with the flighty detective sergeant, Miss Nicks, and Taylor was on track to finally fall in love with her, until Kay withdrew from everything and everyone completely. A nurse came into the room, ending Kay's pleasant day dream of Taylor with civil chitchat and medication.

Kay put her hand up and said, "It's time to cut this down. I need to try and get back to normal, get out there, and I feel good today, so today is the day to start. I feel a little better and I want to live. I want to feel again. He's not getting one more second of my life. Can you speak to the doctor for me and tell her? I'm ready to move on and I mean it!"

The nurse smiled at her. "Take it easy, there is no rush and one good day is a start, but it may not be the end of those dark days. I'll speak to the doctor for you and see what she says, and if you think you're ready, then I'm sure we can get this started." She squeezed her shoulder and gave her a hug, saying, "Welcome back Kay." The nurse really liked Kay and had spent many a dark day and night with her, wiping the sweat from her face as she suffered her way through nightmare after nightmare. She had comforted her and got to know the little bit of Kay that Brennan had left behind. Kay was completely broken and mentally tortured and had been unable to free herself from his grip, terror enveloping every aspect of her life, which in turn stopped her feeling anything, stopping her living, numbness and medication taking over, until today.

Kay smiled as the nurse left and her thoughts drifted back to Taylor. Her touch, her lingering soft and passionate kisses, the pleasure she had shared with this stunning woman breathed life back into Kay's veins. For the first time in months, Kay could almost feel Taylor's tender touch stroking up her legs and over her body tenderly, lingering and caressing longer in certain places. Kay felt warm inside as she began to gently touch herself, her hands softly pushing more firmly as she thought of her first encounter with Taylor. Taylor knew how to please a woman and Kay had found lovemaking with Taylor was amazing, breath taking, exciting and the pleasure, mind blowing. Kay never thought such sensations and level of arousal were physically possible, the orgasms she had experienced at Taylor's touch unimaginable. They lingered and curled all the way through her body, time and time again, and Taylor was a relentless lover. She could sense when she wanted more, and would love and pleasure her over and over until they were completely spent. Kay now wanted to feel that way again, she wanted to be touched again and Taylor was the one she wanted.

Kay wondered what Taylor was doing now and who she was with because she knew Taylor's faults and weaknesses and this was her major issue.

Chapter 36
Taylor Being Taylor

Fran's head pushed back into the bed, pillow crushed up against the wall as she bucked her hips up as Taylor held her where she wanted her to be. Fran was coming and Taylor's tongue slipped over her firmly again and again as she pushed her fingers deep inside her. Fran was gasping for air as this was the third time she had come in around five minutes, her climax getting stronger and stronger. The sensation was overwhelming as Fran moved with her fingers, pushing down harder onto them, her moans guttural as she pulled Taylor up to kiss her, kissing her powerfully and desperately. It had been over a week since they had shared any time, Fran worrying they may not share it again.

She wanted Taylor, she had fallen for her and she knew this was never a safe way to feel with her. Taylor turned Fran over and started to kiss her neck, down her back and onto her perfectly soft exposed bottom. She gripped it with her teeth and kissed and licked her cheeks, her hands stroking over the back of her thighs. Her kisses went down her thighs as her hands stroked firmly down Fran's legs, carrying on the kisses down her calves and onto her feet. Fran twitched and jerked as the tickly sensation was nearly unbearable but also lovely. Taylor pushed herself against Fran, her pussy pushing firmly against her buttocks, her hand now round underneath Fran and pushing over her pussy and delving inside her, Fran wet with pleasure, easing Taylor's fingers on their way, the heat generated between them causing their bodies to slip up and down against each other. Fran's body was still throbbing and sensitive from the last orgasm. She didn't think it was possible to come again but with the motion and pressure from Taylor pushing against her and her nipples brushing over Fran's back, while pleasuring her deeply, Fran was overwhelmed and lost control again. Her body completely let go, experiencing female ejaculation for the first time. Fran gave in to the most amazing out of body experience she had ever felt. She turned her head to frantically kiss Taylor, tongues desperately meeting, mouths devouring each other's moans as Taylor had now also let go. Both of them were in a swirl of pure pleasure, bodies entwined as one in a euphoric state as they started coming down from their natural high.

Both were totally exhausted. They slumped down onto the bed in a twisted entangled mess of body parts, laced with sweat, love and pleasure.

"Wow Taylor. That was amazing! My god, how do you do that?" Fran turned and pushed her face and mouth onto Taylor's and they kissed gently and held each other. Both were now totally relaxed and sharing the enjoyment of physical desire and fulfilment after being so caught up with work, long hours, intense emotions and the trauma of the desperate situation with the kidnap.

They chatted for the rest of the morning, the ease of their conversation relaxing, both sharing their emotions in relation to work, but none entering into the no-go zone of their feelings for each other. Fran did dig Taylor in the ribs and skirted the subject of the flirtation between Taylor and their boss but Taylor just laughed it off. She would have been lying if she had said that the thought hadn't crossed her mind, and still did whenever their paths crossed in the office.

They shared brunch before leaving. Both were heading in for a back shift, both far more relaxed than before and ready to face the trials and tribulations of the day and the further enquiry in relation to the two unsolved murders in the city.

They travelled in the same car, heading through the city as Fran wanted to pick something up in town. They then headed down the cobbled streets into Stockbridge, stopping at Starbucks for a couple of lattes to kick start the shift. Once at Fettes they were laughing and joking in the car park. Taylor leant over to Fran behind the car and mischievously kissed her full on the mouth. She also pinched Fran's bottom. Fran kissed her back and smiled up at her nipping her bottom right back. They then moved apart and walked with what they thought was a safe distance between them.

DCI Sommerville closed the door of her car, a little guiltily, as she had deliberately hesitated, lingering to watch them. She felt a tightening in her stomach and knew that she was jealous of Taylor and Fran. She had begun to enjoy Taylor's presence a little too much.

Chapter 37
DNA

Nathan had read a lot about the investigations in relation to the double murder and related assaults on the television. He listened intently to where the police claimed they were with the enquiry and shook his head visibly. He was aware of the requirement to provide DNA for his age bracket and that it was at present voluntary, but eyebrows would be raised the minute there was a refusal by anyone and further enquiry would be made into why. He was angry at this, such an intrusion into his private life was not welcome and his right to refuse would be scrutinised. He had never been an angel in his earlier years but had never been caught for anything he had ever been involved in, all of which may be revealed from the scrapings from the inside of his cheeks. He buried his hands in his head as he thought of all the consequences that may follow. His family, his near prefect life and the nightmare of his past.

Decision made, he walked off to the nearest station, which for him was Drylaw, his house close by in Silverknowes Bank. He chose to walk, feeling the pending sense of doom and a worry about what this could bring. When he got there he pressed the buzzer and waited to be allowed in, nearly turning and heading away at the slight delay. The door clicked and he pushed his way in and waited at the counter. A bubbly clerk arrived and asked what she could do for him. He explained why he was there and she told him to take a seat, which he did. He sat beside another male, his hair straggly and unclean. He was clearly unwashed and his clothes were reeking of fags and fried food. The man turned to Nathan the minute he sat down and asked if he had a fag on him. His brown teeth were barely stumps with plaque visible and his breath rotten as he sprayed Nathan with saliva as he spoke.

Nathan recoiled instinctively not trying to offend the man, saying "Sorry mate, I don't smoke".

The man just mumbled to himself at the rejection of his request and huddled forwards and moaned about how long it was taking to deal with his fifth complaint that week.

Nathan's hands were sweaty and he was starting to feel uncomfortable and not because of his putrid seating companion. He didn't like anything to do with the authorities. It was one thing working in their buildings but to have them have anything to do with your life was a totally different matter.

Nathan stood up, decision made to leave and walked to the door. He was stuck there fiddling with the lock when an officer came into the waiting area.

"Mr Sloan," the officer asked questioningly as he watched Nathan trying to leave. "Mr Sloan," he repeated as he looked down at the man sitting huddled forward thinking it was him. The man did not flinch but Nathan did at the door and turned and looked at the officer, his eyes wide and his pulse racing. He felt like a trapped animal and was too polite and law-abiding to leave.

He turned to the officer. "That's me, I was just going out for some fresh air," he lied.

The officer was aware that Nathan was agitated and didn't really believe his excuse.

He beckoned Nathan to go with him and was joined by a female officer to corroborate the procedure.

Nathan was taken through to the cells complex, which for him was a first, and it made him feel incredibly uncomfortable to be there. The oppressive thick metal doors of the open cells giving him an unwanted insight into how they looked inside. He didn't want to be in one, ever!

He was lead through to the medical room and invited to sit down as they explained what was going to happen and why and that all DNA would be destroyed once tested and cleared if no criminality was present. Nathan felt physically sick and asked to use the toilet, both officers observing his behaviour and demeanour.

They showed him to the unlockable toilet and waited outside, just in case he needed help or thought about trying to leave, even though the toilet was windowless and all the doors pass locked, although he was still free to do so, just now anyway.

Once back in the medical room Nathan sat down in front of the male officer and was asked to open his mouth wide. He did as he was asked, his mind racing, fearful of where his DNA may have been left and it started to cloud over as the plastic brush scraped the lining of his cheeks, the fear of what this would cost him. The brush went back and forward until they had taken five scrapes on each side.

"That was pretty painless, wasn't it, and that's it, all over," the female officer said cheerily.

Nathan didn't think so. He was now very worried and just wanted to leave, as quickly as he could.

The police confirmed his details and where they could get in touch with him if the need arose.

These words echoed in his head because he knew they would be coming for him and he had to find a way to explain this to Jen.

Chapter 38
Megan Thomson and Natt Spears

Amy was at her desk in her lunch hour, trawling through confidential files, which she had clearance for. There were no cases that sprang out at her, where the offender appeared not to have been convicted. Her stomach twisted in knots as she read the synopsis of a current case the team were involved in and the physical and emotional abuse of two youngsters at the hands of their mother's young partner of two years. The mother had been unaware of what was going on because one child was too scared to say anything and the other too young to talk. Amy had spoken with the mother and she genuinely believed that the mother had no idea what he was up to. He had clearly befriended her, his intention to abuse the children his main reason for choosing her to be his partner. He had come across as a kind and caring man, totally accepting of the two children he hadn't fathered and appeared to be the model boyfriend. He had encouraged her to go back to work part time and he would look after the boys, which she had done two months ago, naively, unwittingly and with trust in this man, who appeared to be a godsend.

Amy shook her head. She was also aware in this case that there appeared to be sufficient evidence, which would ensure his conviction and that if the mother was in the clear, she could rebuild her life with the children, and hopefully regain custody of them.

This fact warmed Amy inside. The abuse had been discovered early enough and there was still a chance for a normal life for both children. They were young enough to block out the memories, or so she hoped. She, unfortunately, had not been able to achieve this in her life. The bitter twist of vengeful emotions continued to live on within her, like a boiling cauldron of corrupted and tormented youth.

She carried on, reviewing the files of other cases, her heart feeling sore as she read detail after detail, until she froze. The name in front of her made her blood run cold. Megan Thomson. Megan Thomson, her biological mother, a name she had not heard for 22 years, a name she never wanted to hear again.

Once she had stopped shaking, she read on. Social work were in the process of arranging to remove the registered sex offender marker from her, as she had reached the recommended time limit. She had also had two other children removed from her years before at birth, a boy and a girl, who would be about 14 and 12 respectively. *My god, I've got another brother and sister and I've never met them,* thought Amy.

She refocused, back to the woman she had hated with every breath she took, every second of every day for the whole of her life and read the address listed for her. Edinburgh, Dumbiedykes, a housing estate that was situated at the foot of the Crags, beside Arthur's seat, an extinct volcano in the heart of Edinburgh, down from the Castle, up from the Palace and a stone's throw away from the Parliament. Anyone wanting to buy here would have to be pretty wealthy to afford anything. It was a well sought after area for people hoping to get a council house, favoured above, Muirhouse, West Pilton, Wester Hailes and Niddrie, a very central location with views across the city dependent on what floor you lived on.

Amy scribbled down the address and made a mental note to tell her brother Nathan all about it, especially the fact that they had a brother and sister.

Finding her mother and what she was up to now, lead her to wonder about Natt Spears. *What is that vile twisted bastard doing now? What's he been doing since he's been out? Is he even alive because he was a fat unhealthy bastard back then,* she thought to herself.

Unfortunately the social workers didn't have access to the same files as the police, and this was a problem that she would have to overcome because she wanted to know where he was now and what he had been involved in.

She didn't like how she was feeling, a sickness buried deep into the pit of her stomach, her mind twisted with the memories or her sad and cruel youth, revenge and violent vengeful aggression taking over.

Chapter 39
DNA results.

Fran had numerous emails in relation to the hundreds of samples of DNA taken from the city's young men. One had a little red flag beside it and she went straight to open it first. She saw that there had been a positive hit and was totally excited about this. She read on. The name in front of her was that of Nathan Sloan. She went skipping over to Taylor's desk, who on seeing Fran's face, clearly with something important to say, gave her her full attention.

"We've got a hit Taylor, and he's local, very local, just down at Silverknowes."

"Who dealt with him when he came in. We'll need to speak to them to see how he reacted. I'll need to tell the boss too. Is she in yet?"

"Yeh, but I think she's in a meeting."

"We'll need to bring him in right away, just in case he has more plans for this evening. We will be completely slated if we don't move on this one!"

Nathan was in the back garden playing with little Millie when he heard the knock at the door. It was a forceful knock and one that made him a little nervous. He felt sick as he thought back to the police station the other day. He knew that they would come knocking sooner or later. In a way he felt relieved, as there was a bit of him that had needed to do this, no more ghosts in the closet. He scooped Millie up from the grass as two armed officers appeared in his back garden. She was frightened. Nathan was wide mouthed and angry at the intrusion that had frightened his precious little girl. He heard a loud crash as his front door caved in under the pressure from the 26 kilo ram, followed by loud shouts of "POLICE" that rang out through the house as they cleared every room. Jen was at work. An officer moved toward Nathan to take hold of Millie and Nathan pulled her back from them immediately.

"What the do you think you're doing, touch her and see what you get!" Nathan rasped through his teeth, trying not to swear in front of his child. He was livid.

The officer tried to persuade him to let them take Millie. They had social workers with them. They had done checks on him and knew he had a child and had taken the steps to care for her if the need arose.

The last thing the police wanted was to upset the child, and when it came down to it neither did Nathan.

"Phone my wife, phone my fucking wife right now. You're not leaving my fucking kid with social services, no fucking danger," he said, terrified at what was going on. All the will he had not to swear now gone.

The officer looked straight into Nathan's eyes and warned him that they were taking him in, holding the child or not, and this was the last chance for him to put her down. The officer asked for his wife's number and said that he would phone her straight away and that officers would keep the child there until she got back, only if he handed her over right now.

"You touch one hair on her head, I swear I will kill you, and I mean it. You better keep her here until her mother gets here or, so help me god, I'll hunt you down." Nathan was raging now and red mist was coming down over him. As soon as he put Millie down the police took hold of him and he completely lost it. He started swinging punches, grabbing, kicking, biting and doing anything he could to get at the police. He didn't like to be touched or restrained, anything that brought back the memories of his childhood. He was like a wild animal and the officers had to call for backup to assist them in arresting him. They could not believe his strength and the ferocity of his fight. Millie was safely out of sight and had been taken straight into the house prior to him kicking off with the police.

Taylor was also inside the house with three other detectives, the search warrant signed and ready to go in her hand as she walked over to the back window and watched four officers struggling to control the suspect Nathan Sloan.

Handcuffs and leg straps were now on, any which way the cops could manage, as they lifted him up face down and horizontal, still struggling with all the strength he had. He knew Millie was still in the house. He could hear her crying because she was being held by a stranger. His heart felt like it was being torn out of his chest as he didn't want to leave his little girl with anyone she didn't know. He couldn't and wouldn't trust any stranger with her, other than Jen and now his sister Amy.

Taylor looked at him through the window. He wasn't a big man but he fought like a lion and had the strength of many. He wasn't what she had imagined. He was a family man, decent house and working. DCs Lomond, Andrews and Brown and DS Nicks paired up and were joined by the specialist search team to go through every inch of the house, to look for further evidence.

Jen put her phone back in her pocket, fumbling because her hand was so shaky. She leaned over and vomited. The voice on the phone had told her of Nathan's detention and that is was on suspicion of double murder and more. She could not breath as her head was swirling with how this could have happened. She got in her car and drove at excessive speed all the way to the house to get to Millie before they took her into care. *How has this happened? Where did they get the evidence? When, how, why, no way! He wouldn't do that, he couldn't.* Her heart felt like it had stopped as she remembered the bruises that he had come home with, the late night walks to clear his head. She hoped these times didn't coincide with anything the police were thinking, because she did not like to lie and she didn't know where he went.

Jen pulled into her driveway, car tyres screeching to a halt. Theirs was a modest drive with room for two cars, a semi-detached house in a decent area of town. She yanked on the handbrake and the sound was deafening. Pulling herself out of the car with purpose, she slammed the door behind her ferociously. Her intention to get answers from the police in her house was clearly evident as she strode towards the doorway. There was an officer at the front door that stopped her entering and it took all her strength not to scream.

"This is my goddamn house and my daughter better be in there. I want you to hand her over right now, and I mean right now, do you understand me? You've taken my husband and you are not taking my child. Where is she? Tell me where she is or so help me, I swear."

Taylor came to the front door and asked her to come in politely, escorting her through. Another officer brought Millie to her. She was no longer upset and had been giggling with the officer that had been looking after her. Jen held out her arms in relief at seeing her daughter was okay and her eyes dared any hesitation from the officer. The officer saw the intent in her eyes and Millie was handed over to her quickly, the female officer fully aware of the look she had received and intuition letting her know what to do.

Jen held Millie close to her, hugged her and started to cry. Millie cried too and Taylor spoke to Jen in an empathetic tone.

"I'm sorry that we have had to do this. I hope they explained what's going on to you when they phoned. You'll need to gather some things for you and Millie because we have to take control of your house for search purposes, and we'll have to search through what you take as well. I am genuinely sorry!" Taylor was sympathetic towards her, and truly felt for her. Her world had been ripped apart. Taylor could see in Jen's face that her shock and emotion was real and very raw.

"Sorry, you're fucking sorry! Really? You've come into my house, taken my husband away on suspicion of murder, fucking

MURDER, and you're sorry! You better have some pretty good evidence to do what you are doing or I will sue you, all of you, I mean it. Do you understand me?" Jen never usually swore in front of Millie but this was extreme circumstances, totally unbelievable, she couldn't get her head around it.

"He's a good man, truly decent. He's kind and gentle, he wouldn't hurt a fly. You must've got it wrong. Please be wrong, please!"

Taylor looked at her and believed she thought he was innocent and did not know anything, but when she had watched her colleagues take him away he had been a little less than gentle with them. Two officers had been injured and he was totally out of control for all to see. Maybe a Jekyll and Hyde character, she wondered .

Chapter 40
No Alibi.

Jen was in St Leonard's police station, the main cells complex for the capital city, Millie safe with her Grandmother at her house in the Clerwood area of Edinburgh, just set back from Corstorphine Hill, with fabulous views of the west side of the city. A female officer had been assigned to take her statement. The officer was tall and confident but with very sympathetic and persuasive qualities, personally selected for the task. There was another officer in the room to ensure that every point and date was covered and nothing was missed out. The statement would either be the nail in the coffin for Nathan or a major part of proving his innocence. Jen went into the last couple of months in as much detail as possible, recounting dates and times as best she could. She was aware of the assaults and murders in Edinburgh because she always watched the news. She was also aware that her beloved husband Nathan was never around in the house on most or all of those dates, and felt sick as her mind fought to not think of the possibility he could be guilty. Nathan did go out a lot though, and more than the dates that had been asked about. The officer then asked about any injuries her husband had ever had, unexplained ones. Jen hesitated, noticed by the officer, as her mind went back to the night he came back with head and facial injuries. He'd said he had been in a fight but no further explanation had been given to her.

The officer prompted Jen to tell the truth and answer honestly. "You need to tell the truth Jen, it is Jen you prefer to be called, isn't it? Any little detail will help us, and help Nathan".

Jen sat back on the uncomfortable seat and didn't speak. She was now aware that every word she said was not helping him at all, the opposite that she had come here to do. She didn't want to think that he could be the person that had carried out all of these savage crimes, although not all the details had been revealed in the press for obvious reasons. Every word she said seemed to make it worse for Nathan.

"I don't have to say any more, you can't make me." Jen said with tears in her eyes.

"No you don't," the officer empathised, as she saw Jen's guilt as understanding dawned that her words were not providing Nathan with alibis, not one.

"He's got nothing to hide, he's a good man, he's never harmed me or Millie. He works hard, he's kind, he's caring and he's not a bloody murderer!" Jen blurted out, her emotions in full swing now, her eyes streaming with tears and her nose running as she sobbed her heart out.

"Injuries, did he ever have injuries when he came back in?" the officer pressed on, hoping that Jen would continue because she could see she wanted to tell the truth but was now fearing the consequence of her words, which were becoming more and more damaging for her husband.

"He did come home with injuries one night but he said that he had been in a fight with some random guy and said that the guy took a chunk out of his face with his ring. I believed him?" Jen exclaimed.

"Did he say where he had been?" the officer pressed on.

"No he didn't. He said he had been out walking to clear his head, which he has done since we met. He had a troubled childhood".

"What do you mean by a troubled childhood? What sort of things are we talking about?"

"Really bad, I think. He doesn't talk about it but he has really bad nightmares and wakes up sweating and he's genuinely petrified," Jen explained.

The officer saw that Jen wanted to talk so she probed a bit more. There could be a motive or reason for these assaults buried deep inside him. Nathan was outwardly a kind and gentle man but one with a dark past and secrets it now seemed.

"Why won't he talk to you about it? I thought he trusted you?"

"What do you mean by that?" Jen bristled with anger and frustration.

"Nothing bad, I just want to try and get into what your husband is dealing with on his own, alone in his thoughts. You know, a private space that may be so bad that he won't let those closest even enter, probably for very good reasons, and I didn't mean to offend you, sorry."

"I think from the state of him after a nightmare, it must have been really bad. He shakes, he is visibly terrified and is physically sick sometimes. I just hold him until he comes out of it, and he is obviously disturbed by what he has just relived." Jen now had her hands in her head as she started to wonder if Nathan could have a hidden side to him.

They continued for several more hours. Jen was totally exhausted at the end of it and could not believe how things now looked. There were a lot of coincidences, none positive, but none of which were proof of any guilt, she reassured herself. She still believed that if you told the truth the justice system would do the right thing.

Throughout the statement, she had not been asked and did not mention Nathan's long lost sister, that she had never known about until a couple of weeks ago. She never gave it a second thought that she was his identical twin, and the importance of that fact.

Chapter 41
What Next?

Nathan sat in the cell, restraints now removed. He was calm but very apprehensive about what was to come and a little ashamed of how he had behaved, but it was a reaction, his protective instinct went into overdrive to protect his little girl after what had happened to him. He went over and over in his head the words, *detained on suspicion for murder. Murder, how the fuck am I here for murder, I didn't kill him did I?*

He put his hands in his head and the realisation of the depth of trouble he appeared to be in, rightly or wrongly was sinking in. He was afraid. *I'm fucked, they seem to think they have me bang to rights; what do they have, what could they have, because they seem pretty certain I've done something really bad here."*

Taylor sat typing furiously, her interview ran into pages and pages of questions, not leaving a single stone unturned. Fran and the rest of the team were gathering and preparing all of the evidence they had, what they called their trump cards, which would hopefully make their suspect admit to his part in the crimes he was accused of. They could also wait for him to give his version of events and then prove them to be wrong, or so they believed. The DCI was pacing back and forth about the office, the enormity of the importance of the interview worrying her slightly. They really did think they had their man here and they had him like a rabbit in the headlights. Their intention was to burst him so he would admit to everything because of the weight of evidence against him.

Fran walked across the open plan office towards Taylor. She knew her lover was totally stressed out. She came up beside her, her movements subtle, as she brushed against Taylor's side, making sure her presence was felt. Taylor looked up at her, appreciating the momentary escape from the task at hand, her stomach fluttering a little as she looked up into Fran's eyes. Fran put her hand on Taylor's and gave it a gentle squeeze, nothing sexual, just supportive and caring. She was stressed to the max with this one. The pressure was immense and a lot was riding on this interview and making sure the danger was taken off the streets for good. Marcus looked up from his desk and smiled at her too. He had a vested interest in this interview, believing that the guy they had in the cells may be a monster to many but he was a saviour to him. His little boy David was only alive today because of him and his actions. Marcus was to come into the interview with Taylor, although Taylor and the DCI had swithered about his suitability for the task, because of his emotional involvement in the case. However, Taylor had worked with Marcus for years. He was one of the best detectives around, very clever, a people person and an amazing talent for getting a confession from many a suspect when others had failed. He himself had mixed feelings on the case because the accused had hurt and maimed people that were capable of the rape, torture and abuse of very young children, and his boy had been taken for that very purpose. Regardless of the suspect's good deed, Marcus would be sure to get the man who had committed extremely violent crimes and needed to be punished but he would also highlight his actions to save the two boys in his report to the procurator fiscal. Taylor rated Marcus highly and had managed to persuade the boss that she would be wrong to exclude him from this interview.

The DCI watched Taylor interact with Fran and felt a little jealous again. Her desire for Taylor that she had tried to suppress was affecting her judgement a little. She watched Taylor talking with both Fran and Marcus and was slightly in awe of the way that others looked up to her and listened and respected her while she spoke.

The DCI went back into her office and closed the door with a little more force than she had intended. It banged behind her causing many in the office to look up and comment to each other about what had rattled her cage. Taylor also looked up at Sommerville, as she looked out of her office window to see the stir that her door slamming had caused, and their eyes engaged. Taylor's eyes questioning the DCI's behaviour, slightly embarrassed for her, as she knew the little outburst had been noticed and talked about. Taylor wondered if it was anything to do with her and Fran being so close. She had already got a hint of attraction from her DCI on several occasions and wondered if the display may have been for her benefit. Taylor made a facial expression, as if to say what was that all about, but the DCI just turned away and slumped down at her desk, Findlay was there, insignificant in his presence, wiping his shirt where he had spilt his coffee when she had slammed the door, waking him up from his normal unfocussed slumber. He hated her being in the office. She was always on at him to check on things and giving him work to do. He was a lazy bastard and had been allowed to be for most of his service but he was one of the old school lads and had got a promotion or two out of it. However, he could not really go any further up the tree without trouble brewing because he was just not able to take on his current responsibility.

Taylor loved the fact that Findlay was now completely down trodden and unable to revel in the success of the work that others did and take all the credit. He could also no longer be lecherous towards the females or bully any of the team because the DCI was most definitely in charge and not him anymore.

"Are you nearly ready Marcus, time is ticking and we'll need every minute possible for this one," Taylor said, standing up from her desk, a bead of sweat now showing on her hairline, a physical display of the pressure she was under.

"Yep, it's now or never. I'm really interested in what he has to say, if he talks that is," Marcus said, hoping that Nathan would explain how and why he did the things he did.

As Taylor walked out of the office, she looked immaculate, fitted three-piece suit, silk white blouse and her hair flowing down onto her shoulders, shining, with a silky appearance. Marcus too was wearing a smart fitted suit, black shirt and colourful silk tie, both of them could almost have been going on the cat walk.

As they left, Fran looked up from her desk at the same time as the DCI came out of her office. The rest of the team watched in a supportive way but the DCI and Fran looked on for other reasons.

Fran looked up at Sommerville with a little jealousy in her eyes. She knew why she was looking because months back she had done the same. She had watched Taylor and Kay, although never with determined intention. She hadn't meant to cause problems between them. She just had an attraction for a very handsome woman.

The DCI stared back at Fran with a deliberate prolonged look, a hint of menace in her eyes. Fran couldn't believe what she was seeing but she wasn't sure. She tried to stare back at Sommerville with an equal warning but the DCI just turned and went back to her office, shutting the door behind her.

Fran sat back at her desk with a sickening feeling in her stomach. Taylor was already becoming more distant, Fran was aware that she still loved Kay and the last thing she needed now was another complication to twist her emotions and lead her even further off the rails.

Chapter 42
Not Forgotten

Amy put down the phone at her desk, her face sheet white and her pulse racing. She could not believe what Jen had just told her about Nathan's detention. The others in the office could not help but notice the change in her demeanour. Amy was usually a picture of calmness and restraint. They asked if she was okay but she didn't answer, she just got up from her desk. She was visibly shaking and the colour had drained from her face.

She ran down the corridor. Her only desire was to get out of the office before she imploded. She was crying, tears streaming down her face as she burst her way out of the doors and onto the pavement outside, gulping in the fresh air. She could not believe that her brother had been taken in for such horrific crimes. *How could this have happened? It was impossible. How could the police have got this so wrong? He didn't do anything, he couldn't have. BECAUSE I DID! IT WAS ME, I DID IT, I DID EVERYTHING, AND I'M NOT FINISHED YET, BUT I NEED TO SAVE MY BROTHER!*

She had already taken files from her work about two very special people. She would try to prove Nathan's innocence by confirming her guilt with a spectacular show of revenge and retribution.

Megan scratched at her backside underneath her pyjamas, unwashed and ill-fitting, with a fag hanging down from her mouth as she leant over the cooker. The stench of fat in the kitchen and throughout her house was ingrained in the walls and furnishings, wallpaper and other surfaces splashed with grease. She was 22 years older, much fatter and, due to her life style and poor health choices, she looked horrific.

"Do ye want sauce on yer butty Mark?" she yelled through to the living room.

"Aye doll, lots," Mark yelled back.

The living room was cluttered with rubbish, filthy clothes and ashtrays that were piled up like pyramids. There were dog ends scattered all over the floor. The walls were amber coloured from nicotine. Dirty, greasy stains covered the furniture, and the floor was littered with excrement from their pets, two dogs and a cat, and nappies. The 52-inch telly was the only visible object in the room, with play station controls stretching back to the couch. The curtains were ripped and partially drawn.

It was the continued chaotic life of a monster, that monster being Amy's mother Megan, who now unfortunately had another child and new partner. They lived in filth and squalor, bringing another innocent life into their world to neglect and ignore, collecting the benefits that came with having a child, none of which the little one would ever see.

A tousle-haired boy came toddling through to the kitchen with an old left over pizza crust in his hand. He tugged on his mum's pyjama bottoms. He was nearly two years old and was clearly hungry as his mum filled her and Mark's plates with greasy food.

Megan lifted her knee up and shoved him away. "Beat it Reecy, you'll get an eggy later. This is for us".

The child fell over sideways and bumped his head on the filthy cupboard, landing hard on his bottom. He was about to cry but, even at such a young age, he didn't bother because there would be no point. He had already learned that they would never comfort him. All they ever did for him were the very basics, to keep him alive and not get charged for neglect. They were clever enough to meet social workers on neutral ground and never after any assaults that had marked Reece, and they always made sure they kept their appointments at the social work building. They never gave the social workers any reason to have to come to the house as there would be no doubt he would be removed from their care instantly.

Megan had been released after five years for her part in the abuse and neglect of Amy and Nathan and had been on the social work department's radar for the next ten years. She had been warned that if she had any children during this time that they would be taken into care without question. She hadn't meant to fall pregnant again, and had thought she was too old, but she had the gift of those who don't want children, the ability to fall pregnant at the drop of a hat, with no change to her lifestyle of booze, drugs, fags and poor diet, and another poor child was brought into the world for a bleak and sad future, as the social workers tried their hardest to prevent neglect and abuse.

Natt Spears sat on the bar stool at his local pub in Easter Road, the Bird in the Hand, a short distance away from the Hibernian football ground. Natt was an avid supporter of his local team, along with the other two men in their late forties sitting at the bar beside him. They chatted about the results and other football matters, his mates totally unaware of his dark past and his desire for sexual gratification through the abuse of children, which in a man's man pub would not go down too well. Natt was one of the lads. He ogled women and joined in with their sexist banter, never showing that he was any different to them but he was; he was cruel, callous and did not care that others suffered for him to get his pleasure.

Natt had served ten years for his crimes against Nathan and Amy. He had been deemed to be the main offender and to have coerced Megan, who was of low intelligence and low self-esteem, a person unlikely to stand up against him and what he wanted her to do.

Natt still managed to commit offences against children. He was from a family where he had access to his nieces and nephew, who were regularly in his company and too frightened to come forward and tell someone what was happening to them because he was a terrifyingly manipulative individual that was able to come across as an alright guy. He had played down his involvement in the crimes against Nathan and Amy, blaming Megan for the abuse, telling his friends and relations that he had been set up by her to take the wrap. He had a strong personality and his version of what had happened became believable and somehow his part was almost trivialised within his family circle. They chose to believe what he said.

Chapter 43
Guilty or Not?

Taylor looked into Nathan's eyes as she had done for the last three hours. She just didn't see the monster in this man; she wasn't feeling it. He was articulate and appeared honest but the nature of the evidence and his lack of alibis for any of the crimes was very apparent and she had been proved wrong before, by falling for the guilty person's story and their ability to have others believe their innocence.

He did not have an alibi for any on the nights in question. He confirmed he came home injured on one of the dates but he did stick to the story about a male assaulting him and that he had been injured from a large ring or a knuckle duster that the mugger had been wearing. He would not budge on any part of his version of events for every time he was out of the house, neither of them proving he wasn't the suspect for either or all of the assaults and the two murders, but his portrayal of his version of events was very plausible.

The interview was going round and round in circles and Nathan would not budge on any detail. That was when Marcus came in with the saving of the children and how this as a father must have made him feel good but, to their surprise, Nathan's response was like a blank canvas, no expression or emotion, no obvious recollection of having done this or any sort of response, just nothing. It was as if it hadn't happened. Marcus and Taylor could not believe how cool this guy was; how could he act like that if he had saved two young kids? Because of the way he acted around his own child, surely there would be some reaction.

Unfortunately, no matter what they felt, there was no evidence to prove his innocence, but there was significant DNA evidence from every crime scene to prove that he was their man. DNA went into millions to one and his was there. He also had no one to back up his version of events, his side of the story. They could only back up that he wasn't in his house every time there was a crime, which just made things worse for him.

The detention time was running out and, the way the interview was going, all they could do was charge him. With so much evidence against him, they had no other choice. Nathan would appear at the high court the next day and a request would be made that he should be remanded in custody until the trial.

Nathan sat in the seat dumbfounded. He couldn't believe what was happening. They seemed to think they had his DNA and it was a match at all of the crime scenes.

"This is impossible! How the fuck am I here? I know I was a naughty boy in my past and that is why I thought you were at my house. Why the fuck would I have come in to give you my DNA if I'd done all this. I just fucking wanted to have a clean slate for my family, never having to worry about my past coming back to haunt me," Nathan stated convincingly to the two detectives, who sat in front of him a little perturbed.

Taylor wasn't happy with this and stopped the tape and excused herself from the interview room. She headed straight to see the DCI, who was at St Leonard's to oversee the interview. Sommerville looked up with a welcoming smile on her face. Taylor explained everything to her and how she felt regarding the suspect and that something didn't add up, except the overwhelming amount of evidence piled up against him.

"Taylor, this is a no brainer! You have to fix him with this, the press and the public will want to hear this. There is no way he can be released on bail. Now go and charge him and we'll have a few drinks after work and chat about it," Sommerville tapped the desk matter-of-factly. Not having been in the interview room with him for hours, she hadn't seen how he had come across.

Taylor had known that would be her reaction but had needed to vent her feelings and thoughts about the accused. It just wasn't how it was meant to feel. She was a little pissed off that she had forgotten to tell Sommerville about Nathan's lack of response when the rescue of David was mentioned, a complete genuine unawareness from him, not even a hint of recollection or reaction. He was either an amazing liar or telling the truth, and Taylor hoped for all of their sakes, that it wasn't the latter. This was a double murder and several serious assaults, not just a simple shoplifting case.

Taylor strode through the corridors and back down to the cells complex and into the interview room with its bare colourless walls, a single table screwed to the ground and a tape recorder. Her face was expressionless but her mannerisms were clearly not happy. She thumped back on her seat, switched the tape back on, reintroduced herself, gave the time and began.

Taylor explained what was happening before Marcus cautioned Nathan and then charged him for all of the offences libelled against him, to which he replied, "It wasn't me, I swear. I swear on my daughter's life, I didn't do any of them. I promise you that!"

Both Taylor and Marcus did not like this. Usually they were brimming with confidence but this time the evidence outweighed their gut instincts.

Nathan couldn't believe what he had just heard and the enormity of the predicament he was now in. He could see no way out.

"Can I see my daughter, I need to see, her. I've never been away from her for a full day since she was born, she's my life, my soul, I need her. Why would I ever do anything that would take me away from her? Fuck, fuck, fuuuucccckk." Nathan was crying. His mouth dribbled as he sobbed loudly into his hands.

Officers came in and helped Nathan to his feet. He wobbled a bit and then walked with them back to his cell.

Chapter 44
Over-indulgence

Taylor and Marcus had just finished the custody report but there was hesitation before they pressed the enter button, which would send it through cyberspace to the fiscal's office, prior to Nathan's court appearance the next day. It was late evening and Taylor knew where she wanted to go and what she wanted to do. She wanted to drink. She was feeling really uneasy about the charges, how honest the accused had seemed, and the fact that she could usually tell a liar but this time she just didn't feel it. There was something wrong here but she was powerless to do anything about it. She wanted to go to a bar and have a drink, a lot of drink. This was a trait of hers, a weakness that she had never managed to shake off or change. She would always seek solitude, no emotional ties, alcohol and if lucky, female company!

Marcus could see it in Taylor's eyes, the blank expression, the emotional detachment he had seen before.

"Hey Taylor, what's up, are you going back to Fran's tonight? She went home hours ago apparently." Marcus tried to ignite her more responsible emotions but he knew he was failing miserably.

"Naa, I think I'll just head out for a bit and stay at my own house tonight. I need a drink Marcus and to be honest, I don't really know what I need. I can't stop thinking about Kay and

I think I still love her. Today was awful; it was like kicking a puppy. I don't know what to do Marcus? I feel hellish, I'm losing it. What do you suggest because this fucking sucks!"

"Okay, okay, I won't stop you because I don't think I could but Fran cares for you, you know, and she is lovely too and she's been there for you over the last few months." Marcus tried to convince Taylor not to do what she was about to do.

"Thank you, I know you care, because you're lovely Marcus, but clearly I'm not and I feel like shit. I'm tired and just want to let loose a little. Are you coming?" she said this half-heartedly because she knew he would be going straight home to Maria and David. That was where he most wanted to be, and she wanted him there too.

Taylor's mind was made up. She went into the rest room and tidied up her hair a little and sprayed on some scent. She was aware she had been in the same clothes all day but didn't care. She hadn't realised how stressed she was. Everything that had happened in the last three months seemed to by swirling round in her head and, after today's events, she just couldn't handle it all. She kept herself active, trying to stop moments like these getting the better of her. She thought of Brennan and the terror she had felt at his hands, what he had done to Fran and Kay, his death, Kay's health, her own infidelity, her desire for Fran - another heart hanging in the balance to be broken, the pressure of this case, the lack of satisfaction in getting the culprit, little David's abduction, the emotional rollercoaster that she felt and couldn't shake off, everything.

She got in her car and drove up to the area known as the pink triangle near the Playhouse Theatre and parked her car on one of the semi-circular roadways just off London Road with no intention of seeing it again in the near future. The four storey luxury flats watched over her as she straightened out her fitted suit. It clung to her where it should, showing off her lean physique and, with her wavy hair flowing casually down to her shoulders, made her a very attractive sight for those who took the time to look. The heels on her boots clacked up the road as she made her way back onto London road, past the pet shop and pubs. She stopped at a bar called The Street, a mixed gay and straight bar where she would sample a few of their drinks, and maybe more.

"Two double Bacardi and cokes please, tall glasses and a lot of ice, thanks," she said smiling at the woman behind the bar. The woman knew Taylor as she had worked there for years and they shared a mutual acquaintance, they even flirted a little once in a while, but nothing had ever happened, both enjoying the temptation, but never acting on it.

"Heavy day, two doubles straight away is gonna hit the spot," the bar tender said with a questioning smile. She had seen Taylor do this before, often. She had watched her scoop many drinks and would usually get pretty pissed and, if lucky, leave with someone.

Taylor moved from the bar stools and walked down the stairs to where there were some comfier seats in booths set back from the main bar areas. She ordered another two doubles from the downstairs bar before she had even finished the first two and struggled to carry them all back to a table in one of the booths.

She threw her jacket down behind her and slumped onto the two-seater couch, another adjacent to her, unoccupied, which she was quite glad of. She didn't really want to be sociable. She just wanted to have her head get floaty and her face warmed with the heat from the alcohol and sit there alone in her little unrealistic bubble, where she wouldn't have to think about anything.

She managed to persuade the barman to bring her another couple of drinks right to the table with a smile and a large tip, to save her having to get up herself, something she would normally do to try and attract some female attention, but tonight she didn't seem to have the enthusiasm to even try.

She slumped on the sofa, the quantity and frequency of the Bacardi already making her feel good, mellow. Her face was flushed and her head was suitably fuzzy, as she had planned from the outset.

As she rested her head back, totally relaxed and a little pissed, she suddenly felt a presence beside her, someone had sat down on the couch opposite her. Taylor was about to say that the seat was taken until she looked up and saw that it was Brooke Sommerville. The DCI was dressed casually but had certainly made a little effort with her makeup and looked pretty nice with jeans and a blouse on. Taylor had never seen her boss's cleavage exposed before and made a very slow point of noticing and enjoying it. Brooke was a little embarrassed at just sitting down beside Taylor uninvited but Taylor wasn't. She knew why the DCI was there and allowed her to feel the embarrassment of this by asking her what had brought her there, watching her squirm a little before responding.

Brooke lied obviously and said she was worried about Taylor and had spoken to Marcus who had told her where he thought she would be.

Taylor smiled and gestured for Brooke to shoosh with her finger pressed gently against her moist and full lips. She kept her finger there longer than necessary, her lips slightly parted and then she gently ran her tongue over them. The action was very erotic and deliberate. She pushed her perfect teeth down onto her bottom lip and then sat up, moving forward and with no warning to take hold of the back of Brooke's neck, firmly but gently. She pulled Brooke towards her and kissed her full on the lips, opening her mouth and letting her tongue enter Brooke's mouth. Brooke was taken aback at just how forward Taylor was but did not try and stop her. This is what she had wanted and why she was there so she responded eagerly, and so did Taylor. She was in that sort of mood, and wanted to take control of Brooke and let her feel a little out of control for a change. Brooke's breath quivered with the excitement of the moment. She had come here wondering and she was going to leave knowing. Taylor was already turned on and her predatory nature was taking over. She could sense that her boss was already feeling a little out of control and most definitely willing to take what Taylor had to offer her. Taylor's tongue met Brooke's, exploring her open and needy mouth, hers gently responding back to Taylor's more intrusive tongue. Brooke let out a little moan at this pleasure, which Taylor heard and made her want to have Brooke all the more. Being aware of her surroundings and how tucked back the booth style seating was, she took full opportunity to touch her boss intimately. She pushed her hand down between Brooke's legs and deliberately rubbed her over her trousers, exactly where she knew it would be felt. Brooke moved back a little and stopped kissing her and looked right at her, her mouth slightly open, a little embarrassed because they were in a public place and at what she was doing, but desire and lust just took over and stopped her worrying and she moved her legs open a little further to allow Taylor's hand a little more freedom to touch her more intensely. Her need to be touched even more was taking over. She kissed Taylor's swollen and sensual lips once again, unable to really comprehend what was happening, how good it felt and how risky they were being. Brooke, who would normally be very much in control, was now suddenly out of control as Taylor's hand pushed harder again, pushing the cloth of her trousers practically inside her.

Taylor leaned into Brooke, her hand now causing Brooke to wriggle a little bit, her cheeks and neck red and flushed, the sensation and pleasure all becoming too much for her. She could barely catch her breath, it was too exciting, almost overwhelming, and she could feel that she was going to come right there in the bar. Her breathing was now quick and desperate and she knew she should stop her at that moment but Taylor's skilled hand knew just how close she was too climax and had no intention of stopping. She continued to push her fingers deeper into the material of Brooke's trousers, while kissing her feverishly. Brooke was losing control. She kissed Taylor passionately. Taylor's tummy flipped and fluttered with pure unadulterated lust. The kiss was intense and thrilling causing Brooke to let go and she moaned loudly into Taylor's mouth as she continued to kiss her, unable to hold back any longer and her pleasure was released. She had never felt anything quite like it before. The power of the desperate pulsating swirl between her legs was amazing and she couldn't believe that she had just let that happen. Her hips raised and pushed against the force of Taylor's hand, making sure she didn't stop, because she wanted more. This was so unlike her to allow this sort of thing to happen but she was under Taylor's spell. Luckily, where they were sitting was out of sight of anyone else and nobody seemed to have noticed what had just gone on.

Taylor leant in to her and said, "Come back with me, come to my house, I want to fuck you, taste you, I want all of you and this time I want to undress you, take my time, and I want to savour every moment".

Brooke's face and neck were totally flushed and she could barely catch her breath to speak but she didn't hesitate to nod her head and let Taylor take her home to her lair, her heart filled with anticipation.

Taylor rose from her seat and reached down to take Brooke's hand and lead her out of the bar. Staggering a little on the way up the stairs, she pushed against Brooke, stealing another deep and lust filled kiss and an intrusive grip of Brooke's bottom, which instinctively tightened at the sensation. They both continued to stumble up the stairs and out onto the street, where Taylor whistled for a cab, totally unladylike, but it did the trick. Both of them teetered as Taylor's lead was a little unsteady from the booze and she was still kissing Brooke as she helped her inside the cab, making sure the heightened emotions did not dissipate on the journey home. Taylor's hands were all over Brooke, and Brooke was fighting all of her emotions to stop her because of where they were, just in case they were seen, but she couldn't help herself. She wanted Taylor and couldn't resist, and Taylor deliberately carried on, fully aware of the emotional struggle Brooke was going through. The taxi driver couldn't help but look as he heard their giggles and loud kisses. He watched in his mirror in delight as two very attractive women made out in the back of his cab, enjoying the view very much. The journey was short as the cab rumbled over the cobbles in town and back to Taylor's home. Taylor paid the fare and got out first taking Brooke's hand and pulling her to the door, turning her round and pushing her up against it, kissing her deeply, hands everywhere. The cab was gone and the foliage in the garden offered a little privacy as she pulled down Brooke's blouse enough to expose her breasts, her nipples taught and inviting as Taylor's mouth surrounded one, then the other, tongue caressing each of them, sucking them full mouthed with her tongue continuing to swirl over her nipples with a powerful pressure causing Brooke to let out another moan which just fed Taylor's desire to have her. Taylor pulled Brook close to her, her thigh between her legs, her mouth still gently pulling down on her nipple as she unfastened her jeans, when Brooke pulled her back a little and said, "Invite me in Taylor, not here, please! Take me to bed, I want you to make love to me in a bed".

Taylor smiled, "Manners, I'm sorry boss lady. Brooke, please come in".

Taylor quickly opened the door and they both almost fell into the hallway, Taylor was quick to take hold of Brooke's hand and led her straight through to the bedroom. The bed was covered with silky linen and several richly coloured tasteful pillows to lean on. The bedroom displayed very much of Taylor's personality, lusty and sensual colours, sexually inviting, a boudoir.

She gently pushed Brooke onto her back and followed her down, continuing to undress her, pulling her jeans down over her lean and muscular legs, which made Taylor smile as she brushed her cheek against them, smooth and silky. She was impressed at how strong they were. Brooke's boots stopped the jeans coming off fully but that didn't bother Taylor; she liked the half-dressed dishevelled look, Brooks' legs were a trapped as Taylor spread them open, her underwear still in place, leaving her totally exposed and completely at Taylor's mercy. Taylor moved up to her navel, deliberately brushing her chin over her pussy, and sending powerful sensations right through Brooke, her underwear moist already. She really wanted Taylor to touch her and Taylor knew it. Taylor's mouth went over her pants again, pushed down on her pussy with her mouth, kissing at the side of the material, over her thighs, her fingers gently pulling at the side of the panties, teasing, Brooke's senses already heightened from before and the intense sensations stimulated by Taylor's mouth. Her warm breath on Brooke as she pulled her pants to the side was intense and the delay and desire excruciating until she kissed her there gently and intimately. Taylor felt Brooke take a deep breath as she waited for the first touch from Taylor's tongue. Brooke was tense, her head still spinning at what was happening. She drew a breath in sharply and the sensory rush exploded inside her as the subtlest contact from Taylor's tongue sent electrical pulses of pleasure rushing and swirling through her. She could feel herself trying to wriggle away from Taylor's mouth as she did it again because the sensation was so intense and she felt like she was going to burst. Taylor's next touch wasn't quite as gentle as she held her thighs down and legs open exposing her, preventing Brooke pulling away from her mouth.

"Oh god, god Taylor! I can't... fuck, fuck, my goddd," Brook's moans and desperate breathing, with lust filled gasps, thrilled Taylor.

Taylor's tongue was joined by her hands. She knew the sensation was almost unbearable for Brooke so she pushed her fingers deep into her. They slipped easily inside, easing the tension from the intense sensation of Taylor's mouth on her pussy. Brooke was holding onto Taylor's shoulders and trying to hold her back. She was struggling to catch her breath and contain herself as Taylor made love to her but as the swirl of mixed sensations intensified, a little less feverishly, she let her go a little to allow Taylor the freedom to push her fingers deeper into her and let Taylor's mouth love her. It didn't take long for Brooke to moan loudly as her whole body tensed up and practically trapped Taylor's hand. Her whole body was gripped with a swirling and powerful orgasm that rushed through her from her head to her toes, explosions of pleasure releasing all through her as Taylor's thrusts remained relentless, knowing how to make sure Brooke's orgasm was fully released, then the next one deep inside her, in quick succession, pleasure rushing through her again. She was gasping for breath. Her body trembled, the release was so intense. Brooke had never experienced anything like it. Taylor pulled her over and on top of her to kiss her some more. They hadn't caught their breath yet and Taylor's desire was unspent. She wanted more; she wanted to make sure that this night would be remembered. Their kisses were erotic and sensual, Taylor's hands exploring Brooke's soft skin, running her fingers down her back and stroking over her well curved bottom, gently cupping her cheeks, gripping where it could be felt, pulling a little and exposing her in a sensual way. Brooke felt the intrusion and liked it. She felt Taylor pull her against her, deliberately creating pressure where it could be enjoyed the most. Brook gave a little moan as she felt Taylor's fingers enter her again, something she didn't expect, but Taylor's arms were long enough to take her from behind and this wasn't a problem. Both hands pleasured her again as their kisses intensified, both mutually appreciating this unplanned encounter. Taylor didn't want to share her own body, she only wanted to take Brooke's and pleasure her. She didn't feel like being loved back, she was already sobering up and the feeling of guilt for Fran and loss for Kay were starting to spoil the moment.

Taylor already knew that she would pay for her unfaithful behaviour, and her weakness, and being the cause of another wounded heart. She was annoyed at her lack of will power.

She turned and kissed Brooke affectionately. She did like Brooke and found her very attractive. The kiss was a kind and polite one that signified the end of any further passion that night but she did pull Brooke close and held her until they fell asleep.

Taylor's phone was on silent but the screen flashed as a second text came in from Fran, nothing pushy, just a hint of concern at the complete lack of contact.

Chapter 45
Hello, Remember Me

Weeks passed after Nathan had been charged with two counts of murder, and several serious assaults with threats to life, and the trial was being fast-tracked through the courts. Both defence and prosecution preparing their cases.

Jen and Millie were just surviving and no more without Nathan. He was their rock, strong and dependable, a loving father to Millie and a really warm and caring husband to Jen. Jen could not believe what was happening. Her heart said he couldn't have done it but the coincidental evidence with no alibis, along with the injuries and the DNA evidence that they said matched his at every scene, was damming. She couldn't help but wonder if it could be possible because of the trauma he went through in his childhood.

Amy on the other hand was devastated that the police had got it so wrong. What evidence did they have? His DNA couldn't be there because it was hers; she was the only one that could prove his innocence by proving her own guilt, but she wasn't ready to do that yet. She knew Nathan and his family were suffering but she had things she needed to do, and her brother would be freed after that.

Amy walked from West Granton Road and round into Royston Mains Street. She had the address etched in her mind from her unofficial look at the files. This was the address of Megan's current boyfriend, not Dumbiedykes as first thought. She had not seen this woman for 22 years and was terrified of how she may react. She stopped dead in her tracks as she saw the door open at the house she was about to visit, and watched as an overweight man bounced a buggy unceremoniously down the steps, unshaven, greasy unkempt hair, his sportswear, which used to be white, slightly misplaced on a man who quite clearly had never played any sport. She tried not to look too obvious as she walked casually by, whilst trying to see when he went out of sight so that she could turn about and head back to make her special visit.

The street was lined with flats, six in a block on one side with red bricked terraced houses on the other side. Most had been freshly painted to disguise the poverty within the walls, although it definitely made things look nicer. The grass was overgrown and there was dog excrement in the garden she was about to visit. It nearly covered every square foot. There were some children's toys in amongst it, the child and dog obviously sharing the outdoor space. Amy winced at this, her heart sore with the never fading memories of her own depraved childhood. She knew her mother's child would not be getting cared for properly. The garden said it all and she hoped her long lost mother was still inside, keeping house and tidying up for her daughter's visit.

Amy walked back quickly, through the gate that was held on by string and skipped lightly up the steps and took a look around her just before she went to the door. Flat 2, ground floor. She could smell the unmistakeable stench of cooking fat and body odour emanating from inside. The door was slightly ajar, the nasty whiff enough to deter any house breaker, but not Amy. Amy's memories reignited with the familiar smell of what she only remembered as hell and her anger started to boil inside her stomach. Her heart nearly bounced out of her chest. She was terrified of a reunion with the woman that had allowed her to be sexually abused, suffering neglect and mental abuse at her and her partner's hands for years. Her fear was not enough to deter her though. She had plans and was determined to see them through, no matter how frightened she was. She gave herself a shake, puffed out her chest and raised her shoulders, taking a deep breath prior to entering the devil's lair, regretting it shortly after due to the rancid smell. The door gently brushed over the only small portion of carpet in the house, and then onto bare floorboards. Amy was a little worried about this because she was bound to be heard. The stench of the house was offensive to her nostrils and almost unbearable to endure. She continued deeper into the hallway, the hair on the back of her neck bristling with anticipation.

"Is that you, that was fucking quick, did you get the weed and the cider and ma chips too?" Megan's coarse and common voice bellowed from within.

There was no answer from the hallway. Amy had stopped dead and stood as still as a statue, trying to work out what to do next. The element of surprise was gone and she couldn't answer back.

Her choice was instantly taken away from her as a fat, greasy, slovenly, pyjama clad woman appeared in the hallway in front of her.

"Why are ye no answering me ya dick, it's ma fuckin' money!"

Megan stopped on the spot, visibly jumping in fright to see a strange woman in her house but that was short-lived as her true colours came bursting out.

"Who the fuck are you and what the fuck are ye daen in ma hoose? Get the fuck oot, can ye no' knock on the fucking door?"

Amy just stood there staring at this monstrosity of a woman. There was nothing, not one tiny thing about her that was nice. She was clearly dirty, unwashed and stinking of BO, fat, with a really bad attitude, missing teeth and a vile and aggressive manner, deliberately intimidating and threatening without provocation.

"A sayed, get the fuck oot oh ma hoose ya deef cow. What the fuck are you staring at anyway?"

"You," Amy replied with a smirk on her face, her eyes locked on her mother. "You, I'm staring at you, and what are you going to do about it?"

Megan had not bothered to wonder who Amy was, her general lack of interest failing to give her that instinctual warning that the person standing in front of her was a viable threat because she usually won the fights that she started, due to her size and ferocity, with no fear of the law or consequence of her actions.

"Who the fuck are you talkin' to ya cheeky bitch, get the fuck oot oh ma hoose before ah tear yer fuckin' face right aff ye, ya bitch."

Amy knew she wouldn't have to make a move because Megan's temper was very short. She came pacing towards Amy, what teeth she had grinding together as she advanced, fists clenched in an intimidating and threatening manner with an obvious intent to assault Amy as she came closer.

As Megan got close enough to touch, Amy gripped the baton tightly and pulled it swiftly from her coat and swung it ferociously at her mother's head. Megan's head rocked back with the brute force; the crunching thud was loud and uncomfortable to hear. Amy watched happily as her mother's face contorted with the force as she fell to the side and slumped onto the floor leaning awkwardly against the wall. Megan was momentarily dazed but not unconscious, a huge lump growing before her eyes. Amy smiled at her as she had fallen close to her feet with a disbelieving look in her eyes, blood starting to trickle down her face. Amy foolishly thought she already had the upper hand but how wrong she was.

"It's me, Amy, your daughter. Remember me, you vile bitch? How could you treat me and Nathan like that, you useless pile of shit, you've ruined our lives and I'm gonna make sure you pay for it too".

Megan looked up, her eyes narrowed and barely visible beneath the blood, and laughed at her. It was a loud and cruel sound, and she knew what this would do to Amy. She knew

Amy hated her mother laughing at her, shaming her, making her feel worthless.

"What the fuck do you think you could do to me? You are nothing but a worthless little slut, you won't have changed, you're weak, useless and you caused me a lot of fucking trouble you useless fucking bitch, and I owe you."

Just then Megan grabbed Amy's ankle and pulled it hard causing her to fall backwards onto the floor a foot or two away from Megan, who had not let go and was pulling herself towards Amy with her leg. Amy was taken aback and could see herself getting into trouble because her mother had always been a force to be reckoned with. Amy had seen Megan assault her stepdad too. He had been fearful of her when she was mad, and she was raging mad now! Amy tried to scrabble backwards away from her but Megan's other hand was now holding her other leg at thigh level and pushing her into the floor. Amy could smell her greasy hair, vile, salt and pepper coloured and stuck to her head with grease and now blood. Megan reached up releasing her first leg and scratched at Amy's face, then came up with her mouth wide open, rotten teeth exposed indicating her intention to bite. Amy was much lighter and more agile but she was pinned down and had to grab Megan's face, her hands almost slipping off from the blood and grease. She pushed and slipped as she fought with all her might to stop this thing assaulting her. Megan, even with a significant head injury, was mentally tough and anger driven, and she was raging at Amy. *How dare that wee slut come to ma hoose and try and get me. I'll fucking teach her.*

The punch crunched into Amy's face and her head rocked back, bumping off the wall behind her, the pain in her nose excruciating and her eyes instantly watering. The second punch burst her lip and she felt her teeth rattle with such force she thought she'd lose them. More punches started to rain down on her as her mother's hefty frame was now up on her knees and over her, enjoying assaulting her daughter once again, this time as an adult, and she didn't seem to be going to stop.

Amy's mind was in panic mode but she still had an ace to play. Her hand tightened round the canister in her pocket and she managed to pull it out from her jacket as her mum moved her knee up and off her coat.

"Fuck you, bitch," Amy cried as she pulled the CS out of her pocket and sprayed it directly into Megan's eyes from only an inch away, the force instantly causing damage and the gas taking immediate effect as mucus and snorters came flooding from every exposed orifice. Amy was also suffering the effects but she had been exposed a lot lately and it was only the residue from the particles on her mother so she fought through it.

Megan rolled backwards like a wallowing hippo, her knees up and her hands covering her face as she rolled about in agony. Amy took her chance and jumped to her feet, her face swollen from Megan's ferocious retaliation.

Amy was filled with hate, any trace of hesitation now gone. She took hold of her mother by her disgusting hair and yanked her head back and hissed at her.

"That was that last time you will ever hurt me, touch me or put me down. You are a fucking disgrace to the human race, you were supposed to protect us."

The words were said with pure hatred and intent and Megan got the threat and, as she moved slowly and blindly round onto all fours, Amy struck her to the temple knocking her back to the ground, stamping on her flabby stomach to wind her. She then sat down on her chest, full weight, as Megan continued to gasp for breath, now visibly struggling to get any. Her incapacitation just spurred Amy on. She knew what she was doing, what she had planned to do, and that was to kill her own mother.

She wanted to look right at her, into her soulless eyes as she stole her life from her; like Megan had done to her. She put her hands round her mother's neck and squeezed, initially a little worried at its width and that her hands might not fit round but, as she used her body weight to push down on Megan's throat, she felt the pressure crunch down on her neck. She looked into her bloodshot eyes with pure hatred and venom, her teeth now gritted at the effort she exerted. Megan could see the blurred outline of Amy's face. She tried to plead with her eyes as she couldn't speak but there was no sympathy or weakness shown by Amy and she pushed down even harder. She knew that Megan would have probably killed her just minutes earlier, had she taken the chance, but now she was at the mercy of her daughter, the daughter that she had neglected and tortured for the first five years of her life. The ill-treatment was etched in Amy's mind for eternity, the nightmares, self-harm, mental illness, failed relationships, distress and fear scarring her whole adult life. She could now finally erase the vermin that had caused her suffering all those years ago.

She pushed her thumbs viciously down in the centre of Megan's throat and jerked up and down several times, causing a hideous snapping sound as the hyoid bone broke. All of the remaining fight in her evil mother was now gone. Amy pushed down savagely one last time, merely in distaste and disrespect for the lifeless body beneath her. She was shaking as she reached into her jacket pocket, her fingers curled round the object, and she pulled it out and held it firmly in her hand as she opened up her mother's mouth. She pulled it down hard until her jaw cracked. The noise was horrible and made Amy wince and a shiver went down her spine. She took the object and shoved it deep into Megan's mouth, totally blocking her throat, pushing it as far back as she could get it before clamping the mouth shut, holding it for a couple of moments to make sure it didn't open up again. Amy wasn't overly bothered that there was a little bit of hair protruding.

She was now physically exhausted, totally unaware of the effort she had had to exert to overpower this formidable woman.

She wobbled as she tentatively got to her feet, taking time to look down at the thing lying there, her mother, the person who was meant to love and protect her but, as she mustered up saliva from the back of her throat, there was no emotion at all for the corpse splayed out in an undignified way. Amy spat on Megan in disgust.

She suddenly heard the unsteady garden gate and she rushed to the door and locked it. She heard the child babbling away with no response from the male, who cursed as the buggy hit the bottom stair, no interaction between him and the boy.

Amy's heart jolted back to life as she looked at the sight beneath her. She couldn't let that little child see this. She ran to the bedroom and took the dirtiest stained duvet she had ever seen from the bed and placed it over her mum, a term she used lightly for this woman.

She hoped the wee boy would be taken into care and adopted by a family that really wanted children because the chances of the child being that guy's were slim to zero, she thought to herself.

She went to the back of the house and left through the back door, glad that the garden was fenced in and the gate appeared to be locked, stopping any chance of pursuit. She leapt over one fence and into a shared courtyard where she looked up as she hurried away. A couple of windows were open, some of the locals leaning out of them having a fag and nosing out at other folk, hoping there would be fight or some police action at some point. It was sometimes better than the telly in this area.

"What happened to yer face doll, was that Meg, did you owe money or something?"

Megan had clearly hurt many previous visitors if they failed to pay for their gear.

Amy just looked up and said "Something like that. How do I get out of this place?"

The woman spoke with a cigarette hanging from her lips and pointed to the gap between the houses and said that the fence was broken down there.

"Thanks for that, I'm in a bit of a rush!"

The wifey just smiled through her haggard face, understanding why Amy needed to run from there; the quicker the better, she thought to herself.

Megan's partner banged at the door furiously. He'd noticed it was closed when he came through the gate and thought Megan was trying to wind him up. The wee boy was starting to cry and was becoming distressed as Mark banged and shouted at the door. Clearly he thought he was the one in trouble and was waiting for the swipe of a hand that normally followed a row.

He bent down and poked the letterbox open with his chubby fingers and screwed up his eyes to try and take in what he was seeing. He could see blood on the walls and the lump beneath the duvet with a blood-soaked hand sticking out. There was no sign of life. The keys were in the back of the door and he couldn't get in. He knew he had to phone the police but he would have to stash his gear first.

Mark pushed the wee boy roughly out of the way, stuffing his large bag of cannabis into the buggy and under the covers to secrete it as he thumbed 999 into his phone.

"Fuck this, oh, aye, eh, police! I think someone has been assaulted," he stuttered.

"Address please, and what is your name?"

Chapter 46 - Break In Silence

Little David sat in the lounge at tea time, engrossed in his toys with the television on in the background. Marcus and Maria came through to the living room to sit beside him and keep a watchful eye over him as he played. Both of them were reluctant to let him out of their sight ever again, to the point that they looked into his room numerous times a night just to check he was still there. Maria still felt guilty about him being taken but she had only gone inside for two minutes at the most and they lived in a decent area. She had done nothing wrong, nothing that any other parent would not have done.

They held each other's hands as they smiled lovingly down at him. David sat cross-legged as he fought with Batman against the Joker, driving the bat mobile roughly into the Joker's lair knocking all the other figures flying into the air. He played happily, not a care in the world, and appeared to have got over his abduction. He never spoke about it.

The music for the news came on and Marcus sat up as the main headlines came on. The top story was the upcoming trial for Nathan Sloan, the major story that had captured the nation's attention. Sloan himself was a victim of sustained and brutal physical and sexual abuse and now he was a killer, charged with two serious assaults and two murders. The headlines started with a picture of the last murder victim, his face took up the whole screen. David looked up and stared right at it, his little

245

eyes widened and he remained in an owl-like gaze. Marcus went straight over to reassure him and was about to take him out of the room to avoid him suffering any distress but both Marcus and Maria wanted to hear what was being said. The newsreader reported about Nathan, the man charged with the murder, and went on to say that he had freed the abducted children from the scene of the murder, where there had been a specially adapted room in the house, a room with padded walls to prevent any noise or screams for help from travelling outside.

"Daddy, what did he say, what did the man there say?"

Marcus was taken aback at how David was acting. He was calm and confused and the fact that he was even asking questions about it was a first and a break in his silence about the abduction.

"The man was talking about the bad man that took you and that's the man that rescued you, it's about his trial coming up."

"What's a trial daddy? And it wasn't that man that saved us. It was a lady. She looked a bit like him though! She was really nice and kind and she bought us both some sweeties, but she said to us not to tell on her, and now she won't be our friend anymore because I've just told you." It was only now that David began to cry; he was crying because he thought he had betrayed the lady that saved him, not because of the abduction.

David had not spoken about his ordeal at all, not once. He had not uttered a word when they tried to interview him. He just clammed up and chose to hide his thoughts deep in his mind but seeing Nathan's face had regenerated his young mind and on hearing something he knew to be wrong, he felt he had to speak up. Like his father, he knew what was right and wrong and when they said it was a man that saved him, he had to let them know that that wasn't the case, even though it meant letting the lady down.

Marcus's jaw dropped at this revelation and he now felt very uneasy about Nathan. Wee Davie didn't tell lies, not that they knew of. Maria came over to him too and asked in a really soft voice, "What did you say there David? Are you sure that it was a lady that helped you, not this man?"

She pointed to the television as Nathan Sloan's picture was shown. It was very clear and his kind eyes gazed warmly out of the screen.

David replied, "Nope, not him, who's he? I said it was a lady, she was really nice, she made us follow her for an adventure and she told us not to tell on her, because she would get into trouble, but she has the same eyes as him, nearly exactly the same!"

"My god, how could we have got this all so wrong? There's evidence though and lots of it, what the fuck," Marcus whispered into Maria's ear. "It never felt right when we interviewed him, you know. He really did seem genuine, and this might be why. It wasn't actually him, shit, shit, shit!"

"Phone Taylor now, right now, before this goes any further for that man."

"I don't think it will be as simple as that, because we still have to disprove all of the evidence we have against him, which we thought was going to be a certain conviction! I'm not sure that things will automatically change that simply on just the say so of a child. They'll say David might have got it wrong because he would have been really traumatised and possibly confused about the whole thing and maybe Nathan had dressed up?"

"Do you believe him Marcus? Because I do, 100%. He wouldn't make it up and that's the first bloody thing he has said about it since it happened. We have to sort this, Nathan has a family and this is not right, phone her, phone her right now, please!" Maria said pleading with Marcus to do something.

Marcus rang Taylor's mobile. She took a while to answer, "Hello, what do you want Marcus, I don't want a lecture, it's a day off you know, is it something important?" Taylor had a headache and the DCI had only just left half an hour ago after another lust fuelled encounter.

"I think we've got the wrong guy Taylor," he said in an exasperated tone.

"We already thought that, because he is such a nice guy, but the evidence far outweighs his nice guy façade. That's nothing new," she moaned .

"David said it was a lady and he was 100% certain. He said that Nathan looked like her though and that his eyes were identical to hers".

"How reliable can a five-year-old be, just how convinced are you Marcus?"

"Very! Wee David says the person who rescued him was a lady, and he is very adamant about it too, and I believe him. It didn't sit right at his interview, we both wanted to believe him, he was straight up as he answered all the questions and his actions didn't appear like that of a guilty person. You felt it too Taylor? Didn't you? I know you did, but the evidence was stacked up against him and our hands were tied. There's no way we could have let him go and I'm not sure we can now? Not without finding another suspect, certainly not just on a wee boy's say so, anyway?"

"What about the DNA? That evidence is rock solid and it was there in abundance at every crime scene and that won't go away either. Could there have been two people? We need to do some more digging about Nathan. There's something not right here, something he's not saying, or that he never thought to mention, who knows?"

Marcus was thinking aloud and said, "He might have a twin, what if he has a twin? That would explain the DNA."

"Only if the twin is the same sex and identical. I think that's how the identical DNA thing works, unless there is one of these billion or so to one exceptions to the rule," Taylor replied.

"It's not an impossibility, his records didn't show he had a sibling so neither of us asked him, we just went with the information we had on him and didn't think to question it. He had been in care for years and sometimes they don't keep siblings together for certain reasons and of course they change their names to hide their identities from their abusers, but there should have been a linked record though, you'd think!" Marcus seemed dumbfounded.

Taylor put her hands on her head, it was already pounding before this phone call and now it felt like it was going to explode.

What they were talking about wasn't an impossibility and she knew it! She would have to research the DNA intricacies and how possible this could be. They needed to delve further into Nathan's childhood and if he had a sibling when he was put into care and what happened to him or her, and where were the fucking records anyway? She banged her hands hard against the door frame at the enormity of this information and what it would mean to the enquiry, and the embarrassment factor and everything else that would come with it.

Their conversation ceased and they both headed to the station to share their revelations with the squad. Taylor would inform the DCI and then get started on further enquiry into trying to prove that Nathan may not be their man after all.

Before they even got to work, their phones were ringing and they were asked to come straight in to assist. There had been another murder in the Royston area of Edinburgh.

Chapter 47
Race Against Time.

On arrival, Taylor put on her forensic suit, gloves, over shoes and dust mask, everything she could. A group of local worthies watched on as she stumbled to the side as her foot caught in her forensic suit. She looked round when she heard them laugh at her as she dressed on the pavement, staring at them with a warning in her eyes, one that said she didn't take any shit and clearly wasn't in the mood either. She knew she had to don her forensic gear in the street, not ideal, but she didn't want to leave a trace of herself at the crime scene. Fran, Marcus and the DCI were also supposed to attend at the scene but she was the first detective there, to the obvious entertainment of those who had gathered. She was tempted to get extra sets down there to check them all out and clear up a few of their outstanding enquires.

Taylor walked in first, signing the crime scene entry log on the way in, time and reason to be there, and protective clothing worn. She tentatively walked in to the hallway. A chubby hand was visible under a duvet on the floor. The scenes examination branch had already been in talking photos and swabs so it was safe for Taylor and the team to search for other physical clues and evidence within. She took the time alone to work the scene. Once the others arrived and were signed in, Taylor gently lifted the duvet off the body and stood back for a while when the final photos were taken of the exposed corpse and the injuries sustained.

"Who is she?" the DCI asked. "What has come back from the checks? Is there anything on her of interest, any reason someone would have done this to her? There needs to be something pretty personal to take a feud this far. She has a little boy for Christ's sake," she said totally unaware just how lucky the little boy was with Megan's untimely death.

Fran stared at the corpse. She had seen the child and partner back at the station and didn't feel any sense of loss for the child as she looked down at the dishevelled woman. She had already looked round the house and felt sad for the little boy that had to stay in a dump like this. There was filth everywhere, barely anything in the fridge, a mattress on the floor, few toys and a lot of used nappies, fag ends and other rubbish lying around the unclean house. She wondered how anyone could care for anything if they lived like this. She looked up at Taylor, who was also looking around, but she had already taken in her surroundings and was obviously trying to avoid Fran's eyes. Fran caught on to this because she had watched Taylor do this before, the avoidance thing, when she had been caught out in the past. Her heart sank into her shoes and she tried her best not to show any feelings but she couldn't help but wonder who Taylor had ended up with this time.

Marcus knelt down by the corpse, noting the trauma to the head, bruising and marks around the neck, petechial haemorrhaging in the whites of the eyes, which was consistent with strangulation and suffocation. He took the time to look at the woman's hands as it appeared there had been a violent struggle prior to her death. There was swelling and bruising on her knuckles, which was still obvious, even though they were naturally large due to her weight, so she had definitely assaulted someone prior to her murder or had been trying to defend herself from the suspect. He looked closer at her mouth which appeared to have hair coming from between her lips. Her mouth was closed but seemed to have something inside it. He leant over and gently pried her lips apart. To his horror he saw a set of blind eyes staring out at him from her mouth. A white face with tight red lips, the cheeks full, with an evil expression, the head of the doll jammed back deep into her throat, put there to ensure that if there was a sign of life, this would put a stop to any chance of survival.

Taylor was on the phone to the detectives back at the station, "Get all of the systems checked, get to the head of social work and retrieve all of the files, everything! I need every stone turned, children, referrals, previous convictions, DNA, anything, previous calls to this address, any other address she's ever lived at, who she's been out with, what she had for breakfast." *That might have been a lot,* she thought to herself. "Don't miss anything because her past most definitely holds the key to this one. Marcus, gonna check with the SEB guys if they have taken swabs from her hands, under the nails, please".

The SEB crew were still outside packing their stuff into the van when Marcus called out to them to ask about the nail swabs as requested by Taylor.

The two of them both turned round with faces of exasperation, "Of course we have, we do that as a matter of course. Tell your boss lady we know how to do our jobs!"

Taylor heard this and initially felt a little annoyed but then realised that she was overly worried about missing something herself so had begun double checking others.

She shouted out from the house, "SORRY, I know you would have done it, I just don't want anything missed, sorry."

The SEB team just shook their heads but smiled at their mini-victory over the MIT (major investigation team). They liked Taylor, and they knew she and her team would be under pressure at the moment with everything that had gone on in the city over the past months.

Taylor then shouted, "Did you do inside her mouth?" a little triumphantly, knowing that they hadn't seen what had been shoved into it.

"Naw, why?" they asked.

"Sorry, if you could just come back for a moment, and bring the camera and a couple more bags please! Thanks," Taylor requested respectfully, not trying to be a smart arse.

The DCI came out of the living room shaking her head at the state of the house and caught Taylor's embarrassment at the little spat with the SEBs, probably more so because of the audience that had seen it happen. Taylor looked up and her face flushed even more as she remembered the drunken liaison with the DCI. Fran walked back into the hallway too and stopped and stared at the two of them. Her stomach twisted into an angry, jealous knot, she knew there was more than a little embarrassment there. She rolled her eyes back in her head, face flushed with rage as she snapped off her gloves and headed out of the door.

"Where are you going?" Taylor asked; she hadn't seen Fran coming in and hadn't noticed her face change.

"I feel sick, the stench in there is giving me the boke, so is the tension between you two, you two-timing shit!" Fran didn't hold back and didn't care about the audience, rank or not.

She pushed past Marcus, and said, "Did you know?"

"Know what?" he replied honestly.

"Them!" as she nodded her head back towards Taylor and the DCI who were still in the hallway, both completely red-faced and mortified.

"Eh, what the fuck? No, no, no way. I knew she was heading out for a drink last night, but no, no way. Really? I didn't, honestly." He questioned the possibility of that being the case because there had never been any mention of any interest on Taylor's part, which was something she would normally do.

Taylor just stood there like a bad child, staring at Fran's perfect little body as she walked towards the police vehicles. She shook her head. *What the fuck have I done? I must be mad.*

The DCI squeezed her shoulder discreetly but Taylor didn't want this. She felt crap, hungover, guilty and undeserving of any affection and lastly any sympathy. She gave a slight shrug, enough for the DCI to get the hint. Marcus disguised his glance up towards them and shook his head in disappointment for Fran. Taylor saw this and gave him a hard stare with her piercing eyes but she knew he was right. She was a complete shithouse.

Taylor turned and walked through the house, actually more like stomped through the house, she was now clearly in a bad mood, caught out again and feeling like shit. She questioned herself inwardly as to why she did the things she did, at the expense of others feelings, just for a short-lived thrill. She shook her head as she opened a large walk-in cupboard. She stood statue still with her mouth open as she looked within. She tried to turn on the light but like the rest of the house they didn't have a light bulb in any room, so she lit her torch. She shone it into the depth of the cupboard, the light glistened off hundreds of sets of eyes, blue, brown, green, all of them seemed to stare straight at her. There in front of her were rows and rows of hideous porcelain dolls, cheap tacky and very ugly, with evil faces, something she had seen a few times before in the last few months. She moved forward into the cupboard and called over her shoulder for Marcus to come. The eyes appeared to follow her as she went, whatever angle she looked from, the eyes just pierced into her. Even to Taylor there was something really frightening about them, something creepy about their presence, almost like they were aware of her.

"Check this out Marcus. Do you think this may be a significant clue in relation to the dolls found at the other crime scenes, possibly a gentle reminder of the terror they may have brought to a young child?" Taylor smiled like the cat that had got the cream.

"I reckon so. These things would give me nightmares. Who would ever want to keep these hideous dolls, they're freaky?!" Marcus replied, a little disturbed by this collection of eerie dolls.

The radio crackled after several more minutes and the officer back in the squad room had vital information to pass on, "To DS Nicks".

"Go ahead, to DS Nicks," Taylor answered and everyone stopped to listen, even Fran from outside.

"You'll want to hear this, guess whose biological mother that is you have there?"

"No idea, just tell me," Taylor moaned a little due to the mini break up she had just suffered minutes before.

"It's Nathan Sloan's biological mother. She and her partner apparently raped and tortured him prior to being discovered. He had been kept hidden in their house. This was all before he was taken into care. Oh, and you'll want to hear this too, she actually had two children, a boy and a girl, and both of them were taken off her when they were five."

"Five, what do you mean five, were they both five?" Taylor quizzed.

"Yep, both five. They were identical twins, even though they were the opposite sex, which I thought was impossible, but obviously not in this case, a biological anomaly!"

"Fuck me!" Taylor didn't know whether to laugh or cry because this explained everything. However, it wouldn't stop the embarrassment and egg on their faces for getting things so wrong. *How the fuck did this not come out in the checks for Nathan?* she thought. However, the information wouldn't necessarily have been openly available to them through normal checks, unless they had specifically known what they were digging for. They would have had to have had knowledge about Nathan's troubled childhood as identities of innocent victims in high profile cases such as his were protected, the less people that knew, the safer the victims were in their new lives.

"We need to find her, we need to find Nathan's sister, his twin sister, and we need a hurry up on the DNA from this place. Please someone call the super to get this rushed through. I think what we thought was Nathan's DNA may end up here at this crime scene and that's impossible as Nathan is still in the five star Saughton luxury prison and clearly couldn't have done this!" *At least this will be enough to free him this time,* she thought to herself. "We'll need to speak to him again though, about his sister and his past, and we'll need to find the male from the initial offences against the children back then and quickly judging by the mess here!"

Chapter 48
Bittersweet Freedom

Nathan walked into the sunshine. Time seemed to have stood still over the last while without his wife and little Millie. He took a deep breath, breathing in the fresh free air, then took several more steps and walked onto Calder Road. He was a little sad that there had been no one there to meet him, until he heard a familiar little voice "BOO". Then the most wonderful giggle followed, as Millie jumped out from behind the hedge. Her mum Jen was right there beside her and he scooped up his little girl and gave her a stubbly hug as she squealed with delight and Jen wrapped her arms around him and said, "I knew you couldn't have done what they said you did, not you, no way. We missed you so much and we love you so much".

"Have they explained to you why I'm out? They haven't told me anything yet but they seem to have evidence that proves I'm innocent," Nathan said with a questioning expression.

"What? They've not even said to you yet, for god's sake, they ruin your life and then don't explain why you can now go free, the bloody nerve of it all!" Jen said as she frowned at him.

"There must be a reason Jen. They must need to keep it a secret for a reason, a reason I can't know! Have you seen Amy recently Jen? She's not been at the prison for the last couple of days?"

"No, I've not seen her, she's not called." Jen shrugged her shoulders. Amy had never been a regular visitor so there was no need to worry that she hadn't been in contact for a while.

"Nathan, there was another murder a couple of days ago, a female in her late forties was murdered down in the Royston area. Did you watch the news in the prison? She was living under a new name and they have revealed her true identity. Her name was Megan Thomson but they didn't say why she had changed her name."

Nathan stopped dead in his tracks, his face went sheet white, his heart started to race and he felt physically sick. He started to tremble uncontrollably and vomited where he stood.

"What's the matter with you, what is it, what's wrong? You're frightening me Nathan!" Jen held his arm and stroked his back while trying to keep hold of Millie too.

Nathan stood up and wiped his mouth, stringy saliva that had dangled precariously from his mouth a moment earlier wrapped itself round his hand. He took a deep breath, tears visible in his eyes as he looked straight at Jen. He looked like a frightened little boy.

She squeezed his shoulder and said, "Speak to me Nathan, please. What the hell is it that's made you like this, you were fine a minute ago?"

"She was my mum, Megan Thomson was my mum, before Amy and I were taken into care. She was meant to love us and look after us and protect us but what she did to us was unspeakable," he said as he wiped his hand on his trousers and took hold of his own little girl and looked at her with loving eyes.

"Where's Amy, we need to find Amy. I think she might be in trouble!"

Chapter 49
Decisions For Taylor

Taylor was back at the office and was sitting at her desk looking at the front cover of several newspapers, *Daily Record*, *Express*, and a couple more. The headline read, "Killer Still On The Loose, As Police Arrest The Wrong Man," and things similar to that on the others.

She slapped it down on the desk as she spun herself back on her swivel chair. She knew this was coming but the evidence they had gathered had been solid, up until the impossible happened. Unfortunately, the public wouldn't see it that way and would really not want to hear that; they quite liked to jump on the bandwagon, up in arms against the police.

Fran sat two desks away, typing away furiously, trying hard not to take any notice of her boss. She was aware the pressure would now be piling on Taylor and she couldn't help feeling a little sorry for her.

She looked up at the DCI's office and could hear raised voices coming from inside. She saw Findlay's overweight frame rise from his chair and walk towards the door. The DCI's voice continued on, raised and angry.

Taylor also looked up from her desk and saw Findlay open the door and leave the office, ruddy faced and looking very sheepish with his head down; it was clear the shit was falling downwards and was coming her way next, although she did smirk to herself at the downfall of her boss. He had made her life hell for years and she was enjoying a little Karma.

Fran couldn't help herself as she looked over at Taylor, just as she looked up in her direction. Taylor gave a sheepish smile back towards her, her eyes were saying sorry. Fran's face just went red as she turned away again, she didn't want to care for Taylor, she didn't want to hear her apologies, she was still raging at her for what she had done to her and how shit she had made her feel. Fran's problem was that she did care for Taylor, she had fallen for her and was in love with her and she wanted to know why she did what she did, so often, even though that's how they had started their affair - behind Kay's back.

"Sergeant Nicks, can you come into the office for a moment please!"

Fran's head snapped back up and looked straight at the DCI, jealous that she could command Taylor's attention, due to rank and authority, and failure on Taylor's part to follow instructions would get her into trouble.

Taylor looked up slowly as this was the last thing she needed or wanted at the moment. She did wonder what the DCI wanted to say and whether it was work related as they had had very little contact since the night they spent together.

She was getting up from her chair slowly, deliberately stalling when her phone beeped. She thought it was going to be Fran, because of the look she had just been given by her a minute ago. She hesitated but curiosity made her lift her phone and look. Her eyes had to double take the name as her heart skipped a beat before sending painful twists into her stomach.

It was Kay, Kay, with all that was going on just now. Her heart fluttered because she knew deep down the reason she had acted the way she had the other night with the DCI. It was because of Kay. She didn't really want to love or truly feel for anyone else because she and Kay still had unfinished business to attend to, and from just looking at her name on a screen every nerve in her body was now tingling and she had suddenly come to life. She didn't read the text. She cared for Fran but she had slept with her boss hurting Fran. However, she now knew that her heart was still with Kay.

She opened the office door and the DCI gestured for her to sit and said politely, "Close the door behind you please."

Taylor sat down heavily on the chair opposite her boss and they just stared at each other, both willing the other to speak first.

"Have you seen the papers Taylor, the top brass are all over this and unfortunately we're in the firing line once again. We need to find this Amy and fast, or our positions here will be on the line!" the DCI explained very matter-of-factly, showing very little emotion or fondness for her colleague. Taylor hadn't made much effort to speak to her boss since their liaison and felt really bad for hurting two women, Fran and Brooke, both of whom she liked and respected very much but she was her own worst enemy. She knew her boss really liked her but she knew Brooke knew about Fran too, and that hadn't stopped her meeting up with Taylor the other night.

Taylor answered honestly and updated her boss on where they were with their enquiries and what the next steps were. They had every detective available on this now and they had located Natt Spears in the last hour and had a car heading to his home address to alert him to the possible danger he might be in.

The DCI was happy with that and leant towards Taylor and spoke very quietly to her. "Have I done anything to upset you? You've not been anywhere near me the last few days?"

"No, no you haven't, clearly it is me with the problem, Fran hates me, you think I'm a user and an asshole and I've just had a text from Kay! I never set out to hurt anyone, I mean that but I've clearly hurt Fran, and I've annoyed you, but neither was intentional, because I think I'm still hurting inside, and that's when I go into self-destruct mode, I'm sorry, I really am, I didn't mean to hurt you, if I did that is, I shouldn't flatter myself!"

Taylor looked genuinely emotional as she spoke with Brooke, "I had a really good time the other night, it was really nice, I mean that, but my heart isn't free to give to you." She hesitated, adding, "you or Fran!" Taylor reached out her hand very discreetly towards her boss and gestured for Brooke to give her her hand, which she did although a little reluctantly because she knew this was the end before it had even had a chance to really begin. Taylor leant forward and kissed Brooke's hand, looked up into her eyes and said, "Sorry, I really am sorry, you are lovely, you're gorgeous in fact and I wish things could be different, I mean that, the timing is just shit!"

Brooke gently touched the side of Taylor's face with true affection and said, "Thank you for being honest, I'm sorry that you're not free for us to have a little more time but the other night was pretty intense and I too had a really good time".

Brooke smiled at Taylor and Taylor back at Brooke. Taylor did genuinely like her boss as more than a friend or a colleague and they both now knew that, it was just the timing hadn't been right for them to have been more.

Brooke then tapped both of her legs and said jokingly to Taylor, "Now go and get some work done before we're both replaced. Both were far more relaxed now and they knew there was a mutual understanding and affection between them, not just a casual one night affair.

Taylor stood up Brooke couldn't help but notice just how attractive Taylor was, both inside and out, her flaws and weakness openly visible to all and very destructive for those who fell for her charm and natural beauty. The contours of her tall slim physique were a pleasure to look at, always well dressed, pristine presentation and she always wore a very alluring perfume. Brooke watched as she walked out of the office and couldn't help but look over at Fran as well but she was no longer at her desk as she hadn't been enjoying the show. Brooke felt for her because she would be feeling just like she did right now, but tenfold because, reading between the lines, Taylor was avoiding commitment from both of them. Brooke had watched Fran for a while now and, just by looking at her, could tell Fran had strong feelings for Taylor.

Chapter 50
A Warning On Deaf Ears

Natt Spear's flat was just off Easter Road on the first floor. Detectives Fran and Marcus managed to get into the communal stair as someone had wedged a yellow pages there to stop the main door closing for whatever reason. They trudged up the stairs. Natt's door was Hibs green and his name was handwritten in a scrawl on a torn piece of paper tucked into the name slot. They knocked loudly in a very police like fashion, their intention not to hide their identity. The door opened and a beer-bellied, unshaven, unwashed man faced them.

"Natt Spears?" Marcus asked.

"Who's fucking asking, like?" Natt said to them in a very hostile manner.

They showed their warrant cards and he tried to shut the door in their faces, but Marcus had anticipated this and had jammed his foot in the doorway. He winced with the force of the door on his foot as Fran tried to hide her mirth at his expense.

"Get yer fucking foot oot of ma door or I'll fucking break it, I've got nothing to say to yoose bastards, I fucking hate the polis and I've done fuck all wrong, I know my rights, now get tae fuck!" he yelled in their faces.

He went to slam the door on Marcus's foot again but Marcus had pushed forward and managed to stop the door with his hands and said politely, but firmly, with a slightly raised but controlled voice.

"Mr Spears, we need to speak to you and it is very important you listen, whether you fucking hate us or not. Do you have five minutes you can spare, please?" Marcus said this sarcastically, nodding his head to the side at Natt as he walked past him into the hallway to avoid the door been slammed on him again.

"You're no goin' any further, ye can say what you've got to say here and then fuck off. Awright?"

"Well Mr Spears, if that's what you'd like, here is fine. Do you remember the two children you raped and tortured 22 years ago?" Marcus said bluntly and with a little hostility, not mincing his words around the facts.

"Eh, what the fuck are ye talking about? I was set up and that was fucking years ago and I've done ma fucking time, so what are ye fucking oan aboot, get tae the fucking point!"

"Well, we believe the girl, Amy, one of the two children, just in case you'd forgotten them; we believe that she may want to harm you, possibly even kill you!"

"What, that little slut? What the fuck could she dae tae me? I'd fucking rip her heid right off, and kill the wee cow if I had too, now fuck off, yer wasting ma time."

"Oh, there's one more thing, remember Megan, the lady you were convicted with? She was brutally murdered yesterday, just thought I'd let you know that, sir," Marcus added flippantly, to at least try to stir up some sort of fear in this coarse and arrogant, unrepentant man.

"What, fucking Megan? She's soft as shite. Who by, de ye ken like?" Natt questioned, with curiosity in his tone.

Natt was fully aware that Megan was far from soft. She was a vicious cow and even though he had beaten her, she had always fought back and he had many scars to prove it.

"Just thought I'd let you know. Oh and Amy might be the suspect and it's just a wee hunch but we think you might be up there for the next candidate for her revenge. What do you think Mr Spears?"

"Right, I get what yer saying but I'm no feared of anyone, I promise you. If she comes anywhere near me, it'll be her that'll need saved, and I'm not scared of you lot either, now get the fuck oot oh ma hoose, before I sue yoose cunts," he spoke with his mouth curled up and pure hatred rasped in his voice and eyes.

He blamed the police for his time in jail; it didn't cross his mind to think that it was his actions and vile behaviour that may be the reason for his custody.

Marcus and Fran were relieved to leave this vile man's house. It stank and he was really quite intimidating, even with all the people they had to deal with, Spears was up there with the very bad ones that made them wary and uncomfortable in their presence.

Chapter 51
Revelation

Amy had made a point of tracing members of Natt's family and was heading to his sister's house. She was still sore from her exertion the other day, she was still sporting a bruise or two and wondered if her appearance may be an issue.

She got off the bus in Leith Walk, deliberately not using her car, as she knew the police would have worked it out by now, because her brother was now free, recently released, and they wouldn't have done that without proof of his innocence or evidence of another suspect. Amy had known from the start of her campaign of revenge that it would only be a matter of time until they were onto her and she knew time was running out before they caught up with her, although she still had an important reunion.

She walked passed Robbie's Bar on Leith Walk and was tempted to go in for a drink, but chose to walk on. She walked a little further up the road and then turned round and headed back and did go in. There were several older men sitting at the bar, and she pulled a stool up beside them and straddled it in the most unladylike fashion as she ordered up a straight triple whiskey, grouse, her favourite. The barman gave her a look on her ordering it and as he handed it to her his eyes appeared a little sympathetic for her.

"Are you okay lady, are you sure you want this?" the barman asked kindly, looking at her bruised face.

"Oh yes, absolutely certain, but thanks for the concern," she replied with a wry smile.

She swigged it back in a oner and the warmth of the alcohol was almost instant. Her cheeks flushed with the inner burn that whisky brings. The older men beside her mumbled at the whisky she had just knocked back and she smiled happily at them as she got up to leave, placing her money on the bar.

A little Dutch courage for her as she continued on up to Albert Street, a cobbled side street off one of the main streets in Edinburgh. The flats were four and five storey stone built dwellings with common stairs on each side of the road.

She got to the main door and looked up the names on the intercom. Luckily for her his sister hadn't changed her name.

She pressed the buzzer named Spears, holding her finger down longer than necessary to avoid not being heard. She waited and buzzed again. This time the intercom crackled and she heard a female voice say, "Hullo, who is it?"

"Hi, sorry you don't know me, but can you let me in, I need to talk to you, please it's really important."

"Aye, come on up then, you'll need to hurry I've got to get the kids from school," the woman said confidently, with no fear at a stranger asking to speak to her.

Amy's heart was racing as she took the steps in twos up to the second floor. The woman was standing in her doorway. She was moderately slim, her hair peroxide, wearing jeans and a cotton top, a bit low at the cleavage, but she was quite attractive and she appeared approachable.

Amy walked up to her, and the woman said, "Well, what is it you wanted to say?"

"Let me tell you who I am, and how I know your brother first. My name is Amy, your brother used to be my mum's partner, and my mum was Megan Thomson!"

The woman's face contorted and she became openly hostile. "That fucking bitch that framed my brother for all of her perverted crimes? How dare you come here. My brother's been through hell and back because of her, he's had more than enough."

"After what he's been through? What the fuck do you mean? What the fuck has he told you? Did he tell you that he had nothing to do with it?"

"Absolutely that!"

"I was one of those two children and your brother was very much involved and not innocently framed as he claims. He was the main offender and he was definitely involved, actively and willingly. He is a brutal vile man that raped, tortured and neglected me and my brother over and over again. It's true, I promise you that. He's an evil bastard and clearly very manipulative!"

"No way! Natt's not like that. He looks after my two bairns all the time. They've never said anything and he does it nearly every week. There's no way he would harm them, he loves them. I don't believe you, she's warped you guys too. Natt's a decent bloke, he has his problems, but he wouldn't hurt the bairns."

"Listen to me, I wouldn't lie to you. I've been kept awake for years because these vivid nightmares never stop, his cruel face, the pain, the fear, it has never gone away and it never will. I'm telling you the truth, ask your kids, check your kids, watch them, save them, take them to a doctor, do something, or you'll live to regret that you didn't believe me, please do it. If you love your kids, you will, whatever you think you believe!"

Amy's eyes were filled with tears as she thought her words were falling on deaf ears but an instinctive mother's mind was already whirring with thoughts and events, incidents explained away and subtle changes in the children's behaviour that had been brushed aside.

Natt's sister Maggie was standing at the door and said, "You'll have to go now, please go, you're wrong, you're so wrong!"

Amy turned to walk away but turned back and said, "Please, please, please check your children, speak with them, ask them, do something if you care for them at all, please do this, for your own peace of mind! Just do something, don't leave them with him again, not until you can be sure he's innocent, please, please!"

Amy went down the stairs, she couldn't do any more. All she could do was hope that she had sown a seed, a seed that would grow in Natt's sister's mind, enough for her to doubt him.

Amy then started to walk the short distance through to Easter Road to make her final special visit of the day.

Chapter 52
Hesitation

Fran's phone beeped as she sat typing at her desk, her heart heavy and her head a little confused at what was happening and why.

She sighed out loud as she reached into her pocket, as she had given up hoping that Taylor would explain or deny what she believed had happened. She unlocked her phone and looked to see who had texted her. This time to her surprise it was Taylor,

"Can I come round to yours tonight, to talk, to explain, please, I owe you an explanation, and I am really sorry, genuinely sorry."

Fran sat back on her seat, and raised her hands to her head in exasperation. She wanted Taylor, she didn't want to hear the reasons why she couldn't have her.

She thumbed at her phone for several minutes and eventually wrote her reply, and then took another ten minutes to send it.

Amy was outside Natt Spears' flat. She stood across the road with a scarf over her head and dark glasses on, secreted in a small garden area and behind a well-placed shrub. She saw a couple of officers sitting in a car a couple of doors down the road to try not to be too obvious as Natt had made it very clear that he hated the police and certainly didn't think he needed their protection.

Natt walked round his flat looking for his keys. He swore loudly as he stomped through to the living room for the second time. Seeing the keys on the floor beside the telly, he marched over to get them. He bent down, the pressure of his rotund beer belly pressing against his thighs causing him to fart loudly. He smirked to himself, proud of what he had done. He scratched at one of the cheeks of his backside as he wandered towards the door, checked his pockets for money for beer and made his way out of the flat. He was totally unaware of what was waiting for him just outside. He had listened to the police and he was not worried about the little girl from the past. *What the fuck could that little rat do to someone like me,* he thought to himself.

He opened his flat door and turned to lock it. Sensing there was someone there in the stair, he clenched his fist into a tight ball.

Amy held her breath and stood as still as she could, her heart beating so loudly she could feel it against her scarf.

Natt spun round and raised his arm up viciously, only just stopping it hitting his neighbour, who was lighting up a spliff.

"What the fuck are you doing man, fuck me, chill out!" he said as he took a long drag on the large reefer hanging out of his mouth.

"Fuck me, what the fuck are you doing hanging around in here like some kind of fucking ghost, a nearly fucking hit ye man, sorry mate, make some fucking noise the next time and stop sneaking up on folk, awright, eh!"

Amy let out her breath as the two cops moved away from where they stood, right in front of where she was hiding. The last thing she wanted to do was be caught before she finished what she came here to do.

Natt shook his shoulders to calm himself back down again after nearly planting his neighbour one for not making enough noise in the common stair. He was a little spooked tonight, nobody liked to be hunted, not even a him.

He pushed on the door onto Easter Road, spotting the police car within a couple of seconds. He walked right up to it but the officers were out walking and watched him with mirth as he turned back on his heels and walked towards them, visibly unhappy that they had seen him march up to the car.

"What the fuck are you laughing at? I told you lot I don't need your protection, I can defend myself, now fuck off and leave me be!"

"There's no need to be like that sir, and you can stop your swearing! We may be here to protect you but if you step too far out of line we can give you a room for tonight that will definitely keep you safe, so enough with the swearing, right Natt? Where are you off to anyway?"

"None of your fucking, business. Don't need you, don't want you, thanks officers, good evening to you," he said as he stomped off down the road.

He walked a couple of hundred yards down the road and into the Bird in the Hand, a popular Hibernian FC supporters bar. He was a regular there and several of the men at the bar nodded and greeted him as he entered. He walked through to the far side of the pub and sat on a low stool at the bar. It was a typical working man's bar, nothing fancy, and room for standing when the football was on the telly. He ordered a pint of Tennent's lager and a large whisky to go with it. He lifted the whisky and gulped it down in one and the fiery warmth swirled down his throat and burned as it landed in his stomach, instantly making him relax a bit. He ordered another straight away and the second chased the first down. He didn't notice the woman walking in to the bar. She was wearing a large woolly scarf covering most of her face. The cops had been distracted by a group of yobs further up the street that were fighting with each other and had headed up to calm things down a bit. Little did they know their deviation from their task would be so costly, but for who?

Amy walked up to the bar, and allowed her scarf to drop from her face as she would have looked too obvious with it up. Natt didn't know what she looked like now anyway and she had made sure that her appearance was significantly altered to prevent any recognition.

Amy ordered a drink and the majority of the men at the bar turned and faced her, as well as Natt. There was a murmur of conversation among them about her, and some passed comment on her looks and lone status at the bar, Nat included, totally oblivious as to who she was, and her intention. They were all a bit leery, bar a couple who were deep in conversation. The words slut, loose and gagging on it were whispered between them, which as always was the exact opposite from the truth. She was just a female wanting to use the same right as others, to be able to come out for a drink in safety without fear of abuse or worse.

Amy had lived life long enough to know she was being talked about and was used to the idle negative chat that many people receive when they walk into places where there was a possessive attitude from a few locals, treating the bar like they owned it and not liking newcomers or strangers. She wasn't overly bothered as she could defend herself and give as good as she got verbally. She had a sharp tongue on her, which her brutal upbringing had given her.

She sat there patiently, biding her time, waiting for her twisted perverted stepdad to take his first piss, which didn't take long. His fat beer belly must have been bearing down on his weakening bladder and inevitably he stood up from his stool and adjusted his trousers and his belt beneath his protruding gut. He was still a strong man even though he waddled a bit, Amy knew what he was like and that he had a ferocious temper but she had to do this, even though she risked being hurt herself. He disappeared through the doorway and in towards the gents. Amy waited to see if any of his mates would join him, which they didn't.

Amy tentatively got up, relatively unnoticed, and wandered through to the toilet. Her hands were shaking now and she started to doubt if she could overpower Natt. Her heart said she could, but her head was having second thoughts. Her desire for revenge could end up costing her a lot more than she had thought it would. She stood in the doorway to the toilet that was ajar. She could see him at the urinals and heard the splatter of his urine as it hit the trough. It turned her stomach, the thought of his penis being exposed in any manner. It also made her remember the pain of her childhood, which manifested in an insatiable rage and enhanced her weakening courage to go through with this.

She reached into her jacket and pulled out a five-inch knife from her inside pocket, already locked in place to avoid being heard. She had taken her time to follow him and he was already finishing taking a piss and putting everything back in his trousers. This was her moment, when his hands were both occupied. She rushed forward with the knife in her right hand and plunged it into his side, once twice, three times but, before the fourth could be administered, Natt had swivelled round, his face contorted with anger initially that someone had punched him when he was taking a leak. Then he saw the small woman from the bar standing there with a small blade in her hand, which had blood dripping from it.

"You fucking bitch, it's you, you fucking dirty little whore, you're gonna fucking pay for that." She swiped the knife at his face and it cut him just beneath his eye as he closed the gap between them and grabbed hold of her face. He thrust a punch deep into her guts, which nearly folded her in two and smashed his knee into her face, sending her head rocking loosely backwards and causing her to fall, stumbling uncontrollably to the ground. She struck her head heavily on the ceramic urinal, rendering her instantly unconscious and completely defenceless. Natt reached round to where she had stabbed him. Even though she had shoved the knife in to the hilt, his girth in that area had prevented him suffering any major injury, although he was now bleeding quite significantly. He was livid. He wanted to finish the job and moved over to where Amy lay and raised his foot above her head. He was about to stamp down on her to break her neck and crush her face into an unrecognisable pulp, but he heard voices coming his way and he heard the word officers as they moved in his direction. His foot still came down hard on her and he nearly fell to the side as he overbalanced, which in turn lightened the blow on Amy's head. He managed to get out of the toilet and headed towards the emergency exit at the rear and back out onto the street. He just narrowly avoided those coming through to the toilets, who were totally unaware of his departure.

Once out in the street he touched his side and wrapped his jumper round the injury and headed off in the direction of Leith Walk, a busy commercial street with a mix of cultural venues and shops. He knew he needed medical attention, and that he may very well have killed Amy. He muttered to himself, *fucking stupid little bitch, I taught that little cow a fucking well-needed lesson, the disrespectful little whore. Who the fuck does she fucking think she is trying to fucking stab me? Fucking little cow.* He moved quickly for someone so heavy and he didn't take long to walk along one of the adjoining streets and onto Leith Walk.

He walked up the pavement towards the town centre and was starting to get a little breathless and thought that he needed to get a taxi to the hospital to get his wounds fixed, so he raised his hand up to try and get the attention of a black cab driving down the other side of the road.

The two officers along with the licensee entered the toilet to see blood over at the urinals directly in front of them, and initially their attention was drawn there. It was only once they had walked right in that they noticed the body of a small female lying on the floor, bleeding heavily from her face, with her facial features clearly damaged. The radio crackled with the words "ambulance, please, female, late twenties, facial injuries, conscious and breathing, but very shallow, we need an immediate response, this woman looks in a really bad way". Both officers knelt down and checked her vital signs more carefully and made sure they monitored them, throughout their time with her. The licensee ran through to the bar to get first aid equipment and they tried to stem the flow of blood coming from her nose, mouth and more worryingly her eye socket. It wasn't long until the much appreciated sound of the siren came into earshot. One officer muttered to his colleague, "Thank fuck!"

"You'll be alright," he said in Amy's ear, hoping his words would make a difference.

Taylor answered her mobile, and she mustered other officers to attend at the scene and the hospital, unbeknown to her that the victim was the most wanted criminal in Edinburgh and that there was another injured party still outstanding. Fran, Marcus, and other members of the team headed out from the station.

Chapter 53
Live or Die

Taylor and her team arrived just as Medic One was leaving the pub, both had got there as quickly as possible.

"Any details of who we've got here and what happened?" Taylor asked the rather shell-shocked cop that was standing outside the door with blood all over him from his attempt to save Amy.

"Nope, no idea who she is Searg, she didn't have any ID on her!" he said, visibly shaken by what he'd just been through.

Taylor took his arm and gave it a squeeze, her way of recognising his efforts and that they hadn't gone unnoticed. She also gave him a smile and said, "Well done" before carrying on with her task at hand, sorting out the mess.

"The bar will have to be emptied and statements taken from everyone who was here, details of those who have been here and since left, CCTV, SEB, all of it, and I know you are up to your neck in it but we need a scene log started, and cordon off this area as best you can, please. Get all the physical evidence you can, secure all the glasses from the bar. I'll go to the hospital with her. Fran, can you come with me please."

Fran turned her head, a little taken aback that Taylor wasn't automatically taking Marcus with her. She was happy with this though, she needed to speak with Taylor, for good reasons.

Apprehension was making her stomach tie in uncomfortable knots, an uncontrollable feeling, also tinged with a little sadness. Taylor was deliberately not taking Marcus with her because she had her suspicions as to who the young lady might be and she knew Marcus was too emotionally attached to the case. It was only down to his professionalism that he had been allowed to continue in the squad, with Sergeant Nicks' full backing.

Both ladies moved effortlessly to the door to leave and all of the males in the bar area turned and watched, both of them very attractive, strong willed and giving off and aura of confidence and control.

The ignition turned over, the car was revved loudly and jammed into gear the crunch uncomfortable to hear. It was driven recklessly up the street, now in second and travelling way faster than the chosen gear, which made the engine whine with effort, until third gear released the power, the acceleration obvious to those standing close by. The car swerved in and out of the traffic, narrowly missing an island, two pedestrians that had to run to avoid being hit and many other road users.

Hand raised and fingers in his mouth to whistle, he was hit full force by the marauding car. His torso took the brunt of the collision, causing his face to smash full force into the bonnet, before the momentum then threw him flying and spinning up into the air. His body seemed to pirouette in the air, everything in slow motion to those watching this surreal situation unfold, with their mouths agape. He spun round two full 360 degree turns before his head crunched down, face first into the road, his already disfigured face smashing loudly as his teeth left his mouth and his skull visibly shattered and bits of brain matter sprayed out and pieces of skull flew up and onto the windows of the shop fronts near to the collision. His heavy frame made the landing even more catastrophic to his slim chance of survival. However, the car which had stopped up ahead momentarily, made sure that wasn't going to happen as the driver now jammed the car into reverse and hit the accelerator hard once again and drove straight back over the already broken body on the road, sending the passers-by that had rushed to help fleeing for their own lives. The sound of his thigh snapping under the tyre was sickening and had every one who had stayed to watch moan out loud and turn away trying to shield their eyes from any further atrocity, as the other tyre crossed directly over the man's face, causing the skin to rotate off with the motion of the tyre. The car was only metres away and the driver pushed it back into first and, to the disbelief of those at the scene, drove forward and over another part of the already mangled body before making off down Leith Walk at high speed.

The car was swerving and weaving around anything that got in its way and headed down Pilrig Street, just far enough away from the scene before those inside bailed out. The driver and accomplice were fully aware that there would be serious heat on the car so they pulled straight into the large graveyard at Pilrig, putting the car completely out of sight of the road behind the high walls, but in a parking area beside several other cars, half a mile away from the scene of the crime. They wiped all the surfaces down that they could, put on normal clothes over their recently bought boiler suits and looked at one another to check that they looked normal before popping on their baseball caps and casually walking down towards the other end of Leith, via Great Junction Street. Both streets had very busy thoroughfares where they would fit in with others dressed similarly. They were able to undress in a common stair unnoticed and dump the boiler suits with hoods in a communal bin not covered by CCTV. They had thought about torching the car but that would have drawn attention to them, leading the police right to the dump site and a quicker pursuit.

Natt's sister Maggie sat in her flat with her two children playing in front of her with their toys, blissfully unaware of their mother's sickened rage, the results of their medical examinations sitting open on the coffee table, revealing the physical evidence of depraved abuse on both of her beloved children. Tears were streaming down her face, the harsh reality of her trust, totally shattered and the pain bearing heavily down on her heart. Her brother Natt, her big brother, an elder brother she had believed and trusted after she thought he had been the victim of another's falsified evidence. Her mind ran wild with the thoughts of what might have gone on behind closed doors, the violation, the cruelty and his depraved needs taken out on her precious innocent little children. She was shaking uncontrollably, terrified of the trail leading back to her but she had been clever, no personal meetings, disposable phones, money drop off and target name and description given, and a little trust that the deed would be done. Luckily there was no issue there, the young guys had been sub contracted from the top guy taking the money, and if they didn't do it, then they would get the shit kicked out of them, so their motivation was their survival. Time would tell if the link could be proved but she knew the police would be coming to investigate what had happened to the children, as social services would have already been called along with the police, after what the findings had revealed from the examination. That would prove a very real motive but, with nothing else, there would not be enough evidence, no matter what the police thought. Regardless of the chance of getting away with it, she was now regretting her actions, the reality of imprisonment and her children being taken into care could happen, and her rage on receipt of the results clearly had taken over all of her clear thinking emotions. Her common sense had gone out of the window in her hurry to seek revenge on this vile man, her big brother Natt. She got down from her seat and cuddled into her little ones and they cuddled her right back and showed her what they were doing with their toys, asking her to join in their game, her heart melting with love for them.

The police arrived in Leith Walk, Marcus about to attend until reminded of possible cross contamination if there was any link between the two events, which with the timings there was a high possibility. A new team had to be made up of those who hadn't been at the previous crime scene and the rest mustered from CID across the city were requested to attend. Roads policing were already there. The road was closed off and the request for tents to cover the body already submitted as it was a hideous sight.

The initial officers attending had checked for signs of life, fully aware there wouldn't be any, and had given a quick cursory search of the victim for ID, finding a wallet in his back pocket.

"Fuck me, is this not the guy that was under our watch?" the young cop mentioned.

"Aye, but I heard he didn't want the police anywhere near him," his colleague said quickly.

"I know, but we'll get the blame though, we always do," he shrugged. "I'll call it in!"

When the radio went, Taylor and Fran listened intently as the name was given, and Taylor shook her head.

"How the fuck did that happen? I thought they had eyes on him!"

Fran replied, a little sarcastically, "I heard he was a complete prick and hated police, and told them to fuck off, on every opportunity he had, and the cops were there. I can imagine just how nice the notorious Natt Spears would have been to them. Remember, he wasn't a fucking angel and there would be a few people out there that may not like him too much," she said a little triumphantly, sticking up for the uniform cops.

"Who do you think we have here up at the hospital? Her face was completely mangled, huge coincidence don't you think?" Taylor questioned.

"Without ID, how are we going to find out?"

"I think we should get Nathan to help, casually of course, but it's the quickest way, if that's who you're thinking it is?" Taylor said quietly.

"You can't do that, and why would he help us anyway, after what he's been through?" Fran exclaimed, a little astonished at the hint of a rule bend from her boss.

"Because it is his sister, and I know he really cares for her, and he will want to be with her, and we need him to confirm who it is, so get on the phone, your own phone and get him to meet us at the hospital and we'll sort something out, and it's not a rule break, he's family and she is really badly injured and it is her right to have her family by her side!" Taylor said with a hint of a gloat, determination and authority, and then a softening of her eyes and a cheeky little wink.

"Fuck you," Fran whispered with a smile back.

Taylor gripped Fran's knee tight in a horse bite action, making Fran jump, but the warmth between them, that had been missing for a while, was back, for now anyway.

"Get the DNA rushed through too, because of the damage to her face, even Nathan might not be able to tell who it is just by looking at her, so fast track it please, with Super's authority, back dated of course." Taylor hadn't even phoned in yet, but hopefully DCI Brooke Sommerville would have been on it.

Chapter 54
Connections

Nathan's face looked shocked and Jen asked him what was wrong.

"They think Amy has been assaulted and they need someone to identify her!"

"Really, they're a bit desperate are they not. I would tell them where to go, after what they put you through!"

"It was fucking shit, but you can see why they went for me, because there was a lot of shit pointing in my direction, in fact, stacked up against me, and I couldn't disprove anything! I would have gone for me too if I was them. If I hadn't thought of Amy and known she existed, how were they supposed to?" he said almost defending the police.

"Anyway I need to go and see her, just to see her if it is her. Who knows if I'll get the chance again without bars in the way, because she won't be seeing blue sky for a long time!" Nathan continued.

Jen agreed with her eyes, a little pissed off with Amy for letting her husband Nathan go through everything he had. But she also understood that in Amy's mind there had been unfinished business, things she needed to do, and for very good reasons.

Fran and Taylor arrived at the hospital. The female brought in by the police and ambulance was now in cardiac arrest and everyone was working hard to save her. The trauma to her head was substantial and very much life threatening.

"Has she been conscious at all, has she said anything?" Taylor asked the cop that had travelled in the ambulance with Amy.

He shook his head. "Nothing, she just gurgled with the blood, she's in a bad way Searg," he said, nodding his head towards the team working on her.

The defibrillator was used between compressions numerous times; adrenaline, fluids, bloods and several scans later, a drill was inserted into her skull and fluid drained to release the pressure. The procedure was successful and Amy was able to be moved to the high dependency unit, alive, but only just. Surgery would have to be planned for the reconstruction of her face once her condition was fully stabilised and no longer life threatening.

Nathan arrived at the hospital and was quickly intercepted by Fran and Taylor, not wanting him to just waltz in there, although there was a cop on the door of the ward.

Taylor thanked him for coming, a gesture of respect and understanding, with an apologetic look on her face and one of genuine gratitude. She explained to him that the female was in a bad way and Taylor explained the situation in which she was found and about the other incident on Leith Walk and who they believed the victim of the hit and run to be.

On hearing this, Nathan was already sure it was his sister Amy that had been brought in, there was too much coincidence there. Nathan knew she wanted to hurt Natt and that was the main reason for her not telling the police about her brother's innocence earlier, because she didn't want the police on to her until she had either killed or seriously maimed him.

"Can I see her, let me see her, how is she, what the fuck has that prick done to her?" Nathan asked, desperate to see his sister and what that bastard had done to her, "Hasn't he fucking done enough to her? I take it he's dead? He fucking better be! Cause there's never been a person that deserves to be dead more than that fucking deviant prick!"

"Who else would want to hurt him Nathan? Because we think Amy was already injured before Natt was hurt," Taylor asked with interest, only realising afterwards that naturally

Nathan would be a suspect once again.

Nathan realised straight away from the question that all of a sudden he would be right back in the frame for Natt's death. His face went sheet white and he felt sick to the stomach and gave a loud deep sigh at his predicament once more.

Taylor saw her error and looked at him apologetically but also with quizzical police eyes. She didn't want him to be involved in this and instead of trying to prove it was him, she would do everything in her power to prove it wasn't. Either way, of course, would end in the right result - the truth, whether it was Nathan or not.

Nathan was very perceptive and sighed with relief when he remembered he had been with Jen and Millie and they had been out for their tea at Pizza Hut at Fountain Park, and he knew there was CCTV everywhere there. He spoke out to Taylor straight away, "I know what you're thinking but it wasn't me! And I do have a provable alibi this time, so please check it out before you drag me in again," he said. "At least this will enable us to be straight up with each other without an agenda."

Taylor smiled, "Aye, you're quick, read my mind! Sorry, I only just realised my mistake after I said it".

Nathan smiled, "I saw your face change, it was pretty obvious, so I thought I would put you out of your misery and free up your mind to find the right person first time this time," he said sarcastically.

Taylor got his sarcasm and thought he was right to be that way. "Thanks for that, c'mon, first things first, we need to see if this young lady is your sister? Because if she's not, then that would change everything, wouldn't it?" Taylor said with humour in her eyes because she saw the realisation in his face and she genuinely felt sorry for him and did not want him to go through any further investigation.

Fran waited outside while Taylor and Nathan went in, after checking with the consultant that it was alright to do so.

Nathan hesitated. The deformity and damage to Amy's face was very obvious and he felt deeply saddened that Natt had done this too her after everything they had been through, but they both knew the risks involved taking on Natt Spears. He looked at everything else, her hands, her jewellery, her ears, and others features, remembering a couple of her injuries and scars from their childhood.

"It's her, it's Amy, definitely," he put his hands up to his face and covered his eyes. He was crying. His sadness was deep and his tears went all the way back to their childhood. In his mind he had failed to protect one of the most precious people in his life. He remembered, as a little boy, that he was always there for his sister when he could be and had always stood in front of her if Natt or his mum was going to hit her or want to do whatever took their fancy on that day.

He looked down at her again, and his stomach twisted tightly with remorse at the damage these people had inflicted on them both, mentally and physically, before and now once again, but he knew she knew the risks when taking her revenge and was willing to face them.

"What happened to Natt then, and is he dead? How did it happen? I fucking hope he's dead, or you may have to investigate me one day!" Nathan's tears turned to rage and revenge.

Taylor was about to give a diplomatic, non-committed answer to him and avoid giving away too much detail but Nathan cut in, mid-sentence with a vicious onslaught of hatred and desire to murder.

He looked directly into Taylor's eyes. "Don't piss me around now Ma'am, is that fucking cunt dead or not, cause if he's not, I'm going to fucking kill him anyway. He doesn't deserve to live, breath the same air as us, he's a fucking child molesting rapist, and I'll tell you now, how the fuck have you lot not got that fucker back in jail, 'cause I know for a fact he won't have stopped abusing kids, it was in his nature. What he did to us, he needed it, and if he wasn't such a lazy fuck, he would have been doing it all day every day. Well, why haven't you? I'm telling you now, he is fucking disgusting and evil! You need to look into who he sees, who he knows, 'cause fuck me, he's a vile beast and there must be someone he's abusing out there!"

"What are you saying Nathan? Nothing has been reported and he's been on the register for years and supported by the police." Taylor stated a little defensively.

"I'm saying, if that fucker has been free for this length of time, he's been busy ruining some other child or children's lives. He is a fucking predatory monster!"

Taylor quickly put him out of his misery. "He is dead, Nathan! You'll be glad to hear. Well, the person they found is dead; they still need to confirm his identity through DNA because he is totally disfigured," Taylor divulged because she knew things would require a little control here if she didn't calm his temper.

"Is he that damaged? Fucking good! He deserves it, this couldn't have happened to a nicer person," he said sarcastically.

Taylor went to speak to Fran but Fran had been in a position to hear it all, as she had put herself in earshot like any good copper would.

Taylor was about to say what had gone on when Fran said, "I heard it, all of it, and I believe him. I don't think he had a clue!"

"That was an assassination today, a hit, so who ordered it and why?" Taylor asked of Fran.

"Sounds like there may be a list and we've missed it but as always, family first then widen the circle, somebody wanted him dead, and we'll need to get results quickly on this one as the shit will come our way," Fran looked back at Taylor, fully realising this.

Taylor phoned Marcus and he answered straight away. "We've got Amy here, Nathan too and a dead man, with no killer! You'll need to do some digging on him, close family, especially those with children. Check with the PPU, social work all other departments. I want medical issues or queries in relation to the children anything that we can work on. Have they got the car yet, have they got anything at all?"

Marcus replied quickly, cutting in, knowing her list would continue. "The public have reported a car in the cemetery with front damage and blood spattered all over it. CCTV from the pub on the corner of Pilrig Street has picked up two young males walking past the pub just down from the cemetery around five minutes after the incident in Leith."

"Have they secured the vehicle and uplifted it? Get a search team there too, cordon off a decent area surrounding it and do a further CCTV trawl down to Leith and also the other way up towards Ferry Road. Who knows which way they went, there are plenty of little cut throughs that we don't know about. Oh and great work," she said thankfully with a wry smile creeping onto her face, delighted her right hand man had got right on it and got results.

Chapter 55
Under Suspicion

Maggie sat with a hot cup of coffee clasped between her hands. A very business-like knock sounded at the door. At first she didn't answer it and sat closer to her children, as if to hide from the inevitable. The knock came again, louder, and a female officer shouted through the letterbox. The words "POLICE," rang loudly in Maggie's ears, amplified and oppressive, her guilt engulfing her with fear until the officer spoke again.

"Margaret, Miss Spears, can you hear me? There's nothing to worry about, we are here about the children, we need to check that they are alright and ask you a few questions about the examination results, that's all, you're not in any trouble," the officer said hoping that to be true.

Marggie stood up and walked through to the hallway, the floor creaking as she went, but stopped dead at the noise she had just made and hesitated once again. She saw the letterbox being pushed inwards and she tried to get back into the living room to avoid being seen but it was too late and the eagle-eyed officer saw her back away as she tried to duck out of sight.

"Margaret, I know you're in there, or someone is! So whoever it is in there, could you please answer the door. You know we can't leave without seeing the children, the door will be forced if we believe that you are seen to be preventing us checking the welfare of those children. We don't want to do that, now open the door please, for the children's sake."

The letterbox was still being held open when Maggie walked back into the hall. The officer outside could see her and encouraged her to open the door with gentle words of reassurance. The officer looked just past where Maggie was standing and saw two young children following her closely, their wish was definitely to be with their mother, with no coercion or strong words, which reassured the officer watching. Actions speak louder than words, she thought to herself, especially when children are involved. The officer did not know this woman but she was glad of what she had seen because no matter how many cases she had dealt with. She could never understand mothers abusing or violating their own children, going against their natural instincts to protect their young.

Maggie eventually opened the door and let the officers into her house. DC Michelle Smith and DC Martin Scholes introduced themselves to her and explained that they were from the family protection unit and what their role was and why they were there. They said they were talking to her face to face because of the results of recent medical examinations carried out on the children and what the findings had revealed.

Maggie started to cry straight away, just hearing someone talking about the results set off an instant repulsed reaction. Her insides twisted and knotted with sickness and rage at what had happened to her precious children, what she had allowed to happen to them at the hands of her brother because of misplaced trust.

DC Smith was very caring with a naturally warm personality and instantly moved towards Maggie to offer comfort. DC Smith was fully aware of the facts in relation to the results for the children, the nature of the trauma and the severity of what they had suffered, silently. She also knew that it was Maggie that was the one that had instigated the medical checks, so this put her at ease in relation to who the culprit wasn't, although they could never be 100% certain.

The officers sat in the comfort of the living room. DC Smith did all of the talking with the occasional interjection from DC Scholes if something was missed. Maggie told them that a woman called Amy had come to the flat a week or so ago and had told her about her brother Natt Spears, his past and what he had done to her and her brother when they were young children, ages similar to her own children. She said that this woman had begged her to believe her and that if she didn't believe her, then to check on the children, get them examined and stop them seeing her brother until this was done. She was very blunt with the facts when she told her what Natt and their mother had done to them. This was after Maggie had said that he babysat for her quite often and had unsupervised access to her children on a regular basis. The officers watched the children and Maggie and their interaction. The children showed no fear or hesitation when going to and from their mother and appeared affectionate and relaxed with her, which was a very significant sign to both officers.

DC Smith had instructions from DS Nicks prior to speaking to Maggie, in relation to the ongoing murder enquiry, as Maggie herself was high on the list of suspects due to her connection to Natt Spears and the very recent and revealing results from her children's medicals.

"Maggie, I'm not trying to shock you here, but are you aware that your brother was killed last night?" DC Scholes revealed quite directly.

Maggie turned round slowly, her face didn't reveal too much emotion but her words certainly did.

"Good, it saves me fucking doing it. I hope that sick fucking bastard suffered in agony and I hope he rots in hell!" Maggie rasped back at them, her eyes filled with hate and angered emotion.

"I also have to ask this question too, I'm afraid. Do you know anything about it? And is there anything you want to tell us?"

"What are you saying? That I killed that fucked up filthy pig? When would I have time to do that? I've got two young kids here that I won't let out of my sight ever, ever again!" The words were spat out of her mouth with pure venom and with a hint of well-practised surprise.

"You have got very good reason to be angry with him. I would be," DC Scholes said to her, willing her to bite and hopefully show some sort of emotion either way, to at least help gauge in their minds whether it could have been her.

Maggie was streetwise and was well aware of what the cops were trying to do, get on her side, agree with why she would be angry, almost making it alright to have been raging enough to murder, but she was a pretty good actress and would not crack or give anything away to them. They would have to link her to the crime with evidence, otherwise there was no way there would be a confession.

Maggie continued, "There must be a fucking queue out there wanting to kill that motherfucker, I must be one of many if this is the type of shit he likes to do! What about the woman that came to visit me, Amy, what about her? She seemed to be well versed on Natt, where he was, what he is and has been doing. She must be right up there at the front of the queue. She said she had a brother, he must want to kill him too if he fucking raped him. He's a man now and that must boil his blood knowing that that fucker is free and continuing with his shit, ruining others' lives. The list goes on, 'cause I'm sure there will be more. My eldest is only five, that leaves a few extra years before that, where he might have made more enemies and you lot haven't found them yet!" She didn't mean to be accusatory about the police's inability to stop him, but she wanted to blame somebody, anybody for what had happened to her little boy and girl, for her naivety, for trusting her brother, her big brother, somebody that should have looked out for her, protected her and her little ones.

DS Smith took over once again and tried to comfort her but Maggie was clearly distraught and as she hugged her, she was sick all down her back, a totally involuntary action. Maggie couldn't help it, she was emotionally broken.

"Oh god I'm really sorry, I just keep thinking of my kids,

how scared they must have been, how vile and depraved this was, the agony they will have suffered. I left them with him, so many times! No wonder that bastard always brought so many toys and treats for them."

DS Smith was very professional, she barely flinched as the watery vomit poured off her back and onto the floor. She understood the revulsion and the guilt, she had seen it many times before, especially how trusting people tended to blame themselves for things that they did not know or could not know were happening, but the predators were very manipulative people, very convincing.

DS Smith focussed on Maggie and revealed what had happened to Amy, that she was in a very serious condition in hospital and that they believed Natt had tried to kill her just prior to his death, although they weren't sure about how they came to be in the same place yet.

Maggie seemed genuinely affected by this. She had only met Amy once but she trusted her, had believed her and she had been right. Amy had saved her children from more pain, suffering and continued violation. Maggie had liked her, she had honest eyes and had taken a risk to try and warn a virtual stranger about the suffering she believed her children were being exposed to.

"Is she alright, what did that filthy bastard do to her, will she live, can I see her? I need to thank her, thank her for saving my children and killing that bastard."

"I never said that she killed him, we haven't established that yet," DS Smith was quick to interject. She also made it clear that Maggie would not be able to see Amy as she was very ill and would be detained the minute she was fit enough, for very serious offences.

Seeing an opportunity to sow a seed, Maggie mentioned, "Well she did say to me that she wouldn't stop until she finished what she started, you can take what you want from that, she just wanted to warn me first!" She said this with honesty as Amy had said this to her on her visit.

"She said that did she?"Smith said taking note. "You will have to come in and give a full statement in relation to where you were last night, your relationship with your brother and the recent revelations, you understand that, don't you?"

"Yes I understand. She did say that. You could tell she was still really affected by him, she clearly still loathed him and she had anger in her eyes and voice, but she didn't come right out and say that she was going to kill him though, she just suggested that she still had a job to do, that's all!"

"Thank you Maggie, obviously we'll be in touch. We still need to have you come down to a station and follow up on a few necessary procedures," DC Smith said truthfully while saying their goodbyes.

As the door shut, Maggie thought that they believed her, and her thoughts turned to Amy, and that she needed to talk to her, thank her and ask her a huge favour but this seemed impossible right now. The kids came up to her and cuddled her legs, nearly tripping her up, their love for their mummy very plain to see. Maggie knelt down to them and cuddled them both tightly. Her eyes were filled with tears of sadness and regret, truly wishing she could turn back time and undo what had been done and save her babies.

Chapter 56
Saviour of Innocents

Amy moaned loudly and sat bolt upright, causing great pain in her bruised ribs and torso. She was screaming loudly, her words incomprehensible. She lay back down on the pillows. She was sweating profusely and very agitated and distressed. It looked like she was in a state of half sleep and she was fighting an invisible demon. The nurses were quick to respond and try and calm her, the officer posted there also paid attention to her conscious state and quickly relayed this to the investigation team. Nathan was still at the hospital and he also tried to pacify her. He was the only authorised visitor due to the severity of her injuries, which could still be fatal.

Amy was lying back, her face so bruised, Nathan couldn't tell if she was awake or not, her eyes swollen shut. Nathan took her hand gently and spoke quietly into her ear.

"Hi, Amy, it's me Nathan, your brother. You're in hospital, but you're okay now, a bit broken, but okay."

"He got me Nathan, he was gonna kill me, but someone was coming through to the toilets and he ran off," Amy said, still obviously terrified of Natt, scared he would try and come and get her. She was very much with it and had full capacity.

"It's okay, he can't touch you now, he's gone."

"No Nathan, I failed. I stabbed him but it barely touched

him, he's that fucking fat. He's still out there, and I think he's gonna kill me."

"No, no you're wrong. He was killed just after he left you, he was totally mangled, very dead, he won't be touching you or anybody else again, ever! They are saying it was a definite hit, no accident and they are wondering how you managed to arrange it. Did you, was this your back-up plan?" Nathan whispered in her ear, making sure the cop at the door couldn't hear what he was saying.

"No, it wasn't me Nathan. I fully intended to kill that fucking fat bastard first time! Are they sure it was deliberate?"

"Very deliberate, the cops say he was run over three times and parts of his body were totally de-gloved, someone did a right job on him."

"God no, she didn't did she?" Amy said gripping Nathan's arm.

"Who, what are you talking about?"

"Natt's sister, Maggie, I went to see her last week, I told her all about him and us and what he did, I told her to get her kids checked out, medically, that is. I know she listened, she was clearly affected by what I said and her face totally changed and the colour drained, she looked visibly ill. I bet she had something to do with this, she didn't look like the type of person that would just sit back and do nothing if someone had hurt her kids. You need to go and see her Nathan, talk to her, see what you think, see if she got the kids checked, what the results were, ask her right out and see how she answers, see her reaction, because there is no way she can get fixed with this. This will ruin all of their lives and I'm not gonna let that bastard hurt anyone else."

Nathan was a little taken aback with her request because he was fully aware that it would be perverting the course of justice if he did what Amy had asked him to do. Nathan did not want to get into trouble with the police again but how could they prove what conversations had gone on there and what had been said between them? He too did not want another innocent family destroyed by that vile predator. He also knew what Amy was accused of, because he had been charged with all of her offences. They were talking triple life sentences at the very least for all her efforts, another death wouldn't make a difference, he couldn't see Amy ever getting out anyway.

The call was received back at the office, Marcus taking it, he stood up instantly and caught Taylor's attention. "Amy's awake at the hospital boss and apparently she's talking in whispers with her brother."

"What? Is he still there?! Fuck me, I thought he'd gone home!" Taylor exclaimed with a contorted disbelieving face. They had all gone home from shift last night, as they had been on for hours, and thought he was away. "We'll need to get up there pronto Marcus, we need to speak to her and see if she will give us any idea as to what the fuck has gone on. Fuck, fuck! We should have made sure he had gone home, or at least if he was there that all conversations were at least monitored. Did the cop hear what they were talking about?"

"I don't think so. He said that they were whispering but that might be because she can't speak very loud because of her injuries," Marcus tried to defend what they both new was complete crap.

"Shit, fuck, piss, goddamn son of a bitch, why the fuck did we not know or bloody well check if he was still there? I thought we were all going home together last night. He must have turned back, not that I think there was anything in it, 'cause I do believe he's a decent guy and just wanted to be by her side. Why the fuck did the cop not tell anyone he was there?"

"Why would he? He'll have thought that we knew he was allowed to be there but he was pretty definite that they were whispering just now!"

"C'mon Marcus, you come with me this time. I take it you have showered and changed your clothes?" She smiled and looked down at his shoes, which were immaculate. "including them," she nodded, making sure that there was no cross contamination.

"Of course I've changed everything," he said with his usual charming and lovable smile.

"Good, let's get up there then!" Both Taylor and Marcus left the office very quickly, leaving Fran and the other members of the team to get on with further enquiry into the two young men seen near to the vehicle that had been recovered. They had facials from the CCTV from a private dwelling house, and they already had names for one, and two other people had given possibilities for the other male. They were now looking to detain the suspects and bring them in for questioning at the earliest opportunity.

The knock at the door was loud and authoritarian. This time Maggie got up straight away, a little irked that they had come back so soon. She went straight to the door without checking who it was.

She swung it wide open expecting to see the police but it was a man standing there, a total stranger right there in front of her. She jumped with fright and wished it had been the police there.

"Who are you, what are you fucking staring at, you gave me a fucking fright, what do you want?" Maggie was still a little shaken at her surprise visitor, her aggressive talk an attempt to show strength and no visible fear.

Nathan had already realised that he had frightened her, which was not his intention and he began to apologise.

"Sorry, I didn't mean to frighten you! I'm Nathan, Amy's brother. Do you remember her? She told me she came to visit you Maggie. It is you isn't it, Maggie?"

"Sorry, you scared the shit out of me." she said starting to smile, her fear alleviating, because she had trusted Amy and her brother had the same trusting eyes, although a minute ago she had been ready to punch him. "You'd better come in then, or did you just come to scare the shit out of me?"

Nathan smiled and went in without a word but instantly looked down warmly as Maggie's children peeked out of the living room, smiles on their cheeky wee faces.

Taylor and Marcus got to the hospital and on reaching Amy's room were met by the cop on duty. He looked a little sheepish, but that might have been because of the way that Taylor had strode up to him in her domineering manner, with her eyes clearly looking right at him, eyebrows raised waiting for an explanation.

"That Nathan guy left just after I called you, he said he wanted to go home to see his wife and daughter, so I let him go, I didn't think there would be an issue with that. Searg, is there a problem with him I should have known about?" he asked innocently.

"Who knows? But you said they were definitely whispering, did you manage to hear anything they said?" Taylor asked.

"No sorry Searg, they were pretty tight in to each other, I don't think they wanted me to hear, and unfortunately I didn't!"

"Was anybody else in the room, anyone who might have heard anything that was said?"

"The nurse that was in checking on her when she woke up, and was still coming in and out, checking her vital signs and all that, she was closer than me, she could have heard something."

"Can you go and see if you can find her please and see if she heard anything? I'll keep an eye on Amy just now for you."

When Taylor had finished, she saw that Marcus was already sitting by Amy's side, holding her hand, and talking to her, but his words were very quiet and clearly only meant for Amy.

"Thank you, thank you for saving my boy, I can never explain how much that means to my wife and I. My little boy David said you were kind and caring and nice to him and to the other little boy, and to me, even with everything that's happened, what you did for my boy means the world to me," Marcus whispered in her ear, because Amy was clearly unable to see him due to her puffy eyes.

Her swollen disfigured lips curled into a definite smile, before she said, "Thank you, but I don't know what you are talking about? I don't know any small handsome little blond boys, that are brave, resilient and helpful, not me, don't know any one like that I'm afraid!"

Marcus squeezed her hand. She had confirmed what he already knew without disclosing anything. He knew it was her and she seemed genuinely happy for his gratitude, but she also knew it was his job to convict her for all of the crimes she had committed.

Taylor came up behind him. "Has she said anything yet?" She saw tears in his eyes as she looked down at him, watching as his hand withdrew from Amy's.

Marcus looked like a guilty child, his eyes looking down and avoiding her piercing gaze. He knew he may have overstepped the mark but he had to do it, for himself, because no matter what this woman had done to others, her crimes, her brutal violence, she had still saved two children from certain sexual abuse, degradation and probably the most vile and depraved death, and he owed her for that forever.

"I was just saying thank you Taylor, I had too, but Amy claims not to know what I was talking about, that's all I've said, nothing else. I was waiting on you for corroboration, sorry, but you knew I had to thank her."

The controller answered the radio to Taylor. "Have a car go to Nathan's house right now to check that he's there. Marcus will relay the address to you shortly. He's just checking his notebook."

Meanwhile Taylor started to speak to Amy, "Amy, hi, I'm Sergeant Taylor Nicks from the Major Investigation Team, we've not had the pleasure of meeting yet, and I'm sorry it had to be under these circumstances." she said genuinely, without sarcasm.

Amy nodded her head. "No problems, I'm just glad that bastard didn't kill me, although he did a good job trying!"

"Can you remember what happened, why were you there, how did you end up like this, why did he attack you?"

"I'm really sorry about this, but no comment. I have nothing to say about anything you have to ask me, not until I can at least see your face, I just need to get better right now. Where's Nathan, has he got my coffee yet?" she said with a hint of a smile.

"Funny that, Nathan doesn't appear to be here anymore, do you know why that would be Amy?" Taylor quizzed.

"Well he does have a family you know, he needed to go and see them." Amy was quick to reply.

"I know, we are checking on him as we speak."

Amy hesitated, and said, "He might have gone for breakfast first, who knows what he was doing?" She said this with a little apprehension but did not show any emotion.

Taylor's radio went within earshot of Amy. "Searg, we have Nathan here at his home address, what was it you needed from him?"

"Thank you, no message," Taylor answered.

Amy's heart stopped racing and relaxed a little as Taylor began to speak to her once again.

Amy seemed to be smiling. Taylor couldn't quite work it out for sure, as her face was clearly not functioning as it would normally do.

Taylor and Marcus took seats beside her and sat talking with her in general, trying to get an impression of the type of person Amy was and of her mental state. They were aware of the level of violence used, the risks taken, her professional position, her access to police buildings and confidential files, cases and other restricted things like CS gas, computer systems and more, but she had never come to the police's attention before, suggesting a high level of intelligence, deceit and intent.

Chapter 57
Pursuit

Marcus's radio was on the joint north channels. His heart leapt as he heard the radio burst into action.

"Vehicle making off," came over the radio from the Leith side, "Permission to pursue?"

"Stand by, I'll check with the top table," the dispatcher replied quickly. "What's your position, follow safely at a distance and report on traffic and pedestrian flow please".

"Roads dry, good visibility, medium flow, low numbers of pedestrians, speed 50 plus and accelerating, taking a right, right, right onto Ferry Road, heading west, straight through a red light, now on the wrong side of the carriageway, can we have roads policing sets join us here please!"

"To Echo Romeo eight two, confirm the reason for the pursuit and do we know who it is we have?" the dispatcher questioned.

"We believe it is the suspect for the hit and run on Leith Walk last night. Do I have permission to pursue, repeat, do I have permission to pursue?"

"Yes, yes, permission to pursue with caution, the roads policing sets are heading into the area, ETA three minutes, withdraw if the risks become life threatening."

"Right, right, right onto Newhaven Road speed 60 plus, left, left onto Stanley Road, wrong side of the road, their driving getting more erratic, vehicle has struck parked vehicles, speed 50 plus, left, left, onto Craighall Road, speed 70 plus, they are really pushing it, right, right, right onto Ferry Road, traffic heavy, vehicle now in the middle of the carriageway still heading west, with no concern for the safety of other road users, ETA for traffic back up, he's taking a left, left, left down at Goldenacre, sorry I don't know the name of the road, right, right, right onto Inverleith Place, vehicle, two white males, 18 to 20 years, light cottons tops, short brown hair, no further description I'm afraid."

"PC Ewar and Blair Romeo Papa three, we're heading East on Carrington Road, request to release stinger".

"Permission granted if safe to do so, repeat, only if safe to do so!" the control room was quick to respond.

"He's still heading east on Inverleith Place, speed 80, I repeat 80 mph plus".

"Cancel the stinger it's too dangerous, I repeat, cancel, cancel, await for a more suitable release sight, the road is too wide and his speed too fast," the dispatcher said with a heightened pitch to her tone, clearly caught in the middle between the cops and the bosses.

"From Romeo Papa three, I have a visual. Fuck me he's shifting," he said to his colleague PC Blair as he glanced over at him with a little apprehension at the direction and course, the approaching vehicle seemed to be taking, which was straight in their direction, a suicidal move at the speed it was going.

"Fucking hell, that little bastard's gonna fucking ram us, fuck, fuuuuuck," PC Ewar rasped through his teeth as he tried to pull his BMW 530D out of the way. His efforts were in vain as the stolen Audi made up the limited ground too quickly and ploughed straight into the driver's side rear section of the police vehicle sending it spiralling round in the air, those inside smashing heavily against the sides, the cop car landing on its roof 20 metres away, its occupants motionless and bleeding.

"Assistance, we need assistance, get the fire service here, right now! There has been a collision, police vehicle on its roof, we're at the junction of Inverleith Place and East Fettes Avenue, we will need medical assistance, multiple casualties, serious injuries I would think."

There was only one responding vehicle in the local area, all others were involved and fully committed unable to break away, although a Public Protection Unit set was in the area and responded to the call due to the nature of the request. These sets were not normally deployed to routine calls but this call was far from routine.

DC Smith and Scholes about-turned and put their blue light on top of their partially marked police vehicle, hitting the sirens as they made their way from the Pilton area of Edinburgh, not far from the collision site.

The response officers that were pursuing the vehicle, Lindsay Simmons and Nick Red, were out of their car within seconds and checking on those within the police vehicle and the stolen car. The officer on the driver's side, PC Ewar, was in a bad way with blood pouring out of his head. PC Blair was trying to get out of the car, although clearly winded and he had injuries to his face from the windscreen and other debris.

DC Michelle Smith screeched to a halt at the scene, he heart thumping at the carnage she saw before her. She saw the officer in the front of the police car was covered in blood. DC Smith was pretty hot on her first aid and was quick to take over from PC Red and tried to stem the flow of blood coming from Pete Ewar's head as he floated in and out of consciousness.

One of the occupants of the stolen vehicle was lying on the ground 20 metres from his upturned vehicle, not moving and his limbs lying in awkward positions, clearly broken or dislocated, with blood streaming down his face.

PC Red looked around and moved towards the vehicle, expecting to find the other male somewhere inside in a similar state and needing medical help.

But no! Within a second of getting to the car, a skinny tracksuit clad young male with blood all over his face, stared back at him, then turned and made off at speed, running like a malnourished cheetah into Inverleith Park.

"Little fucker, how the fuck can that little shit still run?" Nick Red said with an incredulous tone. "Male making off, heading south in Inverleith Park, white, skinny build, 5'10", full grey cottons, white trainers, short dark hair, with blood on his clothing and face," he relayed whilst giving chase and trying to speak clearly enough through his panting so that the controller could understand and pass on the information to other sets attending from other areas in the city.

The ambulances were arriving, along with the fire service. PC Simmons looked at DCs Smith and Scholes to confirm it was safe for them to leave and assist his partner and help give chase. She nodded and gestured to go, steadying PC Ewar's head and speaking reassuringly to him as she pressed harder on his wounds, although she seemed to be failing to stop the bleeding. He looked up at her, fear etched in his eyes, looking at her for some reassurance that he would be alright but DC Smith's eyes were true and honest. She was frightened about how this may turn out for PC Ewar.

"I'm not going to make it am I?" he said quietly to her.

DC Smith swallowed hard, looking down at the level of blood loss already. She looked straight back at him and gave it her best shot to convince him that this wasn't the case.

"You're going to be alright, the ambulance is here, hang in there and I'll buy you a drink when you're better," she said with every ounce of hope she had in her, her honesty being her will for him to live.

"I'll hold you to that," he said as his eyes closed and his head flopped to the side, his breathing laboured and very shallow. DC Smith clung to his hand and tried to get a response from him, but couldn't. Her heart sank and even though she didn't know him, she wanted to be with him, be by his side and see this through together.

PC Simmons was athletic and very fast. He had already made up ground and ran past PC Red with ease. Red wasn't quite as lithe, much to his annoyance as Simmons passed him. PC Simmons, also managed to pass a sarcastic comment about his lack of speed. "Pick it up chunky," rang out as he went by, running as fast as his legs could carry him. He was closing on the male, his motivation the blood streaked face of his colleague now critically injured because of this little shit's reckless behaviour.

Closer and closer he got, so close he could almost touch him, their breathing loud and desperate, their lungs empty and running on adrenaline. PC Simmons threw himself forwards in a last gasp bid to tackle the fleeing man, his lungs burning with the weight of his protective vest and equipment. He had nothing left in the tank, he knew he had to get him now or he'd be off.

His hands missed the man's torso, and he thought that was it, game over, until his flailing arm caught the back of the suspect's heel, sending one foot banging off the other, causing him to trip forward, straight onto his face. PC Simmons himself was now face down full weight on the ground, face throbbing, watching helplessly as the male scrabbled back to his feet and attempted to continue making off, until he was tackled full force by the incoming PC Red, the mighty weight of his body smashing into the skinny lad's ribs and taking him straight to the ground with PC Red crashing heavily down on top of him, face dragging on the ground. A painful grunt was forcefully thrust out of his lungs, to the total relief of both officers, who could barely breath. PC Red quickly turned the suspect over and handcuffed him, cautioning and detaining him in the presence of PC Simmons, who was crawling slowly towards them.

PC Red looked at PC Simmons with dirt all over his face, and smiled at him, "You were saying, mucky chops?" he said as they stood the prisoner up and started walking him back to the scene of the crime, where their car was and the ambulances were still parked. They had to get him checked over before heading to custody because with a collision like that, he must have suffered some sort of injury other than his sore ribs from PC Red.

A voice on the radio came over requesting an immediate update on the casualties.

DC Smith answered, responding with the confirmation from the Medic One response team's diagnosis. "Four casualties, two walking wounded, one PC Blair, two critical, one of those in a critical condition is an officer, it is PC Ewar, roads policing, serious head injury, the other casualties remain nameless at present, no details to pass, broken bones and internal bleeding for one, status not confirmed, all are being taking to the ERI. We'll need fast escorts and another ambulance here please, thanks." Her voice broke as she watched them take PC Ewar away on a trolley, tears in her eyes, fearing he may not make it. She turned to DC Scholes and told him she was going in the ambulance with PC Ewar and that was that. She asked him to sort it with their Sergeant regarding their plans for the rest of the day. She didn't want to leave him on his own. Her partner just nodded in full agreement, a little shocked at the whole incident and fully aware it could have been them in those ambulances.

Chapter 58
Guilt and Innocence

Taylor was in the DCI's office, the atmosphere was a little tense but that was soon alleviated by Taylor's natural relaxed humour, which broke any tension that remained, both mutually respecting one another. They both clearly still liked each other.

"What do we have then?" Brooke asked casually, aware of the basics surrounding the events of the last week or so.

Taylor smiled at her before she started, enjoying that Brooke had the power to summon and demand. "Amy is still recovering well in the hospital and nearly able to be interviewed, so we'll get that sorted asap. Maggie, Natt's sister, has been interviewed at length, she's been questioned in relation to Natt, the children, the results of the medical examinations, her whereabouts, her alibi for the evening of the hit and run, and everything seems to ring true. Regarding the two males from the vehicle, unfortunately one is still in hospital and unable to be interviewed, but of course able to look into compensation through his lawyer, for the injury sustained at the hands of the police, even though he was clearly to blame Ma'am."

Taylor looked up at her boss, who was staring straight at her, exasperation in her face. Poor PC Ewar was still in hospital badly injured and that little scrote was trying to claim from them for his own recklessness. Taylor continued, "The other male burst straight away, giving everything he knew, which unfortunately wasn't a lot, all he said was they were acting on behalf of a woman. He didn't give away who paid them, because he said the person would kill him and, by the way he was acting, I believe him. Nathan is not in the frame at all, his alibi checks out 100% but it is looking like Amy is in the frame for everything. Things there are not quite adding up but we still have to see what she has to say."

Brooke leant back in her seat, her arms up behind her head, her blouse pulling tight on her breasts and the material pulling a little between the buttons. Her features were strong and attractive, her physique that of a sportswoman. Taylor didn't intend to stare, but stare she did, and as Brooke's eyes came back to meet Taylor's, she noticed that her stretch had got the attention of the Detective Sergeant that she thought was no longer interested in her. Taylor dropped her eyes hastily and fixed her own blouse, which also clung to her in all the right places, something Brooke too had noticed. Both women had clearly shared a moment of mutual appreciation, right there in the office. Taylor couldn't help herself, she loved women and everything about them, flirting, chasing, loving them. She had shared an evening with Brooke, which had been very enjoyable but due to circumstances she had not thought it could be repeated, although with their eyes meeting like that, she now knew that it could and might. Brooke smiled at her, an attractively warm smile, one that made Taylor smile back, her predatory gaze making Brooke's cheeks flush with the memories of their evening together.

Taylor stood up and was about to leave as Brooke cleared her throat to speak. Taylor stopped at the door, Findlay accidentally pushing past her as he came back in to the office with his two double filled breakfast rolls. Brooke rolled her eyes at him, at his lack of respect or manners, the smell of his fried food a daily annoyance to her as he always brought it back to chomp on open-mouthed in front of her, like a pig, which she thought was his deliberate way of getting back at her, because he resented her being there.

"You were going to say?" Taylor looked quizzically.

Brooke hesitated, and said "Later, I'll tell you later."

Marcus was back at his desk in the open plan squad room, busily typing up the body of the main report, which was now cross-referenced to several other related incidents. There was a lot of detail to make sure everything was fully expressed in chronological order, with every single snippet of related information and evidence being added, giving the weight of evidence required to secure a solid conviction. The sheer volume of it was   making him feel stressed; he was normally unflappable.

Taylor walked over to him. She could see his exasperation at the task ahead and put her hand on his shoulder for support and reassurance. She pulled up the swivel chair next to him and began to help. Fran also pulled her seat round to help, the three of them all good friends and more. As a team they were a force to be reckoned with. Their collective skill and efficiency would be required to write this one up properly as there was no room for error. Brooke leaned out of the office and was about to call Taylor back in to speak to her, but she watched as her team worked tirelessly to put this mass of evidence in to some semblance of order. The news she had would certainly change how things would be so she made the decision to hold off from telling them.

At the end of a long day, Brooke switched her light out, apologising soon after to Findlay, who was still there, for once staying later than her as she had given him some work to do. She said her goodbyes to the team. Taylor and Fran watched her and each other as she left, Taylor dropping her gaze very quickly to avoid any confrontation with Fran, who was fully aware of their previous liaison.

"Are we having a drink after work tonight anyone?" Marcus asked the rest of the team, knowing that he would never finish the report that night or even that month because they still had Amy's mammoth interview to go into it, which could change a few things.

"Why not?" Tayor quickly responded, along with the majority of the team, including Fran. "We deserve a wee bit of down time and a very large drink, I believe," she said wiggling her fingers pretending to raise a glass to her mouth.

As the Major Investigation Team were freshening up to go out for the evening, DC Smith was back at the hospital, sitting beside PC Ewar's hospital bed as she had done every day since the incident. He had been in a coma ever since. Her visit was nearly over and she was about to let go of his hand once again, a hand she had held for hours every visit. Just as she was slipping hers away from his, she felt a tiny sensation of response. She put her hand back in his and left it there, motionless, waiting and hoping to see if there would be any further movement from him. She waited and waited, wondering if she had actually felt anything at all or just imagined it. She spoke to him, willing him to respond to her voice, to her touch as she stroked his hand. She was just about to give up, when he responded. His hand squeezed hers and this time it was definite, there was a proper grip, not forceful, but a grip, a response. DC Smith rose up from her seat and spoke into his ear and then looked at his face, scars and dressings covering most of it, a face she had never even seen prior to him being injured; their paths in the police had never crossed. His eyes flickered and then opened, brown and alive. They blinked as they met hers for the first time, his brow a little furrowed, as he wasn't quite sure who she was, but he was glad that she was there and he looked straight into her eyes with hope. He saw tears welling up as she introduced herself for the first time. She was overwhelmed with emotion because he had survived. P C Ewar smiled happily through the pain it caused him.

Back at the Raeburn Bar in Stockbridge, the drinks were flowing, the team could see the light at the end of the tunnel. They had all worked long hard hours and missed out on so many things, so much time with their families and friends, just to make sure they had investigated every lead and hadn't missed anything. They tried not to talk about work but it always cropped up and dominated their evening, this case they were on was just so big. Fran had started it and both Taylor and Marcus jumped in with their opinions and theories, all of them clearly wanting to talk about the bits of evidence that didn't quite add up. The main issue for them was finding all of the evidence available and wanting to get the right result. The whole enquiry had destroyed many lives in the present and in the past and there was a continued theory there, lives ripped apart and damaged long term, events that pointed to more lives about to be ruined. All of them had their own theory, none of which had been established or proven. The conversation ended with them all having to disagree on what seemed to be the truth, but agree on the theory of what would be the best outcome for everyone, although that was not yet fully established.

Fran had had enough. She was tired and tipsy and got up to leave. She turned to the group and said goodbye, giving them all a kiss and a hug, her warm personality shining through. She hesitated when she got to Taylor, the whole team staring at them. Taylor looked up through boozy eyes, waiting for Fran to speak.

Fran puffed out her chest and smiled, "Well, are you coming or not?" she said cheekily to Taylor, her posture inviting and tempting.

Anyone who had any doubt about their affair had now just had it confirmed. They all liked Fran and Taylor and watched with anticipation and excited titillation at the unfolding drama before them, waiting for Taylor's reply with bated breath, her eyes warm and affectionate towards Fran.

Taylor just smiled back at her and got up, reaching to take Fran's hand as they motioned to leave and the team gave a rowdy cheer as they left the bar. Fran deliberately pinching Taylor's bottom as she left in full view of the others, who were clearly amused by this.

Fran stopped Taylor outside and pushed her against the wall, pulling Taylor to her to give her a full, open-mouthed passionate kiss, to which Taylor did not hesitate to respond.

Taylor's hands moved over Fran's bottom and pulled her tighter in to her, until their closeness sent butterflies racing to places that were already heating up.

"Come back with me Taylor, be with me. I don't care what you've done, or what you might do again, I just want you, now! I want you to fuck me, and I'm going to fuck you too," she whispered right up into her ear, her hot breath arousing as she licked it, sending shivers down Taylor's back.

Once inside Fran's house, Fran took Taylor by the hand and dragged her through to the bedroom, pushing her face down onto the bed as she followed close behind her. She knelt over her, her pussy pushed up against Taylor's beautifully sculpted bottom, as she undid her blouse beneath her, pulling it open and pushing her hands into Taylor's bra, pulling gently on her nipples as she licked up her back. She bit, sucked and kissed Taylor's perfect neck, causing her to moan out loud. Fran pulled Taylor's blouse aside roughly and casually unclipped her bra with one hand, stopping to look at the lines of perfection on Taylor's back, muscles taut and in all the right places. The top of her white panties were just visible beneath her suit trousers. Fran gently pushed her hand down into the back of Taylor's trousers, her other hand undoing them at the front, allowing her to brush softly against the cheeks of her beautiful ass with the back of her hand. Taylor moaned again as she moved to let Fran get to where she wanted to be. Fran twisted her hand round and pushed it down and under her, feeling her fingers slip into her with ease because Taylor was so wet and turned on. Fran's other hand pushed down the front of Taylor's pussy, slipping skilfully over her as the other pushed deep into her from behind, her trousers now just exposing her bottom, just and no more, but still in place as Fran fucked deep into her, as her hand pleasured her at the front, both working with perfect cohesion to have Taylor willing her to take more from her and make her come.

"God, what the fuck are you doing to me, oh god, oh goddddddd, mmmmm, fuck, oh fuck Fran, I'm coming, goddd

I'm..." her voice cut off and she moaned into the duvet, her face nearly buried as she bit down on it as Fran continued to fuck her, deep and powerfully so that her orgasm swirled over and over and over inside her, both hands loving her perfectly as she kept the rhythm going to bring the next orgasm on with force and unbridled pleasure for Taylor. Taylor rarely experienced what she gave. There weren't many people that could do it confidently but tonight, Fran had certainly taken the lead and was making love to her like a woman possessed, and Taylor was loving it, allowing herself to be taken. Fran felt Taylor's orgasm subside and she kicked her way out of her own trousers, flicking off her panties with her foot as she turned Taylor round and pushed her further up the bed. She too was soaking and in need of Taylor. She pulled herself over Taylor, her nipples deliberately brushing over Taylor's mouth. She dipped them in, teasing her, Taylor raising up to suck them, and lick them feverishly, but Fran could not wait any longer. She moved her nimble body further up and placed her pussy just in reach over Taylor's mouth. Taylor responded straight away delving her tongue deep into Fran, savouring her obvious pleasure. She licked her with a full tongue, aware of how close Fran was already to coming and, seeing how sensitive her pussy was, she pulled her down onto her long fingers and pushed them deep inside her, continuing to thrust deep into her while her tongue took control. Fran flopped forwards panting with almost unbearable pleasure. She fucked down hard onto Taylor's fingers to try and stop herself exploding, her moans needy and desperate, which sent Taylor into a final physical frenzy of effort to make Fran come so hard that it took both of them by surprise. Fran's muscles became taught, trapping Taylor's fingers deep inside her as she finally couldn't stop her orgasm any longer and the swirl of it kept twisting intimately inside her, her hips thrusting over Taylor's mouth, letting her tongue keep the orgasm going as long as she could. Finally Fran collapsed, totally covering Taylor's face. Taylor could barely breathe and had to push Fran over onto her back to catch her breath, but she hadn't finished yet. She pushed her fingers deeper into Fran and fucked her over and over again until Fran was completely breathless and out of control, the depth of her internal orgasm was toe-curling and very obvious to Taylor from Fran's physical responses.

"My god, you are something else," Taylor said as she pulled Fran close for a kiss, then another. They devoured each other, the sweat and moisture between them causing them to slip over each other as they kissed and laughed, two people totally at one with each other.

They crawled up to where the pillows were and lay back at the conventional end of the bed to get their breath back, tilting their heads towards each other to stare into one another's eyes. They didn't speak for several minutes.

Eventually Fran asked Taylor if she wanted a drink.

"Water, just water, I think we need some," Taylor gestured that she was parched to Fran and they both smiled.

Chapter 59
Full Confession

Taylor and Marcus came out of the epic recorded interview with Amy. She had made it really hard work for them, a mixture of no comment answers for some of the offences and a full confession for the last two murders, that of Megan Trainer and Natt Spears. The two people she openly blamed for the trouble she was in now, the two people that had destroyed her life, her relationship with Kerr, the loss of her brother for so many years, everything in her life had been tainted with fear and hate, nightmares and terrors that had haunted every waking moment of her life.

Taylor looked at Marcus and both of them were perplexed at the assault and then subsequent murder of Natt.

"How could she plan that? How did she know he wouldn't die from her initial attack? Is she that clever that she put in a contingency plan? God, it sounds like a police operational order?" Marcus asked of Taylor.

They both had a titter to themselves at that because that was a buzzword used by all hopefuls during promotional interviews. However, both were at odds with the probability of Amy having that much foresight to put everything in place.

"Amy didn't know him anymore and how capable he was of defending himself. Maybe she didn't back herself to succeed one on one and put a back-up plan in place just in case." Taylor suggested.

"She claimed not to know a lot about it, how, when, where and why, as she no commented on that. She said she used untraceable phones and wouldn't say where she dumped them, another no comment on who the middle man was. She didn't know the two lads that took him out. It is possible Taylor, unlikely but possible, and we have no proof to the contrary so we have to go with her confession!"

"What about Maggie? She had a very real motive to kill him, new found hate and she knew all of Natt's habits, his movements, his local haunts and if it was my kids, I'd want to kill that fucking prick too!" Taylor said, putting the cat back amongst the pigeons.

"What proof is there though? There's no proof at all and a full confession and factual knowledge from Amy, which is pretty damning, so even if that's what you think, the jury's gonna convict Amy straight off anyway, with everything else she has done. No matter what her motive, the evidence is pretty comprehensive." Marcus stated.

"Evidence, what, like Nathan's watertight case? I don't want it to be Maggie anyway. She has two young kids that need her, especially now, now that she knows what's happened to them." Taylor said, following her heart and not her instincts.

"How far do we dig to test a hunch though, especially when we have sufficient evidence, certainly enough to convict another to the accessory to murder, why would the jury do that, how often would anyone ignore a confession? Why would we ignore it, we have so much on our plate and we'd be clutching at straws anyway, to what end, 'cause, even if Maggie did do it, I think it would have been a one off, motherly instincts, and not to be repeated."

"We need to see if there is anything to connect them. We need to find out who the main guy is, even though everyone's lips are sealed and clearly not going to give him up!"

Fran walked over to them as they were chatting. "Lunch anyone? I'm starving and they've got some decent specials on at the canteen today."

"Yeh, why not, I'm starving too. I like their baguettes, with everything in it of course." They all got up and walked out, chatting as they went.

Brooke opened the door to her office and welcomed her in, gesturing to the seat in front of her desk.

"Thank you," Kay said as she made herself comfortable.

Brooke leant forward, smiling, aware of the significance of her return and how it would affect the dynamics of the team.

"How are you, ready to break yourself in gently? I certainly hope you're not considering full time hours yet, are you?"

"I'm better, a lot better, I can still feel the physical injuries, but at least my head is back, back where it should be!" Kay said, pleased with the fact she didn't have to speak with lecherous old Findlay.

"Have you been in touch with anyone while you've been absent?" Brooke asked with both professional and personal interest, because she had listened to the office gossip and knew that she and Taylor had been lovers before the capture of Brennan – Brennan who had brutally assaulted Kay, Fran and Taylor before his death, Kay suffering the most traumatic injury.

"I did initially but I cut all ties because I was ill, mentally ill. I was uncomfortable in company, everyone's company, even Taylor's. I started to hate intimacy, touch of any kind, and just wanted to hide away, that's why I had to get professional help," Kay said, with very little emotion.

Brooke knew that she should have warned Taylor the other day, the very day it seemed she had rekindled her affair with Fran, according to the night out gossipers. *Shit, she will not be happy with me, and she's right, I should have told her Kay was coming back this week!*

"Well we're all glad to have you back. Are you aware of the big ongoing case that we're on just now?" Brooke asked.

"I wasn't bothered at first but when I saw Taylor talking on the news after the first murder, I started to follow it a bit, because it's pretty gruesome stuff and very unusual, and now they know it's down to a woman, everyone is interested in the outcome. It's pretty riveting stuff!"

Brooke knew by even those words that her interest was in Taylor and not the case; she would care about the pressure she knew Taylor would have been under and, deep down, she would want to help her get through it.

"When are you starting back? I have it down here as next Monday for four hours, is that right?"

Kay sighed. "Yes, that's right, I need to get back to the real world some time, and I believe it's time now," she said honestly.

"Do you feel you are ready, I mean really ready?" Brooke looked for any hesitation but there wasn't any. "Then if you are ready, I look forward to seeing you back here on Monday. Welcome back Kay." Brooke stood to see Kay back out of the office.

As Kay stood up and went to open the glass door to the DCI's office, Taylor and Fran came bursting into the main office with Marcus trailing behind them. They all appeared happy and were frolicking around. This didn't bother Kay, it actually made her happy to see that things were good, and this enhanced her desire to come back. Her cheeks flushed at the sight of Taylor, still strikingly attractive, beautiful, her face, her immaculate appearance, her lithe body and that gorgeously natural smile. The group coming in hadn't seen her at the office door because they were engrossed in their tales and laughter and buzz of conversation.

Kay watched and, no matter how subtle a touch it was from Fran's hand to Taylor's, she saw it, and from the look between them that followed, she knew that Taylor was more than just friends with Fran.

Brooke watched them too, and she saw it too, but she already knew that they were seeing each other. She also knew that Taylor still had strong feelings for Kay.

Kay moved awkwardly towards the door, hoping not to be seen, but Taylor was drawn to her, her head looked up instinctively, as if she had inhaled her familiar scent.

Taylor's smile was wide and genuine, a true happiness to see Kay. Taylor moved towards her to go and speak with her. Fran and Marcus wondered where she was headed before they too saw that Kay was back. Marcus smiled over at Kay. He was truly happy to see his colleague back in good health once again. Fran was also happy that she was well again but her heart felt like a hole had been punched right through it and someone had kicked her in the stomach, because she, more than anyone, knew that Taylor was still hung up on Kay and maybe even still in love with her.

Kay carried on walking. Her hand gave a feeble gesture of acknowledgement but her actions, as she continued to walk to the door, let Taylor know she didn't want to talk to her right now.

Chapter 60
Guilty, But Only of Avenging Her Soul!

All the evidence had been presented to the jury at the high court over several weeks, in the city's High Street, and the jury had been sent out to deliberate their findings.

The High Street is a portion of Edinburgh's Royal Mile, the prestigious one mile walk from Holyrood Palace to Edinburgh Castle, positioned high on a rock and believed to be an extinct volcano. The street is famous all around the world, playing host to thousands of tourists every year and the International Fringe Festival, where the street comes alive with hundreds of street performers, arts and crafts, a festival that is one of the biggest and most popular in the world. Outside the court, a police traffic cone sat upon the head of the modern bronze statue of David Hume. Set on Clashach sandstone, the Scottish Enlightenment philosopher stood one and half times that of lifesize, right outside the court.

There was a larger than normal police presence surrounding the court, along with the plethora of reporters, hyena-like as they jostled for position outside, their extended lenses banging off one another in an attempt to get the best shot of everyone and anyone involved as they came out into the sunlight for the break. The public galleries had been full throughout the two-week long trial, the public interest very high, their opinions varied and split in relation to the punishment that should be given, as the crimes were so brutal and sadistic, but the perpetrator herself was the victim of unbearable and prolonged neglect, torture, physical and sexual abuse and people could understand why she had taken revenge.

Taylor was the focus of a lot of attention, possibly because of her looks and general presence, but the microphones were thrust into her face with needy ignorance, a desperation to get their story, to do their job no matter what it took, hoping that she would give up a little more information than she should on this occasion.

All she would say was that the jury were deliberating and would come to the right conclusion with the evidence that had been presented at the trial.

She pushed passed them politely and made her way down to the Elephant House on George the IV Bridge on the opposite side of the road, down past the Central Library. One or two of the reporters followed for a bit and kept snapping their cameras at her from behind, for what purpose, nobody knew! Marcus had tagged along with her as he too wanted refreshments and a cake, needing a sugar rush to combat the stress of the trial.

After lunch, the court filled back up again, not a seat left unclaimed, everybody wanting to see what the outcome would be, although there was no doubt there would be a conviction.

The Sheriff came in to the chamber and everyone stood on the command, "All Rise".

Amy stood flanked by two large officers. She looked tiny, defenceless and totally vulnerable, her face still clearly scarred from the assault by the now deceased Natt Spears. Injuries that were clear to see, committed by the man who had scarred her for life as a child, creating a lifetime of mental torture, self-harm and vengeful thoughts. The crimes that she stood accused of had been evidenced over the weeks. They were mind-boggling to both the police and the public because to look at her standing there, vulnerable and alone, tiny in stature and clearly damaged, it didn't look possible that she could have committed any of them.

Look at her, look at that pitiful little creature, how could she have overcome these men, could she have single-handedly brutalised these men herself, could she, did she? Did she? Taylor thought.

Nathan stood alongside Kerr, Amy's long-suffering partner, both watching her. Nathan and Amy looked over at each other, a look that only they knew what it meant. They had an unbreakable bond that nobody else could see or understand, a bond that they had shared since birth. They were born to protect one another, no matter what it took.

Taylor watched Amy, she saw her look straight into her brother's eyes, then she saw a very slight smile shared between them. *Why would she smile, why? She's just about to be banged up for life, without a chance of parole.*

The judge passed the verdict to the clerk of the court to be read out to the accused and those within the court.

"GUILTY of murder on all three counts. GUILTY on both counts of serious assault. GUILTY to the aiding and abetting in the murder of Natt Spears. GUILTY of theft and the possession and use of a section one firearm, perverting the course of justice…" The list went on, guilty on all charges.

"The sentence will be three life sentences, to be served concurrently. There will be a requirement for regular mental health assessments, to ensure that you will be fit to remain in a mainstream prison, and a full programme of rehabilitation and counselling."

Amy stood there, making not a single movement as she digested the information being read out before her. There were no surprises, just relief that there wouldn't be any further victims of Natt Spear's and Megan Thomson's reign of terror and abuse, ever again, and Maggie and her children could live a free life, safe from the evil, the evil that was Natt Spears.

The whole courtroom stared at her as she turned slowly, with tears in her eyes, to walk down the stairs to the cells to begin her lifelong sentence.

She looked like a child, a little girl trapped in horror of her damaged past. She herself, for the first time in her life felt free, free from the cruel tortuous chains that had bound and restricted her in life, every single day, a prison-like incarceration for as long as she could remember. She may be going to another prison but in this one she would be free from the demons that haunted her every thought and dream, free from those vile monsters that took her innocence and spirit, free at last.

Nathan watched with tears in his eyes as his twin sister that was once taken away from him, was taken away again. His heart ached and his stomach twisted, twisted tight with hate and despair, desperation and pain because he couldn't save her from her fate.

Taylor and the others stood respectfully until they could no longer see the accused and they were officially dismissed from the court. They watched as everybody filed out of court. To them it was a job well done, an end to a brutal string of vengeful murders. They had secured a successful conviction. They had got there in the end, Marcus was last to get up. He was the one that had been personally scarred by the events of the past months. The one person that had saved him from a lifetime of regret and misery was to be locked away for the rest of her life and he had helped to put her there. His heart was torn by the human side of Amy, a woman that had risked her life to save others and try and stop the ever growing trend in organised child abuse. She was the one that saved his son and the other boy, not the police, her and nobody else. He owed her his future happiness with his beautiful family and wonderful little boy and he would be forever grateful to her. He made a promise to himself to make sure if he could help her in any way, then he would.

Taylor and the rest of the team chose to leave the court by the back door to avoid a repeat of their earlier media scrum and intrusion into their personal space and they all slipped away into the busy streets. Leaving alone with their thoughts and emotions, away to deal with them as they had to, case after case, personal thoughts, opinions and emotions in relation to each case filed away in their heads, out of reach, to ensure damage limitation, saviour of their own souls, a detachment from the pain and suffering, a required mechanism to deal with the trauma of those who had suffered at the hands of others. All of them just thankful that on this occasion they had all walked away, unharmed, free to go back to their lives and families, when others would not, not ever.

Kerr, Amy's loyal partner was left heartbroken, but happy for her, happy that at last she seemed to be free, free of the demons that had been trapped inside her, stopped her being able to live and love without revulsion. He loved her with all he had and would visit her as much as he could for ever more. He had loved her from the moment he had met her. He had watched the inner turmoil eat away at her soul, stop her from enjoying human touch, true love, trust and affection because her inner scarring had built unbreakable barriers within, a self-preservation mechanism rooted deep inside, one so powerfully set in place to guard against her past and make sure it never happened again that it had prevented any true happiness for her throughout her entire, troubled life.

Nathan went home with Jen. Once in the house, he held Jen and Millie tightly, appreciating what he had and how good it felt. The two new puppies that he had rescued recently were delighted to see them and frantically wagged their tails. While Jen and Millie took the dogs for a walk, Nathan made himself a coffee and went through to the study. He needed time to be alone, time to ingest the events of the day and the loss of his sister's freedom forever.

There on his desk was an unopened letter that Jen had put there for him. She said it had arrived just before they left for court. On it was Amy's handwriting. He hesitated before opening it, its possible contents filled him with apprehension and frightened him. *What has she sent me?*

He peeled open the envelope with care and looked at it with a blank expression, his mouth agape as he laid the contents down in front of him. It was a list of names and addresses and websites, some had star beside them in red.

He felt physically sick as he folded it back up into the envelope and pushed it between two books on a shelf near where he sat. He knew what these people were and why they were on the list. He knew he should give it to the police straight away, but he chose to hang on to it.

Marcus went home to Maria and David. He hugged them both as if it would be the last hug ever. He was clearly emotional, grateful and affected by this case and those involved, especially Amy.

DC Smith pushed PC Ewar along in his wheelchair through the corridors of the hospital to the café. He was still unable to walk from his fractured pelvis. She leant over him and kissed him gently on the top of his head as he reached his hand up to put his on hers with new found warmth and affection.

Kay sat in her living room, sad and alone, staring blankly at the television. She had a glass of red wine in her hand as she went over and over her life in her head. Her head whipped round instinctively as she heard a light knock at her front door. Her heart leapt with her new despised reaction of fear, a sensation that screamed through every nerve ending in her body. Pins and needles piercing her like small electric shocks making every hair on her body stand on end. *Who could that be?*

CPSIA information can be obtained
at www.ICGtesting.com
Printed in the USA
FFOW02n0251240617
37084FF

9 781911 525318